My Trojan Horse Majesty

THE RUSSIAN WITCH'S CURSE
BOOK FIVE

BRIDGET E. BAKER

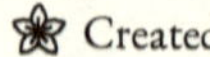 Created with Vellum

What It's About

Breaking a horse is one thing, but can you ever truly *break* a villain of bad behavior?

Izzy Brooks has not always had the easiest life. Her dad died when she was young, and their entire family moved halfway across the country to work a ranch. Strangely, that turned out to be the best thing that ever happened to her.

When she doesn't get into vet school and her boyfriend's facing criminal charges at work, it feels like her life's falling apart all over again. So when she sees a horse that's about to be put down for poor behavior, she decides to take a gamble. Maybe she can train him into something decent and earn the money she needs to help her boyfriend.

But this stallion isn't just a mess—he acts like he's never even *been* a horse before. If he wasn't such a stunning sorrel with a perfect mane, tail, and blaze, she'd release him into the wild and walk away. But she knows what it's like to feel like her options are limited. So when no one's looking, she sneaks him into her trailer and runs away, determined to turn this horse's life around and change her own fate at the same time.

What she doesn't know is that she just stole the world's most powerful magician, who's only temporarily trapped in an unfamiliar horse form, and when he finally breaks free, there will be hell to pay.

For Dora: the real Izzy...

Don't EVER fall for a Tim. BLECH.

CHAPTER 1

Izzy

I was five years old when I told my mom I wanted to be a vet.

On my sixth birthday, I asked for a vet kit. Unable to find one, my mom modified one of the toy doctor kits and added a few stuffed animals. I *loved* it. I took it everywhere. I recruited every stuffed animal in the house, imagining up a whole host of maladies and sad stories so that my services were needed.

By the time I was ten, I knew I wanted to be a large animal doctor.

I love dogs and cats, don't get me wrong, but there's something about the weight, the significance, and the heft in the horses. If I could get away with it, I wanted to treat only horses, but I don't hate dealing with cows either.

After my dad died and my mom remarried, I toyed briefly with the idea of being a horse trainer. For about two years, while I was riding virtually every day, I told everyone I wanted to do both. I spent all my free time either caring for horses, riding horses, or learning how to break and train them. I learned from the very best, too, my new stepdad, Steve Archer.

But eventually, I circled back around to vet, because I didn't want horses—my hobby—to become my job. I wanted to have a job that allowed me to ride for fun separately. I had a few people tell me that I'd have to keep top grades, and that I'd have to study really hard.

The thing is, school was never hard for me.

In fact, I rarely even needed to study.

Other kids often hated me, because I always broke the curve. They *really* hated me when they found out that I did it without studying. But having a solid brain gave me time to focus on horse training in all my spare time. I went to college at the best school that was reasonably close to home—the University of Utah. I didn't get to drive home *all* the time, but I saw my family often.

Other than family and horses, I didn't have much else to cut into my time. I never dated anyone for more than a single date or two. Sometimes it was because I scared them off—horse girls can be a lot. Other times, they freaked *me* out. But mostly, I just didn't really hit it off with anyone.

Until the day I saw Timothy Heaston for the first time.

Gleaming russet brown hair that fell over his brow. Light, almost golden-brown eyes that flashed in the sun. Half a dozen techs and assistants who followed his every order. He was evaluating a horse that could barely move, and then he strode over to the corner to talk to the owner.

"It's what I thought—sepsis in the deep digital flexor tendon."

The owner grimaced.

"But since it happened two days ago, he's a candidate for fenestration." Dr. Heaston was so calm. So forthright.

"That will lower the course of recovery?" The owner's brow furrowed. "Or, why would we do that?"

"It doesn't make the recovery faster, but as I mentioned, damaged tendons heal with irregularly arranged fibers. The scar tissue's less elastic, so the repaired tendon's weaker than it was before. Fenestration—an incision near the injury—will release the initial blood clot, and that should help the new blood vessels to grow into the injured area properly and ensure much greater function after it's healed."

I was at the Bear River Equine Hospital to interview for an internship, and I thought I'd done alright. But seeing Dr. Heaston, watching him diagnose and offer options on the expensive, fancy horse in front of me. . .it felt like I was seeing Taylor Swift in person, only cooler.

He was my version of a rock star.

I'd been interning at Bear Valley for almost a year when he kissed me. In my entire life, I'd never felt butterflies, but kissing an equine orthopedic surgeon that people travelled from hundreds of miles all around to see?

It was more than fireworks.

We've been together for almost a year, now, and even though no one at work knows, I'm still happier than I ever thought I'd be with him.

When he breezes through the door, he smiles. "Did you make dinner?"

I shake my head. "We had trouble getting Chicken Nugget on the trailer, so I didn't leave until six."

"But it's seven fifteen." He frowns. "If you didn't cook, what am I smelling?"

I turn and look at the bag on the kitchen counter. "I picked up Urban Hill. I'd been craving their fried goat cheese."

"So instead of making something, you drove all the way into town to buy overpriced frou-frou food?" He blinks. "Tell me your parents are rich without telling me your parents are rich."

"You're just crabby because you think goat cheese stinks."

He rolls his eyes. "Not only because of that."

"I had to drive into town anyway to check the mail at my apartment."

"Why do you even still have that?" He opens the top of the bag and starts rummaging around. "You've basically lived here for months."

I walk toward him. "My parents don't know that, clearly."

"Where's the goat cheese?" His lip curls. "Did they charge you for it and forget to make it?"

I reach into the bag and pull out the lamb bourguignon, his favorite. "I ate it in my car on the way home, so you won't have to smell it." I step closer. "*And* I already brushed my teeth."

He smiles, then. "Good girl." He reaches for my waist. "Get anything helpful in the mail?"

I sigh and drop my head against his shoulder. "No. Still nothing."

"I thought they'd have sent out letters by now," he says. "Maybe I should call Stetson."

I freeze. "Can you do that?"

He shrugs. "I mean, he's not supposed to share stuff like that, but he'd be able to log in and tell me whether you got in, probably."

"I have to get in, right?" I ask. "I mean, you couldn't recommend me, in case people ever found out about us, but Larry and Dr. Hartfield both love me. They gave me good recommendations, right?" Larry's technically his boss, but only because Tim hates doing paperwork. Tim's the one who brings in the big bucks, and everyone else accommodates him any way they can, including writing letters of recommendation for me when Tim asks. In this case, though, I know I earned them. I've worked hard at Bear River.

Tim leans back against the countertop with his hip and pulls his phone from his pocket. "I'm just going to call him, because if I don't, you'll keep driving down there every single day, won't you?"

I roll my eyes, but I don't argue.

"Hey," Tim says. "It's Heaston."

I can't hear anything from the other line. He must have his volume turned down low. I try to slide closer, but he waves me off.

"Listen, I know this is probably technically against the rules, but can you just take a little peek and tell me, informally, whether one of my interns got into the vet program over there?"

Again, he pauses.

"Right. She's trying to make some big decisions, and she's stressing that the letters haven't come out yet. I told her I'd see what I could do. Sweet girl."

Sweet girl? I slap his chest.

He scowls, and shakes his head. "Yep, her name's Isabel Brooks." He pauses. "Uh-huh." Another break. "Yeah, that's right. Birthday's April fourteenth."

And then he grunts.

"What does that mean?" I whisper. "That sounded *bad*."

"No, I understand. I'll just tell her to keep waiting." When he hangs up, he looks. . .not good.

"What did he say?" I ask. "Are the letters coming out soon?"

Tim sighs heavily. "Look, Peach Pit. I know how much you wanted to do vet school, but if you did go, I wouldn't see you for four years. Logan's a long way off."

What's he saying?

"Plus, you'd never have time to ride if you were working that hard. And if we wanted to get married and start a family, that would be delayed a long while, too. So I know this might seem like bad news, but try to remember—"

I bite off a sob. "Did he say I didn't get in?"

"He told me I can't tell you anything, obviously." He sighs.

"But I didn't."

Tim hugs me. "I'm so sorry. Sometimes life takes us places we didn't expect. Maybe this will turn out to be a good thing."

Tim spends the rest of the night trying to cheer me up. It

doesn't work, but I appreciate his efforts. He's actually singing "Walking on Sunshine" when there's a loud bang on his door.

I straighten immediately, my heart racing. "Who could be here now?" I glance at my watch. "It's after eleven p.m."

Tim shrugs. "Wait here." He pulls a shirt on and walks to the front door of his farmhouse.

I'm not great at doing as I'm told, so of course I sneakily follow him. When he opens the door, I can barely see them from around Tim's broad shoulders. I wish I couldn't see them at all.

Two police officers are standing in the doorway—a woman, and a very large man with grey hair. The man holds out a piece of paper. "We have a warrant for the arrest of a mister Timothy Heaston." He tosses his head. "I presume that's you?"

"What's this for?" Tim asks.

"You're being charged with embezzlement, fraud, and breach of fiduciary duties. You have the right to remain silent." The man brandishes the paper again.

"Anything you say or do may be used against you in a court of law," the woman says. "You also have the right to an attorney."

"Although, I should warn you that your assets have already been frozen, so you'll probably be stuck using the court-appointed one." The man's smiling.

When I found out earlier that I didn't get into vet school, I really didn't think things in my life could get any worse, but boy was I wrong.

And the next day, things worsen yet again. "Based on the evidence I've seen," the judge says, "I think you're a flight risk. I'm setting bail at a hundred thousand dollars."

"A flight risk?" I stand up. "He's a prominent member of the community. You've frozen all his money. There's no way he could buy so much as a bus ticket, much less come up with that bail."

"You're correct, miss." The judge smiles. "Unless he has

some friends or family that trust him enough to risk their own hundred grand on him returning for trial, he's going to be stuck in here until it starts. That's a risk I'm willing to take."

Before they drag him out of the courtroom, at least the officers let me hug him goodbye.

"I have faith in you," he says as he releases me.

"What?"

He leans closer and whispers in my ear. "I know that you'll do whatever it takes to come up with that money. My partners are screwing me, and right now, you're the only one I trust." His eyes are intense, staring right into mine. "Get me out, Peach Pit, and the first thing I'll do once my money's unfrozen is go buy you a massive diamond engagement ring. We can put all the ugliness of this day behind us."

And then he's walking out the door, marching along ahead of armed guards, like he's some kind of psycho killer. It's been a really, really horrible day, but he's not wrong about one thing. I may not have gotten into vet school, but I'm not going to screw this up.

I will get that bail money, and I will get him out of here.

CHAPTER 2

Leonid

The only horse we ever owned when I was a child was a plow horse.

A riding horse, well-trained and healthy, cost close to a hundred times as much as the half-starved plow horses my father purchased whenever we stayed somewhere long enough to need one. Our plow horses probably weren't very well fed, and they certainly weren't well trained. As a result, if our horses didn't bite or kick me, I was having a good day.

I wasn't a big fan of horses.

So later, in spite of having the theoretical ability to shift into a horse, I never did it more than a handful of times. I've always thought it was the most vulnerable form to take, and turning into a horse was certainly the least useful of all our magic. Why would we want to shift into a *prey* animal that we domesticated thousands of years ago?

Only, when something beckons to me from beyond the blackness I've been stuck in and I open my eyes, I'm in my horse form. My very muddy, very wet, massively large horse form. It takes me two tries, but I finally manage to roll to my feet—er, hooves—and then I sense what it was that woke me. I sense it,

8

but I can't figure out what it is. Something very strange is pulling on me, and when I spin around, trotting toward the tugging feeling, I'm able to spot it.

It's a person.

She climbs out of an older silver truck and begins walking toward the house. I shake my head to hopefully get rid of some of the mud, and I focus on shifting back into my human form. I'm certainly not going to get her attention as a horse in a cage.

Only, nothing happens.

I try again.

Still no luck.

I scream in frustration, but it comes out as a very loud, very angry whinny.

Stupid, idiotic magic. I heard Aleks was stuck in his horse form when we awoke, and I'm assuming Alexei and Grigory were, too, but I wasn't.

So why am I now?

I inhale, and I dig down deep, and I think about what my body should feel like, and I push toward that as hard as I can.

Still, nothing happens.

I scream again, this time releasing all the fury that's been bottled up inside since Aleksandr and Grigoriy tricked me with their back-to-back proclamations of surrender.

The woman that's somehow connected to me starts walking toward me. It must be a witch they've summoned to try yet again to destroy me. I created a shield around myself with electricity and water before I confronted them, and I'm guessing it has made me hard to kill. Instead of checking in with any of the others, the witch draws nearer. . .all alone.

And she's smiling.

She must be totally unhinged. Most witches are, so that makes sense. I imagine she can sense my power—the deep well of my magic—even if I can't access it right now.

She reaches through the fence, clearly already preparing to attack. "Look at you."

I snap my teeth at her, pretending I'm not wary of her touch. Acting like a dumb beast often convinces people to lower their guard. They don't expect intelligence when they see idiocy.

Bizarrely, she laughs. "You're a feisty one. I like that."

A man I've never seen before is walking past. "You shouldn't reach through the wire. He's headed for the kill pen. He's just here until they can arrange transport."

Kill pen? They're planning to execute me in this form? Did they somehow freeze me in my horse shape? What spell did they use? How can I force my way around it?

The witch looks utterly appalled. "The—what?"

"Apparently he's a total maniac." The man tilts his head strangely, as if he's looking at something very distasteful—only he's glaring at me. Hardly surprising, if he was brought in by Aleks, Alexei, or Grigoriy. "After watching him just now, I don't even fault the owner. He's *nuts*."

I've literally been awake for two minutes. What's he talking about? Did he mean, because I was sleeping through a rainstorm? I was magically cursed! I want to zap him to teach him to watch his tongue. I want to. . .I realize that for the first time since the early 1900s, I can't tell whether his soul's light or dark. My powers don't appear to be working at all, because I can't tell with the witch either.

Without seeing into their souls, without the ability to detect their goodness or their depravity, I feel. . .off-center. No magic. Stuck as a horse. Somehow already linked to this witch. And I can't even tell whether the people who are evaluating my life are evil or good. I rear back and scream in helpless fury.

"Still. The *kill pen*?" The witch sighs pathetically, her shoulders drooping. "What a shame."

Does she feel sorry for me? Why would she?

"They say he can't even be approached, much less ridden," the man says.

I wish one of them would approach me. I may not have much experience as a horse, but I'm pretty sure I could take either of them down with one solid hoof-strike and still break free. It's this confounded seven-foot-tall electric gate that I can't figure a way to escape.

"At least they could try gelding him first," the witch says. "Maybe he'd calm down."

Geld me? The anger I felt before deepens. Broadens. This time when I rear back, I hold it for a moment, screaming my displeasure. When I finally drop back to all four hooves, the mud around me sprays all over the two idiots in front of me in a very satisfying way. I have so much frustration, so much anger, that I find myself moving again, lest it overcome me. Even with my frenetic activity, and even though she's whispering, I still hear the words.

"You shouldn't be killed. Someone should save you."

I freeze, confused. When I turn back to look at her again, I can't help wondering whether, somehow, I've misunderstood the situation. Why would a witch want to save me? I assumed, based on our connection, that she was some sort of local witch, but what if that's not true? Horses are generally useless, but their sense of smell's quite good. I scent the air, checking for the pungent herbs and strange odors that usually accompany dark mages and witches. I smell none of it. I move closer and try again.

Still no trace.

The girl reaches her hand through the fence again, and even though I worry it's a trap, I move closer still. The ground's so wet underneath me that it's practically boggy, but I ignore that and focus on her. I can sense our connection even more than I could before, but I still have no idea what it is.

She smells of horses, hay, and sunshine, and she's staring at me eagerly. "You can't be that bad, right boy?"

Could Steve, Gustav, Aleks and the others not have told the man or the woman what I am? I imagine they'd want to keep my identity and presence here as secret as they could. Disposing of a horse carcass would be simpler than a human body too, I imagine. But something they might not have considered in a place this small is the impact of external forces, humans moving beyond their control.

Ironically, the quieter they keep things, the more this principle applies.

If she thinks I'm just a horse, and not just that, a horse bound for death. . .might *she* be convinced to save me? If she *did* take me, she'd want to conceal her theft, at least for a while. That just might buy me some time and put me in a position where I can escape and hide safely until my powers return. All I have to do is convince this simpleton that I've been misunderstood and that she can save me.

It's one of the primary failings of all humanity, but especially women, their desperate belief that they're special enough to change someone or something fundamentally. That's the reason Katerina pined for Alexei for so long. It's why romance novels are so popular. It's not their fault—it's what they're taught by society from birth—if you're special, you can fix whatever broken guy you meet and make him someone who will love you.

In this case, I mean to lean in and make her think it's true.

Fix me, I think, as I press my nose against her hand.

She flinches a little, like she thinks I'm going to bite her, and then she opens her eyes wide and exhales sharply.

It's working.

But she won't believe it if I make it all too easy, so I snort loudly, and I shift and then I lean in more, pressing my nose right into her palm, like I enjoy being near her. It must be a masterful performance, because she smiles like a complete idiot.

"What's your name?" Her voice is annoyingly breathy.

I snort again, hoping she'll take it as my stallion-nerves and not recognize it for derision.

"How about Drago?" she asks. "You remind me of a dragon among horses, and I might be about to do something really crazy."

I call to her then, because it seems like she needs a little nudge to just *do it*. I whinny, but I don't snap or do anything aggressive.

"Let's see." Her smile grows even broader. "I wonder whether we might get along. Do you think I could break you and turn you into something worth a hundred thousand bucks?"

A hundred grand? Has she lost her mind? I'm an unridable mess. I bump her so she doesn't realize how much I'm laughing inside.

"It would be better than dying, at least," she mutters. "I'll leave this up to fate. If I can manage to halter him and lead him into the trailer without anyone finding out. . ."

She waits until the man's gone, and then she peers around, checking for anyone else. I have no idea how we're this lucky, but. . .no one else is awake or out and moving around. She disappears into the barn around the corner, possibly planning something horrible, but I'm just thinking, *don't meet someone who will stop you...*

Moments later, she finally emerges holding a ratty blue halter. It looks awfully small, but maybe that'll help me sell this. I have to act a *little* nervous, but seem to be calmed specifically by *her*. I need to exhibit just enough misbehavior to be believable, but somehow also be polite enough that she won't bail and call for help or abort her mission.

When she approaches me, she's as white as a snowdrift in the mountains. She looks like she might be sick at any moment, but after breathing in and out a few times, she lifts her hand, and she undoes the lock and opens the chains. Freedom calls to me, but there's also that strange connection I feel to her. I need to figure out what that is before I bolt. Plus, without my powers, escaping's kind of idiotic. Gustav could catch me quickly and trap me again—or kill me. Which is exactly what they'll work out a way to do if I hang around here. I'm not sure my personal shield can absorb and redirect many more of their violent attempts without giving out entirely.

"This is the test." She's whispering to herself like a crazy person again. "If I can halter him and he loads for me, there's a chance."

The one place I can't scare her off is right here, by the exit. She could change her mind in an instant, slam the gate shut in my face, and my window to an escape will be gone. I consider trotting over to her and sliding my head into the stupid halter straps. That would almost surely freak her out, so instead, I wait. And wait. And wait. She's moving so slowly toward me that I want to scream again. Her hand's trembling, and her mouth's dangling open. When she finally reaches for me, I drop my head just an inch or two, but I make her do all the rest of the work, eyes rolling, nostrils flaring just a bit.

I also shift a bit, just to show her I'm thinking of leaving, but then I don't.

As she struggles to fasten the buckle on the farthest hole, I can't help being annoyed. What horse would stand still and quiet while a person fumbles their way around this much? Am I being *too* submissive?

"You might need a draft size halter with that massive head of yours. Even a warmblood size would fit better than this. Sorry it's so small, big boy."

Big Boy? She has no idea.

Then she rubs my nose. I swear, this whole situation's painfully absurd. I walk beside her, thinking about where she might be taking me, and whether they might have an enclosure from which I could escape. Luckily, as we reach the trailer, I remember that I should be at least a little resistant so she can feel like she's overcoming my objections.

A perfect horse going to a kill lot makes no sense, after all.

I balk at first, when she tries to lead me into the weird metal box, but the second time she asks me to follow her, clucking and cooing, I do. "It's three hours to get to my place. We'll be there before you know it, I swear. And then tomorrow, once you're settled in, we'll get to work."

Three hours? That sounds like a good head start to me.

Thank you, crazy woman, for breaking me out of my jail cell, but tomorrow, we won't be starting any sort of 'work.' Tomorrow, I'll have my powers back, no matter what it takes for me to get them, and I'll be gone faster than you could possibly imagine.

CHAPTER 3

Izzy

Horses were made to run.

Locking them in a metal box is about as opposite of their nature as it gets. I expect Drago, now that he's secured and I've left, to lose his mind—kicking, screaming, and tearing up Steve's trailer. I *hope* he doesn't. But my heart's in my throat, because if Steve or Mom wake up from his screaming and kicking and see me driving off. . .it's going to be very awkward explaining why I'm stealing a horse.

A horse that's destined to die, I remind myself. *It's fine. I'm trying to do something good.*

Only, something good isn't usually something that could also enrich me. I very much need this horse to turn his problems around quickly so I can have the money Heaston needs to get out of jail and start preparing his defense against his horrible partners' claims.

To my shock, the stallion stands completely calm. There's no banging, there's no clanging. He doesn't even shift around or scream. Why would anyone want to put him down, when he's behaving so well?

Is it possible. . .he just likes me?

I've heard of it before—usually in stupid, made-up stories. I shake the nonsensical idea off. Perhaps he's amazing in trailers, but a complete lunatic when anyone comes at him with a saddle. I'm just going to have to approach each step of this whole thing one small problem at a time.

The first half hour or so, I'm so panicked that I drive at ten and two, my hands gripping the steering wheel tightly. I keep expecting my mom to call or the stallion to lose it. Or, once, when a cop car passes, my heart skyrockets.

But that's ridiculous.

Mom wouldn't call the cops on me.

After half an hour, I turn on the radio.

"—very often," the female radio personality's saying. "I mean, it says the last time there even *was* an earthquake in Utah, it was 2022, and that was just an aftershock of the 2020 one."

A man chuckles. "Well, maybe we were due."

Earthquake?

"If we were, I suppose having it happen out in Manila, Utah, of all places, is a good way to go."

My hands go slack, the truck swerves a little, and I have to clamp down to straighten us out. *Manila*? There was an earthquake in Manila? When?

"With a population of just five hundred, the tiny little town located on the Wyoming border isn't going to have much property damage to speak of," the man says.

"Yeah, I bet their cow pastures will recover just fine."

It happened late last night, apparently, a quake that measured five point one on the Richter scale. There have already been three smaller tremors since then, all of them around a two. I'm a little worried that the earthquake might have damaged someone's house—Mandy's? Amanda's? Helen's?—when my phone rings. I glance at the screen. I'd usually be excited to talk to her, but between the news I can't share about not getting into vet school, the horrible mess with

Tim, and now the stallion I'm towing, I feel more sick than anything else.

And, I really, *really* need that horse to be quiet.

Because it's my mom.

My hands are shaking when I hit the green button. "Hey, Mom."

"Izzy?" She sighs. "Thank goodness you're alright. Oliver said he saw you this morning?"

I groan. "Yeah, I woke up super early, and I decided I'd return Steve's trailer, but then when I was almost there, I got a phone call from an old lady client of Tim's. She doesn't have a trailer, and I wanted to at least say hello, but it was urgent—"

"Hey, did you happen to see a stallion while you were here?"

"A stallion?" I ask. "You mean that insane chestnut?"

"Yes," Mom says. "Tell me you didn't touch him."

I snort. "When I tried to pet him, he almost bit my hand off."

"So you didn't. . .take him back with you? Right?"

"Oliver said he was going to be killed. Is that really true?"

"Isabel Brooks, please tell me you didn't—"

"Mom, I'm not insane. But why would you think I'd steal a horse? Did he get loose?"

"I'm not sure when you left," Mom says, "but when we came outside this morning, the gate was open." She sounds like she might cry. "He's gone."

"Oh, shoot," I say. "That's terrible. I mean, he could really be anywhere." I cringe a little. It's not the first time I've lied to my mom, but it's definitely the worst lie I've ever told.

And so far, every time I've tried until now, she's caught me.

She sighs. "He really could be anywhere, I guess."

"Is it really bad?" I ask. "Is he dangerous?"

"More than you could possibly know," Mom says. "But that's not your problem. Good luck helping that old lady, and drive safe."

"I will," I say.

"Wait," she says. "Why do you need Steve's trailer to load her horse? Doesn't Tim have a trailer?"

"He's not at home." Strictly speaking, that's true. "And his truck and trailer are huge, and I don't feel as comfortable driving them." That's partially true too, at least.

"Alright, well, I hope you'll come visit soon, but maybe not in the next week or so. We're really busy here."

"Hey, I heard there was an earthquake. Is everyone okay?"

"It was really strange," Mom says. "We've never had earthquakes here before, but yes. There have been several large ones now. So far, everyone on the family chain says they're alright."

"Really?"

"Donna and Will said there was some damage to their barn, but nothing significant. I guess a window cracked—some kind of shifting under the foundation—but so far everything's alright here, too."

"What about Helen and David's place and both resorts?"

Mom snorts. "They're worried the pool at David's resort has a leak, and to hear Helen tell it, repairing that would be a nightmare."

"I bet Aunt Amanda's happy they didn't put a pool in at their house, though."

"They have that massive hot tub," Mom says. "But she said it looks completely fine."

All the normal talk, and the easy way my mom let go of the idea that I stole Drago, makes me feel much less stressed. . .and also really, really guilty. When she finally hangs up, I have a momentary panic attack.

What am I doing?

Have I gone insane?

If *Steve* thinks the horse should be put down. . .what hope do *I* have of breaking or retraining him? None. Zero. Zilch. I've just taken a horse there's no way I can control, which means it's not going to be worth a brass farthing.

I'm a complete and total idiot.

But what if it was Steve's *client* who was insisting? What if Steve didn't want to give up, but the client won't allow him to keep working with Drago? I should've asked more questions, but I was worried that might be suspicious.

Ugh. Committing crimes is hard.

It occurs to me then that my boyfriend has been accused of a crime he didn't commit—embezzling company funds. In order to get him free of the jail cell he's stuck in. . .I've just committed a real crime.

But as long as I stay safe myself, it's a crime without a victim. The owners wanted the stallion gone, and now he's gone. They won't even have to pay to dispose of his body. I'm really doing something good—giving this animal a shot at life, *and* sparing the owners the vet bills and burial costs of the stallion.

So why do I feel so terribly bad about all of it?

I'm probably just worried that I may be putting Steve in a bind. I flip to the AM satellite radio station, hoping a talk show might distract me. Only, every channel I try has people yapping about more horrible things happening somewhere in the world.

"—wildfires in California and parts of Idaho are spreading. It's strange to see them this late in the year, but if climate change has taught us anything—"

"—another earthquake, this one close to the last. Wyoming almost never sees major quakes, and this one's on the wobble line for what constitutes major, but its genesis is a fault that hasn't really seen any activity in centuries, as far as we can tell."

"—sharply rising rates of violent crime in—"

I shut the radio off, but sitting in silence makes for a very, *very* long drive home. When I finally turn onto the small road that leads to Heaston's property, I'm exhausted. My shoulders are stiff, my head's pounding, and I'm beginning to think this was a very, very stupid plan.

What if, when I go to unload this horse, he doesn't act at all like the calm, sensible guy who got on? What if we're back to the dragon who snapped at me and tried to kill me? What if, instead of being a promising prospect I might sell, this horse tries to end my life, and I'm either injured, or stuck calling Steve and confessing that I've gotten in over my head?

I'm nervous enough that I decide to dose the big beast with Dormosedan before unloading. He's not stomping, he's not screaming, and he's not kicking, but I'm still nervous. He must've been slated to be killed for a reason. It takes me two minutes to run to the tiny office on the end of Tim's house, enter the keypad code, and swipe a tube of gel from the cabinet. As I walk back, I dither about the amount.

Unlike wormer, horses have to absorb the gel under their tongue or on their gums. If he swallows it, it won't work well at all. I'm a little nervous that he won't stand politely and let me give it to him through the window, but if he does, do I give him one or two milliliters? Ugh. Maybe this is why I didn't make it into vet school. I'm just no good at this kind of stuff, and I dither far too much.

In the end, I decide to give him the full dose. If he's a little drowsy, I can stay with him in the stallion enclosure longer. It'll take more time, but that will give me a chance to get to know him better.

Plus, I've had quite a while to get really nervous and second guess this stupid decision. I reach through the window, talking to him while I do. "Alright, boy. I have to do this one little thing, and then I'll unload you. It'll just take one second, and it won't hurt." I pause with my hand under his chin. "Don't bite me. Okay?"

He stares at me calmly. No stomping. No snapping.

I inhale, and then I stick the plunger under his tongue. I

expect him to throw his head up, or toss his face around, or really anything to try and dislodge my tube.

He doesn't. He just stares at me, and it almost creeps me out. He looks. . .more sentient than a horse usually is. He looks like he understood everything I said.

"I'm sorry for sedating you," I say. "I'm nervous you might try to break away from me when we unload."

Now he tosses his head, and he seems to be trying to spit the gel out. Stupid, idiotic horse. Luckily, there's not much gel, and it's a little viscous—hard to dislodge. With the way I smeared it around under his tongue and on his gums, I doubt he could avoid it if he had a compelling reason.

While I wait for it to take effect, he stomps, kicks, and screams.

"I know you're sick of being in the trailer," I say. "And I'm truly sorry. But you're very large, and I'm very small, and if you misbehave, you could hurt me badly." His stomping does lessen a bit, and although he's still got flaring nostrils and rolling eyes, he seems a little less insane.

Finally, enough time has passed that I decide to go ahead and try to unload him. I wish I had someone here to call. I wish I had *anyone* here to call, but I can't explain where he came from, and anyone from the vet practice would have a *lot* of questions for me to answer. Questions I *can't* answer.

My heart's racing as I unclip the bottom of his halter from the lead on the trailer clip. I reattach his lead line and swing the line up over his back. He does look a little drowsy, which is exactly how he should look after taking a full dose. I carefully open the back of the trailer, watching for signs of frustration or anger, but he's standing still and steady. I unhook the latch on the bar that's tied into the middle of the trailer, freeing it, and it swings wide.

Now comes the pivotal moment.

I say a little prayer that he'll back off nicely. I've seen plenty of horses shoot off, damaging themselves or their owners, but he doesn't. He turns his head slowly, realizes he's free, and backs off. Quickly, but not dangerously so.

Then he turns his head toward me.

I snag his lead and start to pull him toward the far right side, angling toward the small stallion enclosure Tim has. His practice uses this as an overflow quarantine when necessary, so I remember him saying his horse setup's a write-off. I was glad he had the property, and I was even happier when he told me I could keep my mare and gelding here. It gives me somewhere to board that's not so expensive I can't justify keeping both my horses close.

And it gave me an excuse to come over more often at first.

Luckily my mare and gelding get along like peanut butter and jelly. They both rush the adjacent fence line as we approach. My mare, Millie, calls loudly. My old gelding, Chromey, simply follows her to the edge.

I had hoped the other horses would reassure Mr. High-strung, but Drago goes the other way. As we approach the gate for the stallion pasture, his nostrils flare, his eyes roll, and he generally begins to act as if he wasn't sedated at all.

"Calm down." I tug on his lead at the same time that I fuss. I should've attached a stallion chain so my tugging would get his attention a little better. What was I thinking? "You're going to be completely safe in there." I gesture ahead. "The devil himself couldn't get through that fence." I laugh. "Not without hands, anyway."

As I take one hand off his lead to open the padlock, Drago loses his mind. I drop the lock and yank sharply, turning him like Steve taught me instead of allowing him to race away, but when he shifts again and bolts, he breaks free.

I might release a string of profanities.

He doesn't care. He's galloping so fast that his tail flies straight up in the air at the top, then streams outward. Chunks of sod spray all over me as I'm completely ditched. He races past the other paddock, ducks around the edge, slowing only infinitesimally to poop, and then picks up speed yet again, racing toward the road.

My heart sinks.

I've *stolen* a horse in an insane long shot to try and help Tim, but my one claim to goodness is that I was going to give him a better life than he'd have had if he was put down. Now I don't even have him in my custody, and the only responsible thing to do is call the authorities and report that I've lost control of a massive, dangerous animal. . .who isn't even mine.

Only, just as he's about to pass out of my view, rounding the bend of the property and high-tailing it up the street—I finally understand that phrase!—he stumbles, falls over, and stops moving. I immediately take off toward him, worried and nervous about something new, but as I draw near, it's clear that something's very wrong.

My massive stallion's dead-still on the shoulder beside the road.

If I didn't know any better, I'd assume he really *was* dead. But horses can't go from racing pell-mell to dead in two seconds, can they? Surely not. . .

I lean down toward him, nervous to find out.

CHAPTER 4
Leonid

After hours in that horrible metal box, a box that still stinks of the excrement of all the other horses who have been stuffed in it, the trailer finally stops. I'm proud of myself when I wait and let the girl unload me. I can't see whether her soul's light or dark, not now, not without my powers, but I can guess. She looks like depictions of Elena the Beautiful from the Ivan Tsarevich fairy tales, and Elena's always the pure and innocent princess.

Even so, I can't stick around here, hoping my powers return.

I have to get away while I can. Once I'm sure I can break free without harming her, as she stoops over the lock on the gate, I sense it's my time. At first, she seems to have anticipated that I might bolt—yanking me sideways, and keeping control of my direction. But there's no way a hundred and fifty pound girl can really control a massive horse. It was never a fair fight.

Once I'm free, I toss my head sideways to swing the lead line back over my neck and keep my legs free, and then I really take off. Racing at full speed in this form has a strange effect—my bowels loosen, and I find myself crapping.

Right in front of that girl I just left.

It feels terribly embarrassing, but I suppose it shouldn't be. I'll never see her again. I speed up once again, moving faster than I ever thought I might when spots start to appear in front of my vision.

Vision that's already extremely strange in this form.

The design for horse eyes is moronic. I can only see with any depth perception in a narrow funnel right in front of my body, but on either side I can see nearly to my rump, and I have to choose which to focus on, only one at a time. At first, the spots seem like flecks of something that has sprayed up and covered my eyes, dimming the light. But then it worsens, and suddenly I can't see.

A second later, I lose control of my legs and crash into the ground.

When I wake up, the girl's back. This time, she's threading a chain through the halter she's already strapped to my face. "I'm sorry," she whispers. "I must've given you too much sedation." She straightens some, squaring her shoulders. "But I'm not *too* sorry, since you took off like a maniac—I guess you needed to be sedated."

I whinny.

"We have to go back to the paddock now. You were very naughty before, but I don't think you'll find it quite so easy to escape this time, not now that I know what tricks you'll try."

I can't help noticing that she's also carrying a large red crop. And wearing gloves.

Delightful.

"I'd rather not use this," she says, "but better safe than sorry." She stands up. "Now, it's time for you to get up, too. Carefully. Slowly." She tugs on the lead she's holding, and the chain tightens down over my nose.

Yowch.

"Stand up, Drago." She tugs again.

This time, I will my body to listen to the commands I'm

giving it, and it finally does. A surge of energy shoots through me, and my muscles ripple, and I roll to my feet.

"You're not so graceful when you're flat on the ground." She snorts. "I'm just glad you don't seem to have done any real damage. You hit the ground hard." She pats my neck. "Now, let's keep this simple. Okay?"

She's nice enough, but I'm definitely not going to let her stupid sedative ruin my bid for freedom. I walk along next to her nicely until we get close to the stallion paddock again. The ground here's tiny pea-gravel, and she won't have much of a chance at keeping her footing when I pull. I yank my head sideways and bolt away from her.

Only, with the chain, she has a much better hold on me.

It *hurts* when she yanks, and I swing out wide, trotting in a circle, the sensitive front of my nose downright crunched. I act like she's convinced me to listen for a few strides, and then I twist again. This time, I do it fast enough and sharply enough that she loses her grip, blessedly.

If I could smile as I race away, I sure would.

My hoof strikes the stupid lead line once, and I slip, nearly slamming into the ground again, but I right myself. I've almost reached the far end of the pasture, her two idiotic horse-friends racing along with me on the other side, when the spots return. Perhaps it's the level of exertion that forces her sedative to kick in.

I slow to a walk, but my vision continues to worsen, and it's nearly black. I stop entirely, but I can hear the irritating girl drawing closer, and that's when I realize I can also *feel* her drawing closer. That connection I felt before, when I woke, it's still there. In fact, it almost feels stronger than it did before.

The spots go away, so before she can reach me again, I take off. But as soon as I reach the road and start moving fast, my vision darkens *again*. It's like she's tied to me somehow, and every time I try to escape, I...pass out. Could that be correct?

Am I effectively *leashed*? If I am, she doesn't seem to know it.

One more course change, and I race the opposite direction, barely crossing her path before she would've intercepted me. Once again, as soon as I pull very far away from her, maybe a hundred yards or so, my vision darkens.

It's very, very vexing, but for now, I don't think I can escape. I'll have to figure out how we're connected and break it before I can get free. Which is why, when she reaches me this time, my sides heaving and my face and neck lathered, I stand politely.

She looks almost as tired as I feel.

"I'm beginning to think you're insane." She wheezes, and reaches for my lead, her hand moving slowly, her eyes wide. "Are you going to bolt again? Bite me? Fall over and crash to the ground?"

I snort at that.

She narrows her eyes. "I think I'm going nuts. I swear you act like you understand what I'm saying."

I bob my head.

"You do?" She arches her eyebrows. "Sure, you do." She chuckles, exhaling. "Now I'm interpreting horse head bobs as affirmations."

I whinny, and I step closer, tossing my head so my choked-down lead will be nearer to her hand. If I'm stuck with her until I can work out why I'm stuck, I may as well be cooperative. The last thing I want is for her to try and kill me off, too.

I doubt she could, but evading attacks gets tiring.

"Alright, the third time's the charm, right?" She arches one eyebrow. "If you don't come with me this time, I'm going to call animal control and let them come pick you up."

I walk meekly, almost like a real horse, right up to the gate.

When she glares at me before swinging the gate open, I wish I could laugh. "Do *not* act like an idiot this time. I'll get fresh hay and water for you as soon as you're through, but I could arrange to have it be moldy hay." She scowls as she opens it. "Remember that."

The villain in my current predicament's threatening me with. . .moldy hay. It's pretty humorous. What's next? A stern talking-to? I sigh as I follow her through.

"Tell me about it," she says. "You think you're sick of this? I'm way more annoyed than you." She reaches for the buckle on my halter, but she stops before undoing it. "I know you can't really understand me. I'm not a total moron. But you *do* act like you're listening, so I'm hoping you can somehow intuit my tone. After all that nonsense earlier, I almost want to leave your halter on and detach the lead, but I worry that with the little scratch on your nose already from your idiocy with the chain, it'll rub." She scowls. "I'm going to take it off. Please don't make me regret this."

She moves her hand to undo the buckle, and I bow my head enough that it slides free.

"You didn't race away," she says. "That's a surprise." She walks forward three steps. Then she turns back toward me and clicks. "Come on. Follow me."

So I do.

She beams. "Okay, a little more." She walks forward again, and I follow. Her wide smile broadens even more.

For some reason, it makes me happy.

Which would be embarrassing if anyone else knew.

I shake my head to remind myself that I'm not really a horse.

"Alright, now we're going to walk and stop." She clucks and starts walking.

I want to walk alongside her, but I can't think of a good reason that I should be doing this, and it makes me feel stupid. I'm not really a horse. Acting like her little 'good boy' just to see her smile is beneath me. I lift my head and neigh. Loudly.

"Alright, alright. You just got off the trailer. I bet you're hungry." She raises her eyebrows and tosses her head. "Water's over here." She takes off at a run.

I could run her over. I could trample her. Her behavior doesn't show a lot of sense. It makes me concerned for her well-being when I'm not around anymore. I hope with other horses, she exhibits a bit more caution. I finally trot off behind her, because I *am* thirsty, but that's the only reason.

It's certainly not because I wanted to see her smile again.

But if I did, I'd be happy to see that she is.

"Good boy." She's leaning against the fence near the water trough when her phone rings. "Shoot," she says. "I shouldn't really be in here if I'm distracted." She sighs as she fishes the phone from her pocket. "I'll call them—"

She freezes.

I can't help lifting my head from the water trough, which tastes surprisingly good given how greenish the water looks. It's easy to glance at the screen, given that I can see in a 320-degree field of vision right now.

It says the Salt Lake County Metro Jail is calling.

That hardly sounds promising. Why would someone in jail be calling her? She taps the phone and whips it to her ear. "Heaston?"

"It's me," a man's voice says. I can barely hear him, but I *can* make out his words. Their eyesight may be whack, but at least horses have decent hearing.

"I thought you could only call once?"

"The sheriff who runs this place is chill," he says. "But that doesn't mean it's not a recorded line." It almost sounds like he's reminding her. "I wanted to see if you'd had any success asking your parents for money."

Someone from the *jail's* asking her for money? From her *parents?*

It hits me then—Steve and Abigail? Is this their daughter? The one I heard them say wanted to be a vet? It would explain why she was there. Maybe this call will explain why she stole me without telling them about it. Most importantly, maybe I can puzzle out how we're linked, why, and how to terminate it.

"I didn't ask them," she says. "It's a weird thing to ask for."

He's silent.

She squirms. "I'm sorry, but they already don't like you much, and—"

"You know, almost every girl in Utah would be delighted to date me. All the parents I've ever gone home to meet have loved me."

He's implying it's *her* fault they don't like him. I don't really like that.

"I know," the girl says. "I'm so sorry."

"Look, Izzy, I'm going to be vindicated, even if I have to rot in here until the trial, but the longer I'm in here, the more my practice will fall apart. The longer I'm here, the more time my partners have to try and come up with bogus evidence against me and the more time they have to turn my clients against me."

What partners?

"I know," the girl, who's apparently named Izzy, says. "I didn't get money from them, but I did retrieve that gorgeous stallion you told me to bring back." She clears her throat.

He's silent for a moment, and then he chuckles. "Oh. Good."

"The problem," Izzy says, "is that I can't find the papers for it. I can't sell *your* chestnut stallion unless it has papers. Papers that show it's a thoroughbred with a blaze. Papers that someone could use to race it."

Again, he's silent for quite a while.

"Tim?" Izzy asks. "Are you there?"

"I'm just trying to remember where I might have put them." He clears his throat. "Remember about six or eight weeks ago? There was that woman who came in with her chestnut stallion, and we were going to put him down?"

"Right," Izzy says.

"But then I convinced her to sell him to me," he says. "And I took him to your stepdad for some training."

She huffs. "Right."

"I think the old woman left the papers with me along with all her other paperwork when she thought we were going to put him down, but I haven't transferred the horse into my name yet. I was waiting until she'd be less upset to sign the transfer."

"What was her name?" Izzy asks. "I'll need to find her file."

"Right." He inhales and exhales slowly. "Hattie? Maddie? Maybe Harriet something?"

"Alright, well, at least that gives me a start." She chuckles again. "But how can I look through your files?"

He's quiet for a moment. "My password's an important date to you."

"Good to know," she says.

"You know, if you're thinking of selling my stallion, I could do the paperwork myself after I get out. A beautiful thorough-bred stallion like that would be a great fit for Anselm Müller. He has more money than sense, so a recommendation from me for a good stallion would be really appreciated. He even told me that not long ago."

Izzy nods slowly. "If you were out, you'd email him yourself."

"Exactly," Tim says. "I'd email him *myself*."

So clearly, he wants her to fake my papers and sell me to the German man. I'm so caught up in interpreting what they're saying that it takes me a moment to realize the important part of this conversation.

Izzy's planning to *sell* me.

Since I pass out when she moves more than a hundred yards away, that's going to be a real problem.

CHAPTER 5

Izzy

"I'm glad you could call," I say. "I've missed hearing your voice."

"Same," Tim says. "But for now, I need you to keep your eye on the prize. If this horse doesn't sell for much, you could sell your trailer. Your truck. Whatever. I'll buy you a new one once this is all over, and you can use my truck for now."

His truck's worth way more than mine, and I wonder for a moment why he's not telling me to sell that. "I can't sell yours, since it's not in my name," I say, "I guess that makes sense."

"Or, if none of that works, you can ask your parents for tuition money, right? You didn't tell them that you didn't get in to vet school yet, did you?"

That hurts. "No, not yet."

"Good," he says. "They've always been great at sending you money for school, so just tell them you need money for that. Later, after we get engaged, you can tell them you've changed your mind. I'll have paid you back, and you can return the money to them."

"I guess." It does make sense, but it feels. . .I don't know. It makes me feel super icky.

"I have to go," he says. "I'm sorry. I'll try and call again as soon as I can."

"Alright." I can't help feeling deflated when he hangs up, and not only because I can't talk to him anymore. It felt like he only really called to try and push me about getting his bail money. He didn't say he missed me. He didn't say anything nice at all. I do get it. He's probably super stressed, and we're on a recorded line, after all.

At least he gave me an idea for where to get papers and a possible buyer for Drago. . .if I can get him into some kind of suitable form to sell. I startle a bit, realizing that I've been standing in the stallion paddock this whole time, right in front of Drago.

Unlike a usual horse, he's not exploring the perimeter of the paddock or even trotting around the center. He's completely ignored the two horses calling to him on the far end of the space, their faces shoved against the fence. Bizarrely, he's standing right beside me, staring for all the world like he was listening in on my phone conversation, which is nuts. Horses obviously don't do that, especially the ones who were just trying to audition for a spot in the Kentucky Derby while running away from me.

I start to sneak past him, headed for the gate, but he follows me.

"Okay." I stop, holding my hand out toward him, palm out.

He shoves his nose against it. It's surprisingly warm, and very, very soft.

"You're sure sweet for someone who tried to destroy me, cover me with your sand-spray, and disappear forever, in that order." I frown. "Repeatedly."

He whuffles against my hand, almost like he's trying to apologize.

"I certainly appreciate the improved manners." I scratch under his chin.

He inhales slowly and shifts away.

Maybe that's not his spot. I move my hand up, up, up and reach carefully behind his ears. It's a very hit or miss spot, but when it hits. . .

He closes his eyes and stretches his whole neck out, his gigantic head reaching closer and closer until it's nestled up beside my boob. If he weren't a horse, I'd slap him. As it is, I just laugh. "Alright, alright." I step back. "I have to go, now. I have some work to do in the house, on the computer. Before I start, I'll get you the hay I promised. Why don't you check out your new space." I point. "Including the shelter on that end. It's not too cold yet, luckily, but we could get a storm rolling through any day. The weather's pretty unpredictable in Utah."

He bobs his head like he understands.

"You do *not* have a winter coat yet." I rub his cheek. "You're way too glossy. I hope you shag out soon, or even a blanket won't keep you warm."

He snorts.

But this time, when I head for the exit, he stands stock still, staring at me. I can't help waving at him.

He tosses his head.

I've barely left the enclosure when a car pulls up in the driveway. It's not one I recognize, and I know most of Tim's friends. It's a plain, unmarked black sedan, but the two men who climb out are anything but boring. One of them's also massively tall. He has to be over six foot five, because I'm five foot eleven inches, and he looks tall, even to me.

The other man's very, very short. He's also not very heavy, but he looks mean, like the pony in the pasture that you have to keep an eye on. He looks like he'd go for the knees and make it count.

Both of the men are wearing all black, including dark sunglasses. For an overcast day, it's odd. But they also start walking toward me together, and it feels aggressive for some reason I can't pinpoint. Maybe because I'm a girl? Maybe because I don't know them. Maybe because I'm here alone.

I really don't like that they're between me and the house.

"Hey guys," I say. "I'm just headed over to get some hay for our new horse here." I point. "Unfortunately, Mr. Heaston's not here. I'm just helping out with the animals until he comes back."

I'm not sure why I say that, except I don't want them to know any more about me than they do. I duck around the edge of the paddock and practically run to the small barn beside the two pastures. I shoot through the door and grab an armful of hay. Drago may not strictly need three full flakes, especially with as big as these are, but it gives me something to do so that I look busy.

Unfortunately, when I come out, they're still out there.

Watching me.

"Yer Heaston's girl," the short one says. "I seen pictures."

The tall one nods, but he doesn't speak.

"We need you to call him now," the short man says. He has a funny accent, but I can't quite place it. Maybe it's one of the odd New York ones I've only heard on television. "Heaston owes our boss a lot of money, and our boss has downright lost his patience."

My pulse starts to pound hard enough that I can hear it in my ears.

This isn't the time to freak out though. *Focus, Izzy.* "Um, that's too bad."

They're both frowning, now.

I circle around them, giving them a wide berth, but they're still moving toward me, their booted footfalls ominously loud as they crunch across the gravel. I move a little faster, my arms starting to complain about being held directly out. Why did I grab so much hay?

"How about this?" I suggest. "Once I have this horse settled,

I'll call Tim and let him know that you came by. He's out of town, but hopefully he'll be back soon."

I'm almost to the paddock, but they're moving faster. There's only a few feet between us. As I see it, I have two options. I could chuck the hay at them and bolt for the house. My fear's that I won't get in and lock the door before they reach me. Or, I could head another direction. With just a few feet between me and the stallion pasture, I could duck in with the hay and hope they're afraid of horses. With my luck, the idiot stallion'll dart out the gate and trample me before the men even get a chance to hurt me themselves.

But when I glance back at the enclosure, I realize that in my flustered state, I didn't close up the padlock on the gate. I could get in quickly, even with hay.

They seem to have figured out what I'm doing, and they take off at a run.

I hurl the hay at them, hoping to buy myself some time, and duck inside the gate. My hands aren't working right, so when I try to lock the padlock. . .I drop it instead.

A terrible swear word escapes my mouth, not that they care.

The fear I feel as the men follow me into the pasture only grows as they get closer and closer. The little man's holding something in his hand, and as he turns, I realize it's a glistening metal gun of some kind.

My heart's racing now and my hands are trembling. Drago has raced along the fence line beside me, and he's standing still at my side, nostrils flared, breath coming in quick, angry puffs.

"These guys are bad," I hiss. "Go." I shoo my hands at the horse. "Run to the back of the pasture, now."

He stomps one foot and whinnies loudly.

"What's wrong with that horse?" the short one asks, waving his gun at Drago. "He sick?"

I nod shortly. "That's why he's in here. He's sick, yes."

The short man pauses. "Can humans get it?"

"Uh, yes," I say. "They can."

The man frowns.

The tall man mumbles something, but I can't hear what he said.

Drago, almost like he's taking advantage of their distraction, bumps me with his nose. Then he drops one shoulder.

"What are you doing?" I ask. "Run."

I can only see his right eye, but I swear he rolls it. Then he drops his shoulder even farther, as if to say, *Get on, idiot.*

"You want me to get on your back?" I've lost my mind. I'm talking to a horse. . .and expecting him to understand me.

He *nods.*

A horse *nodded* in response to my question.

But our reprieve's gone. The men are coming at us again, and I have a quick decision to make. Slap the horse to get him away, or try climbing on his back in the hope they'll be too afraid to follow me on a sick horse.

What's the bigger threat?

Gun-wielding mobsters, or a maniac horse that already tried to kill me once today? I drag a breath in and swing up, grabbing his withers as best I can.

Egads, he's tall.

It's inelegant as all get out, but I manage to scramble onto his back, and what's more, he doesn't flip out or chuck me off, both of which would be very simple for him to do seeing as I have neither bridle nor saddle to help me stay on. Almost as soon as I gain my balance, Drago starts moving, but instead of running *away* from them, he charges.

I chose wrong. I chose wrong. *I chose WRONG!*

We're racing at the men, but instead of shooting us, they duck out of the enclosure, swearing up a storm. In fact, they're both using words I've never even heard before.

Drago isn't satisfied with their retreat. Apparently he wants them *gone.* He pushes past the edge of the gate and keeps after them. I'm pulling on his mane, "Whoa, whoa, there boy."

"Tell your horse to back off," the short man says. "Or I'll shoot."

Drago doesn't act like he understands English now, though. Not at all. He plows forward, rushing right at the tiny man who threatened to shoot us.

BANG.

The man wasn't kidding. A bullet slams into Drago, and I feel the force of its impact. I expect us to crash to the ground, and I prepare to spring away so I'm not rolled flat like pie crust, but he never actually falls. He doesn't even stumble.

Drago keeps moving forward until he's upon the men, and then he rears back and kicks out at the small man, striking him in his hand and sending the gun flying. The tall man runs away, screaming like a little girl. The smaller man falls to the ground, and he's crab walking backward, but only using one arm. His other arm's curled into his body like it's—

Upon closer inspection, the hand that held the gun looks like a bloody, broken mess. I suppose shooting at a maniacal stallion's risky.

The men reach their car *just* in time to avoid a second trampling.

While the tall man turns the car on and the shorter man scrambles inside, slamming the door and locking it, Drago attacks the front bumper with both hooves, striking it over and over. It's all I can to do hold on, but I swear, he's marvelously vicious when he smashes their hood, shatters both headlights, and knocks the bumper off. Their nondescript black sedan won't be so nondescript the next time I see it. I count at least three distinct hoof-shaped dents as they scream backward down the drive.

Once they're gone, I expect Drago to bolt down the road,

ignoring my presence entirely, but he doesn't. He simply turns his head around, eyes me with one big, dark eye, and blinks.

"You were shot!" I completely forgot about it, thanks to his spectacular attack. I slide off his back, no halter in hand to grab him, no crop to guide him, and a massive pile of hay to our right, blowing every which way in the wind that's picking up. I turn toward him, moving slowly, hoping not to spook him. I can't imagine what I'll tell the vet when I call them—the closest practice is Heaston's. Ugh.

But when Drago lets me approach, simply turning his head to watch me, I can't find a scratch on him.

"You were shot," I whisper. "I *saw* it. I *felt* it." I run my hand across his chest and jugular groove, legitimately shocked. "How can this be?"

He whuffles again, brushing his nose against my hair and blowing.

"I can see that you're fine," I say. "I'm just. . .not sure how."

And then, in a move that's almost stranger, he waits while I gather up all the hay I can, and then he follows me right back into his enclosure and stands patiently while I close the gate.

"Maybe you were hangry before," I say. "I should've put hay in your paddock first." I'm just. . .I'm reaching. But I can't think of anything else to make sense of the last half hour. "Why would *anyone* kill a creature as spectacular as you?"

His snorting sounds almost like laughter.

I pat his neck. "Eat, you amazing beast." I lean against him, scratching the line of skin just underneath his mane. Nearly every horse likes that, and he's no exception, freezing in place other than turning his head slightly to the side and *stretching*.

"You're my hero today, Drago. I mean it."

He finally turns then and eats some hay. He looks almost put out by it, but I can't figure out why he would be. "I'll bring you grain for dinner tonight," I say. "It's the good kind, too. You'll be happier about that."

He snorts.

Probably just clearing his nose.

I'm sure all this interaction is all in my head, but I'm going to pretend it's not. After the day I've had, I deserve it. "Who can blame me for thinking you're brilliant?" I ask. "You did just save my life."

He tosses his head again, and I scratch his shoulder.

"I guess you know how to be ridden, or at least you're okay with someone getting on your back. Maybe it's your stallion instincts. Either way, I feel better about my crazy idea than I have all day, so thanks for that."

Now I just have to go inside and dig through Heaston's files until I find the stuff from that lady with the chestnut stallion. I remember Heaston being pretty upset when he had to put that one down. If he somehow has her papers, it would be a miracle, especially if the markings are even somewhat similar to Drago's.

Then again, when someone as good as Tim Heaston needs help, it makes sense that the stars would align. I'm happy to play my part in it. One day, when we're telling our kids about this, it's going to be quite a story. I look forward to hearing why those men showed up—probably something to do with his partners setting him up. They're going to have a lot to answer for.

CHAPTER 6

Leonid

I hate this Heaston guy.

Even without seeing him, I can tell he's got a dark soul. The odds of two men like that coming after someone good are quite low, but with the way he spoke to her on the phone. . . I don't need my powers to see that he has bad things coming to him. But why can't the girl see it? She seems bright, so how did he dupe her?

I have a lot of things to worry about, most importantly, regaining my powers and ensuring that Kristiana and her brother Gustav can't ever challenge me. With Aleksandr, Grigoriy, and Alexei behind them, killing them's the only sure way to keep myself safe. But before I deal with them, I'm going to eliminate this Heaston guy for fun. He deserves to die, I'm almost positive.

My best bet at regaining my powers and being freed is to cooperate with this girl. She's smart, she's kind, and I'm even more sure she's good than I was before. To figure out what's connecting us, I'll need to spend more time with her, so I've decided to be a 'good boy' for a while. Plus, if she tries to abandon me, I'll pass out again at the very least.

Could I die if she keeps moving away after I pass out? Would she even notice? What if she leaves me in here to go to the store?

I'm not really keen on finding out.

She's planning to 'train' me, so I need to be good enough to keep her interested, but not good enough that she thinks she can sell me yet. For her to really try and work with me, she can't be afraid of me. I hate thinking how far I set back her trust with my ill-advised bolting, but taking that bullet must've helped to restore her faith. Unfortunately, it also absorbed the end of my protection spell. Another hit like that one, and I really will be gushing blood from an open wound.

Until I regain my powers, an injury like that could kill me.

"Alright, boy. You eat and rest. I have some work to do and some emails to send, but I'll be back out in a few hours. I was going to give you today off, but I'm kind of in a hurry. Maybe I'll come back out this afternoon to see what you can do." She smiles softly, and I know it's just for me.

It makes me happy in a way I can't explain, and I hate it. I can't be giddy about some little girl smiling at me. I'm not really a horse, and it's vital that I not forget my purpose here.

After she disappears inside the house, I try to focus on my next steps. I pace back and forth while I review them. First, I need to figure out how I'm connected to Izzy Brooks. Then I need to figure out how to sever that connection. And finally, I need to make sure that once I'm free of her, I can still regain my powers. I should have control of all five elements now, but when I reach for them. . .there's nothing there.

When I try to shift back into my human form, it's the same.

It's so frustrating that I want to kill people. At home, it was easy to round up petty tyrants, murderers, and mob enforcers. Here, though, there's no way to vent my fury. I could shout, but when I scream as a horse, people, namely Izzy Brooks, think I'm unhinged. I drag my hoof through the dirt and realize that I've been pacing back and forth all over the hay Izzy brought.

Why do horses have to eat dead grass dumped on the ground?

Since we're in *Utah*, there's no live grass right now. Everything's brown or gold. It's so disgusting that I'd rather just die than eat it. . .until I involuntarily take a bite and my teeth start working, and suddenly the dry, dirty bits of hay—why don't they rinse it before drying?—are disintegrating in my mouth and it's actually not that bad. How have I never realized how delicious grass could be? I was probably biased by the fact that I walked around on it. It's a little embarrassing when I realize that I've eaten nearly every speck of hay that was piled up, and now I'm using my enormous, floppy lips in conjunction with my air-blowing nostrils to try and sort dirt from hay so I can find just a few more bites.

How pathetic have I become in less than one day?

I force myself to walk away from the hay, and just to kill time, I walk to the other end of my paddock and finally greet the horses who have been watching me this entire time. The mare whinnies and tosses her head, her mane rippling in the breeze. The gelding, clearly much older, paws at the dirt beneath his hooves and shrieks.

I whinny back, but it's not like I have much to say. Within a minute or two, I find myself walking back and snuffling around on the ground for more shreds of hay. It's so undignified. The only things worse are the piles of poo that just sort of *pop* out whenever they feel like it. At least when I finally go pee, I appear to have impressive equipment in this form.

The downside is that, even though I stretched my back legs out as far as I possibly could, I could still feel pee splattering on the front of my back legs and on the back of my front legs. I'm trying to work out a way to wipe it off that doesn't involve my nose when I hear the door to the house open.

It's a little embarrassing how excited I am to see Izzy again.

But at least she can't really tell. After my initial reaction, I drop my head and go back to nosing around in the dirt. Then I start to wonder whether being attentive to this tiny, powerless human or being a dirt-nuzzler is more pathetic. When Izzy disappears into the barn, I know the answer.

I call out for her involuntarily, almost. It's not really my fault. I sensed the bond connecting us easing as she drew near, and then it tightened again as she walked away.

"I'm coming." Her voice is sing-songy in a way I've never noticed with anyone else. "Be right there, Mr. Whiny Pants."

Whiny *pants*? I don't even have pants. What's she saying? Maybe it's an American phrase I simply haven't heard yet. She emerges a moment later, lugging a saddle, a bridle, and a thick, ugly saddle pad.

"I stole you in Manila, Utah." She huffs, clearly winded from carrying such a large saddle. "I'm guessing any training you've had has been Western."

She's cute, but also kind of dumb.

I never understood why humans like those dumb, ugly dogs, but maybe this is like that. I like her *because* she's so dumb. She unlocks the paddock and picks the saddle and gear up again, shoving her way through with it into my enclosure.

"Alright." She sets it down near the fence, and then she approaches me with a halter. "Let's see if you'll let me handle you this time without any evil henchmen nearby trying to beat money out of me."

I shy away twice, just to keep her on her toes.

"Does it take the threat of danger for you to behave?" She frowns. "Maybe I should go pick up—"

I shove my face into the halter and stand still. Can't have her leaving to pick anyone up. I ought to shift and stomp around a little to sell my unease, probably, but her feet look really small. I'd hate to clip one.

Not because I care about her.

Just because a wounded Izzy won't help me get any closer to

discovering how we're connected. She'd probably go to the hospital, and I'd die while she was gone.

"Normally I'd tie you up now."

She's always got a running narrative. It's kind of cute. She must know I can't understand her, in theory, but she's clearly not someone who has trouble rolling with the unexplainable.

"But if you flip out, you might hurt yourself trying to get away, so I'm going to hope you'll stand still and pray I can duck out of the way if you have a crazy moment."

I blow air out of my nose and stomp once.

She looks suitably nervous, but then she picks up the saddle pad and slowly moves it toward me. When I don't react, she places it on my back. After a moment, she smiles.

Again, for some reason, that makes me happy.

So I chuck the saddle pad off and into the dirt.

She throws her hands up into the air. "You know, I used to think I was good at everything." She leans against the fence. "I used to think I was smart—brilliant, really. I got perfect grades in school. Teachers all sang my praises. Once, when I was in first grade, they gave me a test called the CogAt. It's supposed to measure your cognitive abilities." She snorts. "I got a perfect score, and they called my mom to tell her I was one of only two students in the entire country who got a perfect score."

I lower my head a little and turn to the side so I can see her better.

She smiles. "You have no idea what I'm saying, which is why I'm saying all this to you. You'd think I'd be happy to find out I was smart, but it wasn't good, not really. My siblings all got mad about it, for one, and for another, everyone had all these expectations. So if someone else failed a test, oh well. They just didn't study enough or had a bad day. If I failed it was like, 'whoa, Izzy, what's going on? You're not fulfilling your potential.' And my mom would kind of freak out."

She kicks the saddle pad.

"And then if I did well, no one was like, 'nice work, Izzy. You worked so hard.' Because I'm a super genius, and I didn't work for that, so you know, nothing I do really counts." She huffs. "That's why I like breaking horses so much." She holds out her hand.

I press my nose into it.

I'm rewarded with a smile. "All it takes to break a horse right is patience and time. That's it. Horses are a problem I know how to solve. With enough patience, with enough hard work, you can always take a horse and make him something useful. You can take a horse that might be a danger to himself or other humans and make him safe. Only, you're a little different." She tilts her head, and she moves her hand up my face to rub the flat part between my eyes. "You—I'm not breaking you. I'm trying to figure out what you know, and what deficits there are in your education that make you dangerous." She grimaces. "And the hardest part of all is that my stepdad, Steve, he's basically the best trainer I've ever known. He never gets overly emotional. He's hard-working, he's fair, and he's an amazing rider." She sighs. "If he agreed you were a lost cause, then what am I doing?"

Her shoulders slump.

"I should just call my parents and beg them to loan me money. That's the safe thing. But if I tell them what I did—that I stole you? There's no way they'll help. So now I'm stuck. If I die trying to train you, then what will they put on my tombstone? 'Here lies an idiot criminal who also sucks at training horses'?" Her laughter sounds a little. . .off. "They'd be right."

She picks up the saddle, and I jump back.

"No, no, I'm not coming at you with this. Maybe you had a bad experience with a saddle. So let's not work on that for today. You let me on your back just fine last time. Let's see if that was a one-time miracle, or if it's the saddle you don't like." She puts the saddle near the gate, and she grabs the bridle, slinging it over her shoulder. "I'm going to take this halter off. If we aren't saddling, I don't need it." Her hands are steady as she reaches up and lifts the strap and releases the buckle, freeing my face. Then she buckles it instead through a chink in the fence so it just hangs there. "Alright. Now let's see whether you're scared of bridles and bits."

Before she can try to stick that metal bar through my teeth, her phone rings. She rolls her eyes, but she whips it out of her pocket. Her eyes widen. Whoever she thought was calling, it's clearly not them. She shoves it back into her pocket, her face falling.

I bump her hand with my nose. Then I blow air on her pocket.

"If I really was crazy, and I thought you could talk to me and understand what I was saying, I'd assume you were asking me why I'm disappointed." She chuckles. "I was hoping it was Tim." She groans. "Which is silly."

She picks up the bridle and shows it to me, holding it just far enough in front of me that I can see it with both eyes at once, which means I can see its shape and depth as well. Clearly she knows something about how horses see.

"My parents don't like him. My friends don't like him. In fact, they all complained about him so much that I just stopped talking to them about our relationship at all, really." She shakes her head. "It's tiring."

She sidles around the side of me. "I'm going to try and put this on you and see if you'll let me lead you around with it."

I snort, but otherwise I don't move.

She rubs my nose again, and she says, "Okay, here goes. Let's hope no one slammed you in the teeth with a bit, because that just makes this way harder for all of us."

But when she bridles me, I stand utterly still, opening my mouth as the bit comes closer. She slides the leather straps up my face and over my ears, and then she beams. I can only see it from my left side, of course, but it still makes me happy.

"See, you were amazing for that. You're a stunning horse. You're clearly athletic, and you're really smart. You took the bridle like a champ." She sighs. "But no one else sees it."

She frowns.

"It's just like my relationship. Tim's amazing in so many ways. He's handsome, rich, smart, and at the top of his field. He's decisive, and he knows just what he wants. And anything he wants, he just goes and gets. My family and friends dislike me dating him because he's older than me." She scratches behind my ears. "But I'm sure his are just as frustrated that he's dating a loser like me. He's just so far out of my league."

She doesn't realize how great she is—that's her problem. I wonder why, but if I had to guess, I'd place blame somewhere around *Tim*.

"And it's only getting worse." She sighs heavily. "I just found out that I didn't even get into vet school, and he's not only a vet, he's an equine orthopedic surgeon—the best in the state. But he's patient with me, and he never acts like he's too good for me, even though he is."

I'm sick of hearing her talk about this guy like he's a saint. Clearly he's the problem. I toss my head.

"Yes, I'm sure you get it—you're just like that. They didn't understand you either, and that's how you wound up headed for the kill pen."

I stomp my foot, hard. I hate that's she's comparing me to that jerk.

"I'm just as upset as you," she says. "Is that it? You're frustrated?" She has a bemused expression like she's just playing a game.

I shake my head.

"There aren't any flies, you know." She laughs. "I swear, if I didn't know better, I would think you were answering me." She leans against my neck, holding the reins in one hand. "The thing about dating someone who's, like, ten times better than you, is that you always feel like a loser. It's worth it to be with him, but imagine how the moon would feel, dating the sun." She lifts the reins, showing them to me closely. "All the stars keep telling me to dump the sun, but the moon can *tell* the sun is the best thing out there. Can you fault her for wanting to be near its magnificence, even if it makes her light not look so bright?"

But stars are also suns—I've learned that since waking. She's just too close to the situation to see how he intentionally dims her light. I wish I could talk. I'd tell her what she's missing.

Sounds like plenty of other people have already tried, though.

"I should lead you out into the courtyard where I have a mounting block," she says. "But I'm too worried you'll bolt." She glances at the water trough. "I could maybe climb up on that, but I swear, if I ever told anyone this story, they'd think I was certifiable. I absconded with a horse who was going to the kill pen, and then he knocked my saddle over, so I just climbed on him bareback. Easy peasy."

I whuffle her hand.

"You and I don't make sense," she says. "There's no way anyone would understand what I'm about to do, but when I learned to train a horse, it was with liberty. It's a method that's about seeing and interpreting what the horse is telling you. It's about communicating in whatever way works, and I swear, it feels like you understand me. It feels like I can trust you *not* to hurt me." She laughs. "Which is stupid. You're a horse. Your primary directive is to keep yourself safe, and you're scared of everything. Bags. Trash. Wind. Small dogs that couldn't even get their mouth around your ankles." She sighs. "Nevertheless, here we go."

She leads me over to the water trough, and I stand, still as a lamb, while she hoists herself up on the metal rim with one foot, the other floating in the air.

I take one small step closer to her and turn my head to watch.

Her smile's brilliant. "Aren't you a sweet boy." She slides her leg over my back. "And such a lovely top line." She runs her free hand down my back and side.

A shiver runs through my entire body.

I want her to touch me *more*.

Which is crazy. Why should I want her to touch me? It must be something about our connection. That's probably why I feel this way.

"Alright." She pats my neck. "Now let's see what cues you know."

None. I know no cues. I've never been ridden by anyone—at least, not in this form.

When she tightens up on the reins, I become acutely aware of the strip of segmented metal between my teeth. She's not pulling, but it's like I can *feel* her hands right there in my mouth. It's strangely. . .intimate. Someone on my body, telling me what to do with her hands.

When she bumps my side with her feet, I shoot forward. That was almost. . .intuitive. I don't really like anyone telling me what to do—never have, but for some reason, I don't hate this.

"Okay, that's a trot," she says. "Good. But you don't have to shoot off when I ask you to move. You can simply step off." She pulls back, just a hair, on the reins and the bit pivots on my tongue.

I stop.

"Good boy." She pats my neck. "Alright, now let's see if you know how to move over."

A moron would get this one. She presses on my left side with her left foot, so I move away from the pressure, shifting to the right. It takes me a minute to realize that when her foot is forward, she wants the front part of my body to move right, and when her foot shifts back, she wants my butt to move over.

"Good!"

Aaaand, we're right back to me feeling annoyed at how happy I am to have pleased her. For the czar of Russia, I sure am pathetic.

It's all a means to an end, I remind myself.

But I can't think of quite why I need to be good at letting her ride me, except I like to see her smile. So if I'm a little squirrelly, and if I take off at the start a few times, well, I suppose I've always been rebellious at heart. We work for a while on walk, trot, walk, trot, stop. And then, she drags in a breath. "I think it's time to see what you can do at a slightly faster speed."

But she doesn't do anything. She doesn't lean forward. She doesn't bump me. She doesn't click. She sits perfectly still.

I swivel my head to the side and eye her.

"I know." She sighs. "Is it bad that I'm nervous to ask you to canter bareback?" Her hands tighten on the reins. "If you can't be saddled, maybe I should call it a day."

I whinny—I wish there was a better way to tell her that I won't be crazy, but after my bolting and dashing. . .

"My sister Whitney would be making fun of me right now." She leans down low over my neck, dropping to a whisper. "She's the fearless one. She's the one who does crazy things all the time. I'm the one who plays things safe. I'm the responsible older sister. I don't do insane things, like steal horses and lie." She stiffens. "Except, this time, I did." She sits up, and she gathers the reins again, and she slides her left leg back just a hair. Then she squeezes with her right leg, bumps me with her left, and kisses at the same time.

"Let's see what you know."

I don't really know what she's asking, other than more speed, so I take off at a run. She tugs back on the reins just a little, so I slow to a jog.

"Whoooo," she says as I slow up. "That was a little scary. You sure can move, though." Once I realize what she's asking, I maintain the speed, jogging along in big looping circles.

She starts and stops me a few times.

"You don't seem to know your leads, but that's hardly surprising. It feels like you were meant for speed, and they don't bother with leads much on the track." She exhales. "Which is good, I guess. But. . .I wonder what you'll do if I ask you to really go."

She bites her lips, and her eyes squint up. "This paddock isn't enormous," she says. "But it's pretty big." She walks me slowly to one end. "Let's see how fast you move when I ask you to really go."

I barely wait for her to ask—for some reason I want to impress her.

She crouches low over my neck, her body moving with mine, her hands staying impressively steady. We race from one end of the pasture to the next, faster with each run, as I figure out how quickly I can stop and as she becomes more comfortable with my movement and being bareback.

When she finally stops, I notice something odd. Her leg seems to be *shaking*. She digs around and pulls out her phone.

Of course. Maybe being a horse has damaged my brain.

"Ugh, it's that same number. They called six times while I was working you." She groans. "I guess I'd better see what's going on." She cringes. "But what if it's Steve's client?" Her hand trembles for a moment, and then she swipes to answer. "Hello?"

Again, I can barely hear the voice on the other end of the line. "Is this Isabel Brooks?"

"Uh, yes." Her free hand tightens on the reins. "That's me."

"Your boyfriend, Tim Heaston, told me to call you. I guess he's out of town." The man has a German accent.

"Yes." She clears her throat. "You must be Mr. Müller."

"I am," he says. "Tim said to email you about a horse you're working with, but I thought calling would be faster."

"Oh, well, sure. Good." Izzy relaxes a little, clearly pleased it's not someone calling to yell about me being here. "I'm actually out with him now, but maybe I can call you back later."

"Actually, I was able to pull up the feed from Tim's paddock cam, so I've been watching you ride."

"His—what?"

"A few months back, I had one of my horses at Tim's for a week. He gave me the website address to watch his paddock cam, so I could check in on my rehabbing stallion."

"Oh." Izzy sounds confused. "I didn't even know he had one."

"Well, he told me that he wasn't sure how talented this horse was yet, and he wasn't sure how broke he was either, but I think both are clear from the video footage I just saw, and I don't want him to reach out to anyone else."

"About—you're saying. . .I'm sorry. What are you calling me about? Tim said people would call me with questions."

"I want to come buy that stallion you're riding, Miss Brooks, before someone else snatches him up. I can bring the money in cash tomorrow."

Izzy drops her phone.

I think about stepping on it, but I'm not sure that will solve our problem. Mr. Müller sounds pretty determined, and if he shows up tomorrow with a fistful of cash and Izzy hands me over, I'm going to pass out before I can kill her criminal boyfriend or anyone else.

I might even die.

This is very, very bad.

CHAPTER 7

Izzy

All I've wanted for days now is to come up with the money Tim needs. I've called friends, I've gone to the bank. I called credit cards to see how much I could get as a cash advance. It turns out, when your job as a vet tech barely pays above minimum wage, and you've just graduated from college, you aren't worth much. In fact, I've never felt more worthless in my entire life. Yesterday, it prompted me to do something very, very stupid.

I stole a horse.

A horse I knew nothing about.

It got worse when I pulled papers from a *dead* horse to pass off as the stolen horse's from my boyfriend's files, and then I emailed the German businessman about him from Tim's account. I mean, Tim basically told me to do all that, but I'm the one who did it. I'm lucky the stallion didn't kill me when I unloaded him in a strange place, when I climbed up on his back without a saddle, and when I asked him to really move.

But what's really lucky is that the German guy—Müller— happened to see us and wants to buy him. Actually, he wants to do more than *buy* him. He wants to pay a hundred grand for him, which is just insane to me.

I know a lot of the horses Tim treats are worth far more than that. I've helped him with quarter-of-a-million-dollar, and even half-million-dollar horses. He's regularly called in to consult on horses with insurance policies that get close to a million. It's the reason he can charge what he charges for his services. People with five-thousand-dollar horses don't pay twenty or forty thousand dollars for surgeries. Not the sane ones.

So of course he'd know people like Anselm Müller.

People just like him probably make up most of his book of business.

I vaguely recall meeting this particular man at some point, about five or six months ago. He's short, he has bushy eyebrows, and he's in banking. But the thing I remember most was that his brother, who has even more money than him, got into horses years before he did. Anselm's desperate to beat him and beating him with a stallion that could sire a whole winning line would be even better.

I'm sure that's why Tim suggested him.

I shouldn't feel guilty about selling this horse to Müller. He probably takes great care of his horses, and clearly Drago's both sound and can really run. He's also such a common color—chestnut—that even with his shocking height and sleek, muscular build, I doubt anyone could ever come back on me. I even scanned him for a chip, just to make sure they can't prove he isn't who I'm saying he is. Blessedly, he didn't have one. Thankfully, neither did the dead horse.

I do worry that he won't be quite as amicable with a new owner as he has been with me, but that's probably my own ego talking.

The papers Harriet Parsons left for the horse that Tim medically eliminated list the horse as an eight-year-old chestnut stallion with a blaze. The markings are almost perfect—right down to no socks of any kind, but there are probably lots of chestnut stallions with blazes. The concerning part's going to be the age. Not many thoroughbreds start their racing career at eight. In fact, I haven't ever heard of any. But every horse born the year *after* this dead one was born had to be chipped or they couldn't be registered.

At least the papered name's pretty cute. Catchup if you Can. Thoroughbred names are often kind of goofy, thanks to all their rules and the fact that you can't have living horses with the same name, but that one. . .for some reason it makes me think of french fries, but then it's spelled wrong for the delicious kind of ketchup. In any case, when I finally walk out to feed Drago breakfast, I feel uneasy.

It's probably because of all my criminal activity in the last two days.

Or I could be nervous that Drago will act like a lunatic.

I keep hoping Tim will call—I have so much to talk to him about and so much to ask him. It's not like I can talk about the shady guys who came by looking for him on a recorded line, but I could beat around the bush about my concerns with selling the stallion. I could also maybe get some guidance about negotiating with Müller. That's not illegal—selling a horse. In the email I sent pretending to be Tim, I said we wanted a hundred grand, but I didn't elaborate.

Müller didn't *say* he was going to haggle.

But don't most people do it when they show up?

And what if, when we try to trailer Drago, the idiot horse bolts again?

All these things are running through my head as I dump grain for Chromey and Millie and walk toward the stallion pen to feed Drago. "Morning." I yawn. "Looks like you're already awake. I hope you got your beauty sleep, though. You need to look pretty for today."

He tosses his head, his mane flowing like a bronze waterfall.

He probably doesn't even need beauty sleep. He's so fabulous he could stay up all night and still look great.

When I dump the grain in his bucket, he drops his nose into it and sniffs around, the air puffs from his nostrils blowing a tiny cloud of dust and detritus up and into my face.

"Whoa, there," I say. "You're making a mess."

When he lifts his head, I swear he's glaring at me.

"What? You think I should have cleaned your bucket before dumping your grain?" I lean closer and set the grain scoops on the ground. "News flash. No matter how pretty you are, you're still a horse. This isn't the Taj Mahal."

Though if we sell him for a hundred grand today, maybe he should be headed there. And as I look around, I can't help noticing the massive piles of poop all over—I should try and clean this up a little if people are coming to look at a horse worth a hundred grand.

"You're pretty fancy for a horse." I lean against the fence and fold my arms. "Today, I really need you to look your best. I can't have you ruining this chance for me. It's the whole reason I saved you."

I spend the next thirty minutes with a muck tub, gathering up all the poop in the pasture I can easily reach, and then hauling it out of the field. By then, Chromey and Millie are screaming for their hay, and I'm not sure what time the buyers are coming to look at him. I decide to drop the muck tub in the back of Tim's truck and deal with it later.

Drago watches the whole thing, seemingly a little confused. Maybe they had a poop spreader at his last barn. While I'm heaving the muck tub into the back of Tim's truck, he snorts, spins around, and races to the corner of the paddock—the low spot—the only place that isn't pristine.

And then he rolls.

When he walks back, a blob of mud dangling from his forelock, I swear, he's smirking at me.

"I hate you," I say. "You just had to do that, right as I finished cleaning all the poop—you decide to look like manure yourself. Is that it?" I glance back at my horses in the farther pasture. "Do you see Chromey over there?" I scowl at Drago again, as if he might actually care. "I'm going to give him more hay and more scratches because he keeps himself clean."

He whuffles. . .just like a human might laugh.

"I do need to sell you," I mutter. "But even if I didn't, I'd want to do it. You're turning me into a crazy person, thinking you can understand what I'm saying."

He tosses his head, his nose moving up and down rapidly, mud *sliding* slowly down his face.

"Yep. I'm crazy. You're right about that."

One glance at his bucket shows me he never ate his breakfast. It's been twenty or thirty minutes already. I worry that he's not eating because of a tummy ache. Combined with the rolling I thought he was doing to be irritating, it could be a really bad sign. Skipping food and rolling for horses usually means colic. After I stare at him for a long moment, he finally drops his head into the bucket and starts eating the feed. He's messy, and it spills all over the ground, but I gave him enough that he can waste a little.

"Good boy," I say. "I'll bring some hay out in a bit."

Thanks to the time I spent on pasture cleanup, Millie and Chromey are already pacing, waiting for theirs. I always feed alfalfa in the morning along with the orchard grass, so it takes me a while to get it all distributed, but I finally finish with theirs. When I reach the stallion paddock with my arms full of Drago's hay, he's waiting by the gate.

For a brief moment, I worry he's going to try and push past me, bolt, and disappear. He doesn't, thankfully. He's as polite as he has been the last few times I've gone in, following me slowly to the far end where there's a metal hay bin. "If you're not messy, you won't have any dirt mixed with your hay. Be a smart boy, alright?"

He's glaring at me when I walk toward the house, I just know it.

I'm not sure why, though.

I gave him all the things horses love, but he was definitely still irritated about something. He's barely circled back to the hay bin to munch on his hay when a large, red truck pulls up, dragging a very nice, very shiny Logan Coach trailer. I should've guessed—they're based out of Utah. It's pretty much the king of trailers around here. Their trailer makes the one I borrowed from Steve, a very nice Lakota, look like a bargain basement hauler.

When they stop, Drago lifts his head from his hay and starts to prance back and forth along the fence line, his tail flying out behind him. I didn't even have time to clean him up, so he's still covered in mud, and he looks agitated at best. At least he's moving with beauty and grace, even if he looks pretty homeless.

Unsurprisingly, Müller's not alone. A tall man with a strong jaw climbs out of the driver's seat.

"Isabel." Müller waves. "This is my trainer, Josh Averett. He's as excited as I am." Müller's so excited that he's practically bouncing. He reminds me a little of the shaky, wiry little dogs that wet on the floor when their owner comes home.

Averett does *not* look excited. He looks wary. He tosses his head at me in acknowledgement, but says nothing.

"Look at him." Müller's already moving toward the stallion pen. "Isn't he spectacular?"

Averett scowls, and I wonder whether he's the one who will be doing the negotiating. A quick google search taught me that the first rule to successfully negotiating a good price is not to act too excited. Good luck doing that, Averett. Your boss is peeing all over the linoleum already.

"It's a small setup," I say. "So yes, you've already identified

Drago." I cross toward the gate. "He's not done with breakfast, but you can see that he moves quite well."

"What's his deal?" Averett narrows his eyes. "Why did Tim decide to buy him? And why does he think he'll do well on the track?"

I'm not sure what to say. Mr. Müller hadn't asked about any of that, and I stupidly didn't even come up with a story. To my knowledge, Tim's never bought a horse. I cast about for any possible reason Tim might have bought him, and I can't really think of anything.

"I'm assuming he bought him from a client who couldn't handle him," Müller says. "Or maybe he saw him while treating another horse and fell in love?"

I shake my head. "That's sort of true," I say, improvising badly. "He did buy him from a client, and he was actually slated to be put down. I fell in love with him the moment I saw him, and I thought I could handle him even when the older woman he bought him from couldn't." I cringe a little. "I know that sounds terrible, but it's true."

"Why are you selling him, then?" Averett narrows his eyes. "Why not keep him?"

"I need money for vet school," I say. "And he turned out to be a nicer horse than we expected. It seemed silly for me to use him on skijoring." I shrug.

"On what?" Averett's frowning.

"You've never heard of skijoring?" I ask. "It's racing horses, but pulling a skier behind you. We go over jumps, through obstacles, and—"

"Oh, no," Müller says. "You can't waste a magnificent creature like this on that."

"We do mostly use quarter horses," I say.

"Plenty of horses are put down that shouldn't be, so that doesn't upset me," Averett says. "The terrible part is asking a hundred grand for one of those damaged but still salvageable horses." He's glaring, now.

"It's not that we're questioning the value, mind you," Müller says. "It's just that—"

"My job's to make sure my client's enthusiasm and optimism don't overwhelm his pocketbook." Averett points. "I'm assuming you'll breeze him for us?"

"If you don't want him, Tim will email others who might. And if no one does for that price, I'll just keep him for myself." Number two rule of negotiating, according to Google, is never to act like you *need* them. Always have something else on the back burner. "As to breezing him, I don't exactly have a track handy, but—"

"Right here's fine." Averett points at the long strip that runs the length of the property, from the edge of the driveway to the road that abuts the end of the paddock area. "I'm sure we can get a good feel for how he moves and how much speed he can handle."

"Uh, sure," I say. "I don't have a racing saddle, but I could—"

Averett's looking pretty smug when he cuts me off. "Anselm tells me you were on him bareback yesterday. Sadly, the feed's a livestream, so I couldn't verify how he looked myself."

"Sure," I say. "Of course. Just let me grab the bridle." And a curry comb and a brush or ten.

This time, I also lug a mounting block out to the ground outside the paddock. I can't count on Drago to align himself with a water trough every time I want to get on. Most of the mud has at least dried, and thankfully, he allows me to halter him, curry, and brush him off so he's not nearly as ragamuffin-looking. My heart rate slows to a less terrifying pace when he lets me bridle him. Once I'm on his back, it'll be harder for him to race off—at least I should be able to turn him.

Unless he chucks me off.

When I lead him out of the gate, he throws his head up, ears swiveling, and my heart takes off at a dead sprint again. I keep seeing the image of him bolting away. Two different directions, even. "Okay, boy," I whisper. "Please, *please*, don't kill me, and don't run off and make me look terrible."

He lets me lead him to the mounting block, and he stands stock still while I hop up and swing my leg over his back, shimmying my way into place.

"Tim needs a taller mounting block for horses like you," I mutter. "You have to be almost eighteen hands."

"What's that?" Averett asks.

I shake my head. "Nothing, but I better warm him up a little." Why didn't I think to use that for an excuse to do all this inside the paddock? Idiot.

Miraculously, he walks for me just fine, and even when we get close to the edge of the property, he makes no attempt to run. As we circle back around near the men, I ask him to trot, and he does. It's as springy and hard to sit as it was yesterday, so I don't keep him trotting for more than three laps before I ask him to canter.

It's not very good to cut his warm-up short, probably, but he's been out all night, at least. I doubt his muscles were entirely stiff with all the pacing he was doing earlier. When I ask him to canter, he seems to remember what we worked on yesterday— namely, not bolting.

"He looks like a show pony," Averett says. "What did you say he was used for?"

"Nothing wrong with racehorses having manners," I say. "Not enough of them do."

"Yes, but he's already eight years old," Averett says. "I don't want to depress you, Anselm, but I think he's too old. He looks stiff to me."

"I told you I mostly wanted him for breeding. I want to shake things up—try something new. A bloodline that hasn't been overbred but shows promise. That's what Gunther did. Besides, he didn't look stiff yesterday," Müller says. "Have her gallop him, and then decide." He's smiling at me broadly.

I swing him around, and I bring him to the edge of the property, near where I pulled the trailer in yesterday. When I ask Drago to go, he picks up some speed, but not much. Compared to yesterday, he's practically crawling.

"That's it?" Averett sounds disgusted.

Part of me's actually relieved. Now that we've come down to it, I don't really want to sell him. I mean, I'm probably just nervous about selling a horse I don't own. The illegality of it all has me concerned, I'm sure, but I should be panicked that he's disinterested.

I need that money. Tim needs that money.

If I don't sell him, where does that leave us?

My only other play is calling my parents, but if I don't sell him, how will I explain Drago to them? I can imagine just what I'll say. "Oh, yep. You *do* recognize this horse?" I would laugh. "Funny story. Oliver told me he was going to be put down, so. . ." I could throw my hands up in the air and pretend I thought it was a big joke.

I doubt I'd get much laughter.

Ugh.

I'm hauling on Drago's reins and turning him around when a car on the road behind us backfires. The noise is so loud and so unexpected that both Drago and I spook.

He takes off like a devil's on our tail.

We *fly* past the two men so fast that I can barely see Averett's face at all, but it's enough. His jaw's dangling wide open.

When I slow Drago down, he scans the area carefully, probably shocked that we aren't under attack again. I can't blame him. Those two guys from yesterday had guns, and that backfire sounded almost the same. It was also right behind us, which had to be confusing, too. If it motivated him to bolt right when I needed it, well, maybe God's on my side. That would be nice.

"You're right," Averett's telling Müller. "He can really move."

Müller's back to hopping up and down like some kind of strange cartoon villain. If he had a mustache to twirl and didn't smile so much, the similarities would be uncanny. "Yes, yes, so you're on board?" He tilts his head.

"Fine," Averett says. "I wish Tim was here himself, but if you're worried someone else will snatch him up, I can't fault you. He's got something special. I'll admit that much."

But as I hear the words, I realize something.

It wasn't just simple relief when I thought they didn't want him. I don't *want* to sell Drago. I really, really like him.

Which is stupid.

I know nothing about him.

I can't possibly keep him without telling my parents what I've done, and I *cannot* tell them this.

And the biggest problem is that selling Drago was my solution to a major issue. I have to get Tim out, and fast, and I have no other way to come up with this kind of money. I have absolutely no business saying what I'm about to say, and yet, I find myself saying the words anyway. "Oh, shoot." I whip out my phone. "I'm so sorry, but I just got a message from Tim."

"You did?" Müller sounds as confused as Averett looks.

"Yep," I say. "He said we can't sell him after all. Problem with—" I cough. "—the paperwork. It's a long story."

"How did you even know you got a message? You said that before you got your phone out." Averett's scowling.

"Uh, it came to my watch." I gesture at my plain black watch that's not smart in any way. Hopefully they can't tell. "I'm *so* sorry to have wasted your time today."

"Not at all." Mr. Müller takes a step closer and holds his hand out toward Drago. "If anything changes, anything at all, call me. I'll come right back." He looks up at me then, and I almost feel bad. He looks like he'd have loved Drago almost as much as I do.

Wait, do I *love* him? A horse I just met? A horse I *stole?*

As Averett stomps over to the truck and Anselm Müller walks over, turning back and gazing at us wistfully, I realize that I do.

I pat his neck. "I am such an idiot. You know that?"

He turns around and rubs his cheek against my boot, like he knows I just decided not to sell him.

"I needed that money," I hiss. "I needed it, and my boyfriend *really* needed it, and I should have sold you. I could have sold a horse that was supposed to die for *a hundred grand* and I said no." I smack my forehead. "A hundred grand." I exhale. "I must have lost my ever-loving mind."

Drago just whinnies.

"How am I going to get that money now?" I wail.

But as I slide off his back, I have an idea. Now that we have fake papers we can use, if I pay for the expedited transfer on his paperwork, maybe I could race him myself and keep the prize money. I put him back in his paddock, and I lock the gate.

"I have some work to do," I say. "We have some races to win, Catchup if you Can."

He looks very, very confused as I walk away.

Which, he should. He is, after all, a horse. And his new—illegal—owner is a grade A moron. Let's hope I can find some other way to get Tim out, or my parents won't even be the first ones in line to kill me for this.

CHAPTER 8
Izzy

<u>Isabel Brooks' Assets:</u>

2018 Ford F-250

Quarter horse mare, Millie. Papered. 11 years.

Quarter horse gelding, Chromey. Papered. 19 years.

A lot of pretty saddle pads. (Too many, but I'll never admit it.)

Three saddles; two western, one English.

Six bridles. Various conditions.

Kingsley riding boots.

Some jewelry from Mom.

Lucchese boots from Aunt Helen (2 pair).

Various used clothing.

A Tiffany's necklace Mom and Dad gave me when I turned 12.

Used furniture: bed, nightstand, chest of drawers, table, four chairs, sofa, armchair, coffee table.

* * *

As I stare at my meager list of belongings, I'm not sure I could find a buyer for any of it, and even if I did, there's no way I'll get to anywhere near a hundred grand. Plus, I'd die before I'd sell Millie or Chromey. Does that mean I'm not devoted to Tim? Does not selling Drago mean that same thing? I mean, I barely know the new horse, so why was I so emotional about it? I still feel a little sick about sending Müller away, but I felt worse about selling him that beautiful, quirky, misunderstood stallion.

Why did the judge set Tim's bail *so* high? It's so unfair, especially since they froze all his assets.

I wonder whether I might be able to sell his trailer or truck and just tell the buyer we'll sign the paperwork later. I doubt anyone who wasn't shady would agree to something like that. Which reminds me of the men who came over looking for money. Could they be somehow related to his partners who are screwing him over? Maybe they lied and told the guys *Tim* owed them money in their place.

The only way I can think to possibly earn a hundred thousand dollars in a quick timeframe is totally insane. I know there are a lot of horse races in California, which isn't *that* far away. I've never even raced a horse—I'm no jockey. Aaaand, I'm five foot eleven and a hundred and forty-six pounds. Hardly jockey material.

Maybe I could find someone else to ride him.

Not that it solves my documentation problem. I have papers for another horse, a dead thoroughbred stallion, that maybe I can get an expedited transfer on so he's in my name? But then I'm back to forging signatures from a woman whose horse really *is* dead. Plus, I'm going to have to do some digging to discover if there even *are* any horseraces with big purses this weekend.

The night before, I sent an email from Tim through my phone to the Müller guy. I know his login for work so I can help with paperwork from time to time. But now, if I want to look all this stuff up, I need to do it on a computer. Pecking at the keys on my phone's too slow. I try to login to Tim's computer—what did he say about his password? It's a date that's important to him? I try the date we met—nope. The day of our first date. Again, no. Our anniversary. Nope. I try various configurations of those dates, with and without the year. Still no dice.

Finally, I try his birthday.

That works.

His password is. . .his birthday? Really? It's so obvious. But at least I'm in. My fingers fly over the keys. Within two minutes, I discover the Breeder's Cup is this weekend! It would be nuts, but. . .oh, snap. I can't even enter. It's invite only. The Breeder's Cup Festival week has quite a few races I *could* enter.

Which means I need to see how quickly I can transfer ownership, so I'm clacking away and then poking around on the Jockey Club website. It looks like, with expedited processing. . .I'm peering at the screen, trying to figure out what I might be able to do, when an email notification pops up for Tim's outlook.

I glance at it, barely paying attention until I notice my own name. The subject line says Izzy's Recommendation. And it's from Doctor Hartfield. She's the vet I've been working with almost five days a week for two years, now. My fingers are trembling a little as I click on the email. It's not to me, but it's *about* me.

I think I'm entitled to read it.

I can't think of a single reason she'd need to email Tim about me. When the email opens, I can barely breathe.

* * *

Tim:

* * *

I still can't fathom what circumstance precipitated your request, and I hate that I honored it. Izzy Brooks has been nothing but a phenomenal vet tech, and her help has been absolutely pivotal on several cases. She always goes above and beyond. She cares about what's best for the horse, and she approaches clients with care and consideration. I feel that people like her, who truly love the animals, are the very best candidates for vet school.

No one I've met would make a finer veterinarian than Isabel Brooks.

I'm ashamed that I wrote her such an ugly letter when she asked me to recommend her. All I can say is that I trusted you and your judgment. Now, knowing that you've stolen from all of us, knowing what kind of debt you've gotten yourself into thanks to your personal proclivities, I'm sickened. How could I have been such a bad judge of character? How could I have let you convince me that I was helping the world by keeping her out of vet school? I didn't agree when you told me she had bad judgment but I thought her boyfriend—of all people—would know. I thought, based on what you said, that she must be an alcoholic or something, and you just didn't want to say it explicitly.

There's nothing I can do now. My recommendation was already submitted, and I'm sure the vet schools are making their decisions even now. But I hope, for her sake, that USU has more discernment than I had. And I hope you know that I won't be helping you out ever again. I hope Mark, Greg, and Julie roast your carcass on a spit before this is all said and done.

* * *

Becca

* * *

Holy guacamole.

I stare at the screen in disbelief. Could she have lost her mind? Could she. . .Tim couldn't possibly have asked her to give me a bad recommendation, right? It can't be his fault I wasn't accepted.

It can't.

He's my boyfriend.

He's been helping me for years.

But why would she send that email if he hadn't done as she said? She sent it to *him*, not to me. It's. . .

It occurs to me then that the title of the message is '*Re*: Recommendation.' She was replying to something Tim sent. My stomach flips as I click on the expand button to read his original email. I force myself to focus on the words from my boyfriend himself.

* * *

Rebecca,

* * *

We've been colleagues a very long time. I hope you'll understand that my message comes from a good place, both for you and for Izzy. I know she asked you to write her a recommendation letter. I'm counting on you to help me out with something very important.

She's not ready to be a vet. She may never be ready. She has some personal things that would make it impossible for her to even attend school, much less excel, and I'm worried that if she gets in. . .it will be catastrophic all around. Trust me on that. The best place for Isabel Brooks right now is precisely where she already is.

I'm more grateful than you know to have people I can trust around me, people I know will help both me and Izzy navigate these difficult circumstances in a way that will keep her safe and happy.

* * *

Tim

* * *

His signature block reminds me, with all the initials and letters behind it, how qualified he is to make a determination about my fitness to be a vet. Even if Becca's mad at him for all the things his partners did to frame him, no one should be better at gauging my potential success as a vet than Tim.

It hurts, reading that he thinks it would be 'bad all around' for me to follow my dream. Did he just think I was an idiot the whole time I talked about it? When I doodled little signs that said Dr. and Mrs. Dr. Tim Heaston, was he laughing? Is that why he marked out the second doctor and just left *Mrs.*?

But then Becca's words come back to me.

No one I've met would make a finer veterinarian than Isabel Brooks.

Who's right?

I suddenly *need* to know why Tim thinks I'd be a bad vet. I know he'll be furious the sale fell through—that I don't have his bail yet—and I know it's going to be awful facing him about that, but I'm too upset about the email. I have to know why he sent it to Becca.

Without even seeing him yet, I can guess how he'll react when I ask.

"Are you kidding, Izzy? I'm in *jail*, and you storm in here, not to see me and support me, not with bail money to get me out so I can defend myself, but to yell at me? To ask me about *your* inadequacies? Well, I don't have time to deal with your stuff right now. I'm up to my eyeballs in *my* stuff. And mine is a way bigger deal. Mine is my whole career—you don't even have a career."

As I think about what I'm sure he'll say, I start to wonder. . .

If someone said that to Whitney, if they said it to my mother, I would be livid. I'd never let them tell my sister she didn't have a career, even if it was true. Why would I put up with it for myself, even if it is all true?

And now I'm convicting him before I've even confronted him.

I tear the page of my assets off the notepad and throw it in the trash, and I make a new list.

<u>Questions for Tim:</u>

1. Why did you tell Dr. Hartfield that I'd be a bad vet? Why do you think that?

2. Why are bad men coming to your house and threatening me—*shooting* at me?

3. Why are your partners accusing you of things, and why does everyone believe them? What's really going on?

I freeze then, my pen poised over the notepad. Am I questioning his innocence? Am I worried that maybe, just *maybe*, the man who has thugs coming to his house with guns, the man who told my boss to dis-recommend me. . .might be the bad guy after all?

Because if he is, how stupid does that make me?

The only way for me to find out is to confront him. I know him well enough to tell whether he's lying, or at least, I hope I do. I grab my jacket off the hook by the door, and I throw my purse over my shoulder. I have no idea whether the jail allows visitors, but I'm about to find out. I hope they let me in, and I hope they record our meeting, because if he really did screw not only me, but all his partners, I'm done trying to help him.

In the doorway, I pause.

I should call my best friend Paige. She's never liked Tim, though, so I already know what she'll say. She'll jump on the email and the nefarious men, and she'll call for his head. Until I'm sure, until I'm absolutely positive that I've been wrong about him, I should keep this quiet. He's in a delicate position, and if there's any chance I'm wrong about this stuff, I shouldn't make things worse. Mom and Paige could never forgive all this stuff—the charges and the men and the email.

I have to decide what I think before I tell them about any of it.

I'm almost to my truck when Drago spots me. When he sees me open the door, purse in hand, he loses his mind. He's bucking, he's screaming, and he's kicking the side of the fence. I'm worried he'll destroy it or himself in the state he's in. He looks almost exactly the same as he did that first morning, before I ever tried to halter him.

He looks insane.

I glance at my watch. It's not even eleven in the morning. I have plenty of time, even if the jail officially 'closes' at five. I sling my purse into the cab, and I jog across the two dozen yards between me and the nutso stallion. "Drago," I say. "Calm down, idiot."

He drops to all four hooves, which is an improvement, and he snorts, pawing at the ground.

"I have a quick errand," I say. "I have to leave for a little bit, but I'll be back." Yes, I'm now talking to a horse like I think he understands me. I'm not sure when I accepted it, but here we are.

He tosses his head, and he screeches.

"I know you're worried." Actually, I do feel like he is, and I'm not sure why. I reach my hand through the fence. "You couldn't see me before, when I was in the house." I tilt my head. "Did you know I was in there? Could you see me through the windows?" I squint at Tim's house, not sure how he possibly could.

He sidles closer to the fence, leaning against my hand.

I scratch his shoulder, and he stretches his head out. Then he tosses his head at the gate and throws his nose up in the air repeatedly.

"I can't come in to see you right now. I'm sorry, but I have to run an errand, no horses allowed."

And he's screaming again.

I yank my hand back, worried he might bite me.

He stomps, pawing at the ground, churning up aggressive furrows of earth, then he rears back and slams his big front hooves into the ground again. When he tosses his head, his nostrils are flared and his eyes rolling.

I can't help my laugh. "These tantrums aren't very attractive on such a handsome guy." I tentatively reach my hand through again. "And you may not have learned this yet, but in our world, horses always have to wait around for the humans to finish their stuff." I drop my voice to a whisper. "You guys think you run things, but you don't. And sadly, when I decided to keep you, it cost me a lot of money. Then when I went inside, today got even worse." Any human would judge me for being melodramatic, but a horse can't do that. I drop my forehead against the fence. "It's actually been a very, *very* bad day for this human." I can't help my frown. "And now I have to go somewhere they only allow humans to talk to the other human I'm mad at."

He steps toward me, head bowed, seemingly calmer. I press my hand against the flat front of his face. He sighs. It's so cute, it actually makes me smile.

"I wish I could take you with me," I say. "I wish you were a man, just for the afternoon. Then you could come—and I'd be happy for the backup, believe me."

A jolt of what feels like electricity shoots up my arm and

knocks me back on my rear end in the dirt. When I finally regain my bearings enough to sit up, Drago's *gone*.

There's a painfully beautiful man standing where he was.

A very dirty, very *naked* man.

I really should not be looking, but underneath the dirt, and the smug smile, he has a *glorious* human body.

CHAPTER 9

Leonid

Utah weather in the fall is nothing compared to a Russian winter.

In fact, in the time I've been here, I haven't even needed a jacket. The temperatures have dropped quite a bit in the last few days, and still, I'm fine. In fact, as a horse, I've been quite comfortable. When the weather becomes colder overnight, my fur fluffs up and I stay comfortable enough to have no cause for complaint.

I have a newfound appreciation for the ingenious design of a horse's coat. Because right now, now that I'm naked, I'm completely *freezing*, and I feel far, far too exposed.

Not that I'd ever show it.

"Isabel Brooks." I shake my head. "Finally I'm able to speak."

Her lovely blue eyes widen even further. "You—you can speak?" She shakes her head and stands, averting her eyes. "Of course you can speak. You aren't really a horse who just turned into a naked man. Who *are* you, and what happened to Drago?"

"I *am* Drago," I say. "Or rather, you called me Drago when I was in my horse form, but I'm actually Leonid Ivanovich, Czar of Russia, currently visiting America for the first time."

She coughs and turns toward me, her eyes meeting mine and then dropping downward. Her entire face flushes bright red again.

I can't help my smile.

She's not a child, and yet she's so innocent about everything.

"Now that I'm in my human form, if you would be willing to loan me some clothing, I can accompany you on your errand as you wished."

"As I. . ." Her jaw drops. "If I loan you some—" She nods vigorously. "Yes. Clothing. You obviously need clothing. Wait here."

I spread my arms. "I can't go anywhere else. You've locked me into a pasture, have you not?"

She gulps. "I mean, you were a *horse*. That's what people do with horses."

"We do the same in Russia, yes." I'm smiling again. "I'm not angry for the way you treated me, given what you knew, but clothing would be most appreciated."

She nods and sprints away, stopping about halfway to the house. She turns around slowly and then looks out toward the road. "I—I can't just leave you out here." She swallows. "Not *naked* like that." She points down, at the parts she's trying not to look directly at.

I can't help my smile again. "I doubt I'd be harmed by a small wait, but I'd be just as happy to follow you inside." I bite my lower lip. "I promise not to *bite*."

She blinks, nods slowly, and then jogs over to the gate. She keeps her eyes intently focused on the lock until it's open, and then she's careful to look at the ground as we walk back toward the house. "You must be really cold."

"I could do with a hot shower, if you have time to allow for it."

She opens the front door by entering the number 0735 on a keypad, and then she waves me in. "Of course. You'll find a shower there, on the left." She points. "I'll find you some clothes and leave them outside the door."

The bathroom's small, as befits a man as unworthy as her boyfriend, but the hot shower feels heavenly. It's interesting that even the lowliest of men in the present age live better than the kings did in my time. Hot water at the turn of a knob. Prepared foods of every taste and variety, frozen, fresh, or dried, stacked up in row upon row at grocery stores. Fruits and vegetables out of season, still readily available year round.

When I reach through a crack in the doorway, I can't help noticing that she's watching me from the corner of the family room. When our eyes meet, she squeaks and backs away until she's out of sight.

I can't help my smile.

With her blonde hair and her bright eyes, she's like the sunshine the room lacks, thanks to the closed drapes. My solnyshko. My very own sunshine.

The clothing she left for me isn't exceptionally fine, but it's manageable. The jeans appear to be worn here often by males, and the shirt's a nice, deep blue. It's not overlarge on my lean frame, which is nice. When I emerge, dressed, I'm almost disappointed. I knew she wasn't going to blush and stammer anymore.

But I'm not prepared for her not to even notice I've emerged.

She's too busy staring at the computer in front of her. I walk closer, my feet clad only in socks. No shoes were provided, so my steps are also virtually silent. It gives me a chance to study her a little, and not from the perspective of a horse in a pen.

Izzy Brooks is absolutely beautiful.

I'm not sure I'd noticed that before. I blame the fact that I was stuck in an equine form, but until this moment, I didn't even realize quite how stunning she is. Her hair's cut into a short blonde bob. Her eyes are a bright, light blue, and they're focused entirely on a news report. . .about *me*. She may not have been waiting on me, but she was studying me in her own way.

I sigh with a little bit of pleasure.

She jumps, shoving the chair back behind her. It's loud as it rolls, but she's off-balance, and she nearly falls. I grab her arm to steady her, and she spins, almost crashing into me.

Then she straightens abruptly. "I'm so sorry."

She's nearly as tall as I am then, maybe only three or four inches shorter. It's a nice change from all the terribly short Russian women I've been surrounded by lately, and even worse, the bossy, pint-sized Latvian women who've plagued me. "Are you alright?"

She nods and extricates her arm from my grasp.

The news anchor's yammering on. "—an extraordinary individual for an extraordinary time in Russian history." She beams at the screen. "Now we're going to interview some people here in Times Square to see what they think of Leonid Ivanovich's visit."

A small woman with a child beside her looks a little startled when she's asked. "Um, well, he's really, really good looking," she says. "And he seems nice enough." She frowns. "I'm not sure about all the people he's killed, but at least they all seem to be bad men."

I snort.

"You killed people." I feel her eyes on me. "Is that really true?"

"That's your first question?" My lip twitches.

"Well, obviously I want to know how you were a horse and what on earth you were doing at my parents' house."

"I was touring the farmlands of America," I say, "when I happened on some very bad men."

"Did you kill them?" She folds her arms.

I shake my head. "I didn't kill anyone—but they trapped me in my horse form."

"You keep saying that, like you can turn into a horse whenever you want."

I shrug. "It's true, though I rarely exercise that ability."

"Wait." She throws her hands up in front of me, her fingers nearly touching my chest. "My brother Gabe used to carry around these old comic books he made, and in them, there were Russian people who could turn into horses."

"You don't say."

She shakes her head. "This is *so* weird."

"Weird," I say. "I agree."

"So can you do it right now?" she asks. "Turn into a horse, I mean?"

"Something happened to me," I say. "When you found me, I had already been trapped, penned up like I really was just a stallion."

"I know. Oliver, one of my dad's grooms, said you were going to be killed."

"They were going to try," I say. "Normally, they'd have had no chance of killing me."

"Who?" she asks. "Who wants you dead?" She drops her arms.

I can hardly tell her that her own mother's among them. I hate doing it, but I change the subject. "The bigger issue is *why* they want me dead." I tilt my head. "I have a lot of magic, you see. Transforming into a horse is the least of it, I assure you, but it's currently been suppressed somehow, by someone. I don't know who, and I don't know how." I step closer, her face just inches from mine. "But I do know that you're involved somehow."

"Me?" She blinks, and her eyes distract me. . .again. She's so surprisingly beautiful.

I have to focus, though. Now that I can talk, we can finally try to discover how exactly we're linked and consequently, how we can undo it. "There's some kind of magic tying you to me. On the day we arrived here, I tried to run away from you."

"Yes." She backs up a step and narrows her eyes. "I remember."

"You thought I passed out from the tranquilizers you tried to administer, but I assure you, that wasn't the reason."

"No?" She arches one eyebrow. "Why, then?"

"If you draw farther from me than this house to that road." I point. "Then I fall unconscious."

"That makes no sense. I wasn't anywhere near you until I saw you that morning a few days ago. There's no connection between us, I swear."

"When you've been a part of my world a bit longer, you won't struggle with things that make no sense quite as much. Most things make no sense until you uncover the truth of them."

She shakes a little, like a dog divesting itself of water. "Okay, but I really do have an errand to run. I have to go talk to my boyfriend."

"The loser who's in jail?" I can't help my scowl.

"He's not—well, he is, but it's complicated."

"So he's no longer in jail?" I raise both eyebrows. "How did you come up with the bail, when you refused to sell me?"

"You understood all that?" She exhales, pointing one finger at my face. "I knew it."

"Yes, if you'd trusted your judgment a bit more, we might have gotten here faster."

"Why?" She cocks one hip. "Would you have written something in the dirt? Tried to change me into a horse too?" She laughs then. "This is such a weird day."

"What do you need to do at the jail?"

Her entire face shutters.

"Please tell me that you're dumping your boyfriend."

"Dumping him?" She frowns.

"Is that not the correct word here? Breaking up with him?"

Her scowl deepens. "Why would you assume that?"

"You are staying at his house," I say. "Which isn't promising, but while you were here, he encouraged you to illegally sell a horse to someone using false papers. That exposes you to criminal prosecution, does it not?"

"Well, it was my idea." Her lips compress.

"And he's done things bad enough that men have come here, threatening you. You either must pay his debts or be punished in his place."

"Did you get shot?" Her eyes brighten. "I swear, you got shot, right?"

"I had a residual protection spell that prevented it from harming me, but yes, the man shot me."

She backs up a step, shaking her head and making a strange sound, almost like a horse whuffling. "I knew that, too. I swear, I have felt so crazy, but—"

"I know you think that stealing me was insane on your part, but I'm sure you felt the connection between us. That's why you felt compelled to act as you did, and it's also why you trusted me even when you knew nothing about me."

"Maybe." She looks like she wants to argue with me, but it's hard to argue when she saw me turn from a horse into a man.

"I'll ask again, since you appear to be disinclined to answer. What business do you have at the jail?"

"Well, for one, Tim's going to be royally ticked that I don't have his bail money yet."

"It's not reasonable for a criminal like him to expect you to clean up his messes."

She sighs. "Well, that's another thing I want to ask him about. Until today, I hadn't even considered that he might be guilty of what he's accused of doing." Her shoulders slump. "He's not the kind of person who would ever need to break the law. He's got everything going for him—" She shakes her head. "It doesn't matter. I need to ask him about something I saw, and he's going to be really upset when I do."

"I'm already upset," I say. "I don't think you should go. Don't give that man another moment of your time."

"You sound like Paige."

"Paige is clearly both intelligent and wise," I say. "Who is she?"

"My best friend." She grabs the rolling chair, yanks it over, and sits down. "Or, you know, she was. I don't see her that often anymore. She hates Tim, and no matter what I said, she wouldn't change her mind about it."

"Okay, so we've decided. You won't go to the jail. We'll stay here."

She stands. "No, we haven't decided that at all. You can't just tell me someone's bad—just because you think it, or Paige thinks it—and expect that to be that. This is an important person to me, and I never let people in my life down. No matter what questions I may have, that's not who I am."

She's magnificent.

I'm not sure I've ever seen a woman stand up for a terrible guy quite so vehemently. "Alright."

"Alright?" She blinks. "Alright, what?"

"You want this man to be released from jail, and you require a hundred thousand dollars to do it. Yes?"

She nods.

"I'll pay the bail for his release, and then you can confirm that he's not worth your time. After that, I'll kill him so you can focus on me."

She laughs. "Sure. You'll kill him."

"But I need to go by a bank first."

"Wait." She peers at me. "Why aren't you laughing? It's a joke, right, the killing thing?"

I force a smile. "Sure. It was a joke."

She stares at me for a long moment before deciding it must have been. "I can't possibly let you pay for his bail, but I can call the Russian Embassy for you. I'm assuming you lost your phone in the 'stuck-as-a-horse' debacle. The media hasn't mentioned that you're missing, but you're either a crazy impersonator, or you're really their new czar." Her brow furrows. "At least if the Russian embassy comes and picks you up, my parents don't ever need to know I stole a horse from them." She still looks sad, though.

"I'm serious about the money," I say. "It's nothing to me, and then you can stop scrounging around, trying to sell your meager belongings or earn the money in other ways."

"You hate him even though you haven't met him."

"You work with horses a lot, right?"

She frowns, but then she nods.

"Have you ever watched someone having a problem on a horse, and it's been plain to you exactly what's wrong?" I wait. "Maybe they have no idea what's going on, or they're blaming the horse, but you can see what's happening, and it's their error?"

"Are you saying I'm an idiot? That even a stolen horse-man can see that my boyfriend's a jerk, but I can't?" She scowls. "Because—"

I lower my voice until she can barely hear it. "*You* said he was like the sun and you're the moon."

Her eyes widen and she rolls several feet away from me. "I—I wasn't—you were a horse when I said all that."

I step closer, almost stalking her now. "You said you were the moon, but I think that's wrong. I think you have no idea how brightly you could shine if he wasn't actively dimming your light. I've known enough men like him that I don't even have to meet him. Hearing your conversation on the phone was enough."

"You're saying that you hate this guy, and you think he's trash, but you'll just *give* me a hundred grand to save him?"

"Not to save him," I clarify. "To save you from him. While he's tied up in there, you're tied up on him."

"So to help *me*, someone you barely know, you'll just drop a hundred thousand dollars."

"It's a smart move for me," I say. "I'm connected to you, and you recently saved me. But you're distracted. You've been distracted since whatever connected us connected us. I need you to focus, because I need your help. I have to regain my powers *immediately*. I can't have you distracted anymore, and I'm willing to buy your attention." I lift both eyebrows.

"Do we have a deal?"

She stands. "I want to test your statement."

"What?"

"I want to see you pass out when I walk away."

I roll my eyes. "For the—you must be kidding. What possible reason could I have to lie about that?"

She shrugs. "It's easy to test, is it not?"

"Not if I don't fancy going face-first in the dirt."

"I'll sit you in a chair," she says. "I just want to see whether we're really connected like you say, because if we aren't. . ."

"Then I'm just a creepy horse-man who's pushing you into doing things and giving you large sums of money for inexplicable reasons."

"It seems odd," she says. "I know you say we're connected, but I can't feel it, and I can't see it, and I have no idea how we possibly could be when we'd never even met."

"Fine." I grab the chair by the back and pick it up on my way out the front door. I have to set it down to rummage around for a pair of shoes from the rack near the door. In addition to being an idiot, Mr. Heaston's also got terrible taste in shoes for his small feet. I finally manage to shove my feet into a pair of ghastly sneakers, and then I pick up the chair and continue outside.

After watching my shoe troubles with a half-smile, Izzy trots after me. "Okay, so I'll leave you here by the house, and I'll jog off, and then if what you're saying is true—"

I point. "Set up your phone over there. You can run the video so you can see up close exactly what happens when you move away from me. I'd hardly have time to tamper with it while you run back. I'll be unconscious."

"That's actually a pretty decent idea."

"Because I'm telling the truth." I drop the chair and sit. "But I want you to do something for me, too. A show of good faith, if you will."

She stiffens.

"Not something gross. I want you to try and *feel* a connection between us when you jog away. I want you to try and sense whatever it is that binds us, so you might be able to work with me on figuring this out. I need a partner, not a jailer."

"Fine." She nods. "Sure." And then she sets up her phone, and she jogs away from me. I spin around in the chair a few times. Then my vision starts to darken and then everything goes black.

Moments later, when I wake up, I'm flat on my face, and she's tugging me over onto my back. "Sorry." She's grimacing. "I really thought you'd slump—I didn't think you'd fall forward like that."

I brush the dust from my borrowed clothing. "It's fine." I stand. "Are you ready to head to that bank now? We have some forms to fill out, I'm sure."

Izzy once again grabs her jacket, heads out the front door, and locks the keypad with a sequence of numbers. Only this time, instead of seeing her from across the property and panicking, I'm walking beside her. It's a much nicer feeling. Not that I care about her, of course. It's just not a great feeling to have her moving away from me. Watching that made me panicky, and I haven't felt out of control like that in a very long time.

Which is why, a moment later, when I circle the car and finally see the same stupid sedan parked behind Izzy's truck, I say a very bad, very rude word. The men who were here to collect money from that criminal Tim are back.

And I don't have my powers.

I'm barely better than useless, which makes me very, very angry.

CHAPTER 10

Izzy

The day Tim kissed me, it was very, very cold.

Ironically, I doubt it would have happened if not for Paige, my best friend. . .who hates him. Paige is a skier. She and I had very little in common when we were matched as roommates our freshman year of college, but over time, we became more and more similar. In fact, we became partners when our largest difference became our biggest connection point—I loved horses, and she loved plowing through snow on sticks.

By her sophomore year, we had realized where our interests connected and decided to try skijoring, on a lark mostly. She had a ski team friend who mentioned that they had a friendly competition the following week. Paige decided she wanted to try it, but she needed a horse to pull her with a rope through the ski course.

At forty miles an hour.

Millie probably would have killed us, but I convinced Steve and Mom to bring the horse I learned barrels on, Chromey, and he was a champ. Running in the snow didn't scare him. Racing past screaming crowds gathered along the course didn't faze him either. The only part that made Chromey nervous was the flag we had to carry for our college.

All in all, though we didn't get close to first place, we were almost as far away from last. We decided to do it again.

And again.

And then again.

After my tenth or twelfth run, we started rolling Millie into the lineup. She was bred for reining, so I didn't think she'd be great, but she got the hang of it quicker than I expected. The flag never even fazed her.

By my junior year, I'd been working for the Bear River Equine Hospital for a few months already. I knew most of the vets there. So when I showed up at the Heber City Utah skijoring competition, I wasn't even surprised to see they were the vet for the meet. I was actually proud to introduce them to all the friends I'd made in the bizarre sport I'd fallen in love with.

"And this is Timothy Heaston," I said to Paige. "He's our orthopedic surgeon, so I'm not sure why he had to come."

"I wanted to come," he said. "I love things like this, and when I heard you would be here, I didn't want to miss it." But he was staring at me, not Paige.

"I know everyone here's a potential client," Paige said. "But you'll have to cheer the loudest for us." She winked.

Tim stepped closer. "Izzy's the only one I'll be cheering for. She's the only one I even see." Then he winked. . .*at me.*

"At first I thought it would be fun flirting with him," Paige said. "But I didn't think he'd actually like you. He's way too old for you." Paige glared as he rejoined the Bear River team.

"Let's just worry about the race," I said.

It was the first time we'd ever taken first place, and it was very, very exciting. We even won some money. After all the photos and the interview with the local Heber City paper, I was finally walking Chromey back to my trailer when my "Girls Just Wanna Have Fun" ringtone alerted me that my mom was calling.

In the process of trying to answer, I almost ran into someone. I dropped my reins, Chromey spooked, and I fumbled my phone. Chromey reared back, which was very uncommon for him, and he was hovering over me, blocking out the sun.

The person I almost plowed over was Tim.

He gracefully caught my phone, snagged Chromey's reins before he could bolt, and swung me around behind him to keep me safe. "Careful, champion."

I swear, the whole thing played out like a scene from a movie. He was in the right place at the right time, and without missing a beat, he set my horse at ease, kept me safe, and prevented my phone from breaking. I was in *awe*, even more than I had been before.

"It was exciting, watching you in your element," he said.

"It was your cheering that did it, I think." In spite of the cold, my cheeks felt warm. His arm—still braced around my lower back—helped.

"You were spectacular. Really." His eyes dropped to my mouth.

I inhaled.

And then he kissed me. It felt like everything in my world dropped into place in that moment. Sometimes, when things feel hard, I think back on that moment. When I was in trouble, he swung me around and shielded me with his body. At the time, I remember thinking it might be the closest thing I'd ever experienced to having an actual white knight.

When the men who shot at us before show up again, my heart races, and I realize I'm in more danger now than I was that day, when Chromey panicked and I was almost trampled.

Sadly, Leonid Ivanovich is definitely not a knight.

He's also not dressed in anything remotely close to white— he's not even wearing his own clothes. But whereas Chromey could be calmed with a steady gesture and a smooth voice, I doubt anything like that will work here. In fact, as I take in their expressions and their approach, I notice something. Something very bad.

"Leonid," I whisper. "He—he's got a gun."

No matter how many times you watch a heroine on a show stand up to someone bravely, no matter how many times you run through a life-and-death scenario you see in a movie or read in a book, nothing really prepares you for facing the rounded end of a metal weapon that's pointed at your face in real life.

I remember the sound of the *bang* when they fired last time.

I remember how Drago—Leonid—flinched.

And I remember frantically checking him over after he charged them and finding no damage at all. I hadn't understood it then, and I'm not sure I really get it now. He said it was because of the remnants of a protection spell, but what does that even mean?

Harry Potter's not real.

Twilight? As far as I know, there are neither werewolves nor vampires. But yesterday, I'd have sworn there was no such thing as a man who can turn into a horse, and clearly. . . If any of that existed, now would be a great time for a shirtless wolf-man to show up and twist this gun into a hunk of deformed metal. Bopping the guys on the head for good measure wouldn't hurt, either.

When the short man swings his gun around to point right at my head *again*, I panic. I should duck. I could scream. In fact, I ought to dive behind the truck.

But I don't do any of that.

I stare at him wide-eyed and dopey, my heart hammering.

Until Leonid yanks my upper arm back, stepping into place in front of me. "Put that down."

The small man smiles. "Before she had a big, scary horse racing to her aid." He snorts. "Now. . .just you?" He shakes his head. "I'll be honest. I was way more scared of the horse."

"Then you're a fool," Leonid says. "Because I'm the czar of Russia. One word from me will end not only your life, but also the lives of every person you've ever cared remotely for." I can only make out the side of his face, but the brutality of Leonid's smile chills me to the bone. Definitely not the white knight I was looking for. Honestly, he looks a lot scarier than the shirtless wolf-man.

And yet, this man, this scary man with his posh British accent is facing the two who are threatening me, and he has no weapons at all.

"The czar of. . ." The small man's laughter grates on me, like a dentist drilling on a molar. He slaps the tall man on his side. "This fake British man says he's the czar of Russia." He sighs. "That's very interesting, because I just found out that I'm the queen of bloody England."

"Oh, I think not," Leonid says. "Queen Camilla has better personal hygiene, and is both much prettier *and* much smarter than you." He curls his lip. "I'm also more afraid of her than I could ever be of someone who breathes through his mouth like you do."

The little man may be uncouth, but he understands the insult. He takes one small step closer. "I don't know who you are, but you're on Timothy Heaston's property, and you're with his girlfriend, so in my book, that makes you fair game."

"Game?" Leonid doesn't even look one percent scared. "Game for what, exactly? I feel like chess would be beyond you —checkers, maybe? Can you keep the difference between black and red straight? What if we stack up one of the checkers? Wouldn't you get confused?"

"Why does he sound British if he's supposed to be from Russia?" The tall man's frowning. "Because I do feel like I saw him on TV."

"My English tutor was British," Leonid says. "A tutor is someone who teaches you things. Unlike the two of you, I'm quite bright and pick things up right away, so hiring tutors makes sense."

"If you really are Russian, you must be stupid," the tall man says. "Here in America, we know not to insult people who are holding guns."

"Was I insulting you? I thought I was merely stating facts—facts I didn't think you could comprehend." Leonid steps toward them, his right hand holding me behind his back. "What's most entertaining to me is that here in America, the scariest thing you can imagine is a gun."

"Oh please," the short man says. "What could be scarier than a gun?"

Leonid turns toward me slightly, just enough that I can see his profile. "Turn me back."

"Into a horse?" I hiss. "How would I even do that?"

"I don't know. How did you turn me last time?"

"What are you two talking about?" The small man shakes his gun at us. "Stop it."

"If you don't," Leonid whispers, "I'm not sure how—"

But the small man's out of patience. "I'll show you why we're scared of guns, big talker." He shifts so his eye's just behind the barrel, and then he pulls the trigger.

It all happens so quickly that I'm not sure exactly *what* happens. The bullet never hits us, and somehow, instead, the two men catch fire. The short man drops his gun on the ground, and it goes off again. That bullet never reaches us either, but the screams from the two men as they burn?

They must be able to hear them in outer space.

Their bodies burn on and on and on. I'm not sure I'll ever be able to stop hearing their screams and smelling the odor of melting flesh.

"What on earth happened?" I'm casting about for someone else—anyone, or anything—who could have set them on fire.

"Did the gun misfire? Did it spark or explode?" But how would they *both* go up in flames like that?

Leonid watches them with a tilted head, utterly unconcerned, for another two minutes or so until they've burned down to nothing but two smoking piles of ash. It's unlike anything I've ever seen before. Then he slowly turns around, smiling. "I just discovered that thanks to our connection, when I'm touching you, I have full access to my powers."

I leap backward. "Are you saying. . ." I swallow. "Did *you* just incinerate them?"

He looks utterly unfazed. "Of course I did. Did you think it was a terrible sunburn that just spiraled out of control?"

Is he making a *joke*? "Two men just died."

"I'm pretty sure they only qualified as men in the loosest sense of the word. If you'd seen their faces, the way I see them, you'd know I was doing the world a favor."

"You—what? Their faces?"

"When I asked you to shift me into a horse, I tried to do it myself, and I felt the ability. That's when I began to wonder if I might be able to do more. . ."

"So you got your powers, and then you just *killed* them?"

"Oh, don't worry," Leonid says. "There's no body. Even in America, they need a body to convict you. And besides, I have diplomatic immunity here. Neither of us will be in trouble."

Great.

I'm somehow linked to a *psychopath*.

CHAPTER 11

Izzy

Leonid walks past me, snaking the dangling key out of my hand, and hops in the driver's seat. "You coming, love?"

"Oh, no, no. I'm not going anywhere with you," I say. "You need an English lesson."

"Are you upset I took the keys?" He swivels back outward and half-slides off the driver's seat. "You want to drive?"

"No, I said *English* lesson. Let me elaborate. When I say 'an outfit cost me an arm and a leg,' I don't really mean that. I have both my arms, and I have both my legs."

He frowns.

"And when I say 'it's raining cats and dogs outside,' it isn't *really* raining dogs or cats. That just means it's raining a lot. I could also say the rain's heavy. It would be unbearably grotesque if actual animals were falling from the sky."

"Okay." He narrows his eyes at me. "Get to your point here."

"So when I say I'm so hungry I could eat a horse. . ." I pause.

"You aren't really going to eat a horse."

I nod. "Good. You do understand some things."

"What are you so upset about?" Leonid asks. "Those men tried to shoot us—no, they *did* shoot us yesterday. If I hadn't been protected by the end of my precautionary spell, we might have died then. And today, without my magic, which I was only able to access through you seconds before they fired a gun at us, we'd also both be dead." He leans closer. "Tell me you understand that. The men I just roasted, they were very, very bad men who intended to do eminent harm to both you and me."

"Two wrongs don't make a right."

"What about fifty wrongs? At what point does eliminating the originator of those wrongs make a right?"

I'm shaking my head. "You don't get to decide that. The government has to make that decision."

"Did you not hear me? I'm the czar of Russia. I *am* the government."

I scowl. "But not here you aren't."

"Actually, I still *am* the czar of Russia, even when I'm here. But take your phrase, the 'cats and dogs' one. It makes absolutely no sense. And similarly, two negatives do make a positive. Two wrongs being eliminated *is* right." He stands. "In fact, in this world, the only thing you *can* do with two wrongs is right them."

"Well, I'm not sure what to say about all that. You have a remarkable way with words for someone who learned English as a second language."

"Fifth language," he says. "My dad was certifiably nuts and thought I was destined to be the czar of Russia, so he taught me several in my infancy."

Is he mocking himself? "I—I'm glad we didn't die," I say, lamely. "I just think—that was horrible, watching that."

"I'm sorry," Leonid says. "The next time I have to kill people, I'll do it in a less messy way and just bury their bodies so far down in the earth that no one can ever find them."

"You'll—what?"

"The earth power's new to me, so I was nervous I couldn't do it without leaving a very noticeable mound of dirt. I didn't want that leading to questions for you or your reprehensible boyfriend."

"Your what power? What about Tim?" For some reason, it almost feels like he's switched to Russian. But then something he said clicks. The next time he has to kill people. "Do you plan to kill more people?"

"It's the most useful part of my magic," he says. "Before, when I encountered evil people, I had to endure their wickedness. My only other option was to run away. Now, I can eliminate them and the threat they pose to the rest of society."

"You're saying you're like a first strike strategy? Brutal, but the best way to keep people safe?"

He blinks. "First strike's a reference to the cold war nuclear arms race."

"It is," I say. "The thought was that if we could hit them first, we'd be safe. Take out the bad guys before they could take us out."

"I'm nothing like that," Leonid says. "Those were threats—a plan of attack. I don't threaten anyone. I simply eliminate the danger before they can harm innocent people, like you."

I'm pretty sure my stepdad Steve would love this guy. "Well, in America, we believe in innocent until proven guilty."

"So what does shooting us—twice—make them, if not guilty?"

I stomp around the side of the truck and get in. "Are you still going to give me money to bail Tim out?" Because frankly, after watching this guy incinerate two men, Tim feels like a Nobel-Prize-eligible bunny rabbit.

"Of course," he says. "And I'm more encouraged than before by this turn of events. Now that I can access my powers again, even if it is only with your help, we're clearly making progress.

The next step is figuring out how we can do it so I no longer need you."

"But right now, you believe you have to touch me to kill people?" That sounds. . .made up.

Actually, all of this sounds made up, so maybe that's not a good barometer anymore. "Why are you driving?" I ask. "You don't even know where we're going."

"Do you know?" he asks.

"A bank," I say. "You didn't specify whether we needed a certain one."

"International," he says. "My money will be arriving by foreign wire."

"And how exactly are you going to get it?" I examine him. "Or did you sprout a wallet and identification card while I was busy watching those men burn?"

The curl of his lip makes his face look even more unbelievably beautiful, and that annoys me for some reason. "You certainly express your disapproval freely." Leonid turns the key over and starts my truck. Only, as usual, it doesn't start right away. "In this case, since you think I'm a crazy killer, I'd think you might keep your judgment under wraps."

For some reason, Leonid doesn't scare me. He probably should—he just incinerated two men—but he doesn't. I'm more irritated at him than anything else. "You should let me drive my own truck. She's temperamental."

"The single best thing about the changes in the world from when I was born and now is that we no longer have to rely on temperamental creatures for our transportation. You need a new car. One that listens when you command it."

"Command?" I chuckle. "What, are you a hundred years old?"

He grunts, for some reason.

"If you turn it just a little and then all the way and pump the gas pedal at the same time, it'll start."

He tries.

I mutter, "Usually."

But just then, it finally roars to life. I pat the dash. "Atta girl, Rita."

"Rita?"

"For margarita," I say. "Never mind."

He frowns.

"There's a Bank of America about three miles from here."

"Tell me where to turn."

The rest of the drive, Leonid says nothing. In fact, he's so intent on driving and the road that it's almost alarming.

"You know, if I didn't know better, I'd think you hadn't been driving very long."

"I was a chauffeur for a while," he says. "But I didn't drive cars that could go quite this fast, so I've only been driving at this speed for a few years now."

"What?" I ask. "Are cars in Russia slow?"

"Not now. But since becoming the czar, people act like I *can't* drive myself. Before that, well, I drove myself places. . .sometimes."

He's a very odd man. Maybe it's because he's Russian. Even so, I can't help sneaking a glance now and again. I may have spent most of my formative years in a town of five hundred, but I've met a lot of men since starting college. I even dated quite a few of them. Over all of them, Tim stood out as the handsomest. He has gleaming, wavy hair that falls around his face. His light, golden-brown eyes are somehow also commanding, and his broad face and athletic build made him a standout in every way. He's also tall, at around six foot. That's important to me, since I'm five eleven.

But Leonid—he makes Tim look shabby.

His hair's immaculately cut, not a hair out of place, and it's a half dozen shades of shining, golden blonde. It's the kind of color that no one has without paying a fortune. I used to have hair that color, until it darkened as I aged. Now I have to pay for highlights like his. Something tells me he's not paying to look the way he does. His eyes are a bright, vibrant shade of green I'm not sure I've ever seen, more like the grass in Easter egg baskets for children than anything I've seen in nature. His skin's a deeper, brighter gold than a burnished apple or a rich autumn leaf, and it perfectly complements his hair. He looks. . .well, he looks like a cartoon drawing of a Prince Charming come to life.

No wonder our whole country's lost their mind for him. In a world that grew up knowing that Disney princes didn't exist, a young, handsome, rich one has turned up on our doorstep.

Or in my case, the driver's seat of my car.

It's a pity he's a psycho.

Then again, those men were trying to kill us. "Here's what I don't understand. If they wanted to collect money from us, why did they try to shoot us?" I ask. "Oh, make a right turn here."

He does.

"Because it's not like they can collect any money for their boss if they kill the people who owe him, right?"

"Ah, but *we* didn't owe them," Leonid says. "Your dear, beloved boyfriend owes them for who knows what. Killing us would send him the necessary message. Pay up, or lose something else, something more valuable."

"I guess." I'm not sure Tim would see losing me as a huge hit right now. He's in prison, and it's been days, and I've done nothing to get him out. "Turn left at the next light, and it's around the corner."

I should've just told Steve and Mom I needed money. Maybe they'd have been more reasonable than I thought. Maybe they'd have loaned it to me right away. Maybe then, I wouldn't be shackled to this nut with some kind of invisible magic harness.

"What are your powers exactly?" I ask.

But we've just pulled into the parking lot of the Bank of America, and even more than learning about his powers, I'm really hoping that he can make good on his claim to wire me the money I need.

"You know what?" I put my hand on the door handle. "Tell me later. Get me money now. That'll feel like a massive super-power already."

"So you're more of a gold-digger than a superhero fangirl." Leonid's chuckling as he hops out of the car.

"World's least successful gold-digger," I mutter. "Net worth of negative two horses and one horse-man pyro."

"Don't forget this truck that barely starts."

"Hey, Rita's seen me through some things," I say. "Don't diss Rita."

"Diss?" He frowns, but I don't have time to get into that one.

There's no line to see a teller, so we walk right up to the counter. "I have a weird thing to ask," I say. "This guy." I toss my thumb in his direction. "Has a lot of money, but he has no iden-tification."

"I need to access an international account," Leonid says. "I have the requisite codes and passwords, and I'll pay the one percent surcharge gladly."

The short man with the blocky glasses shoves them up his nose. "Let me grab my manager."

Three minutes later, we're being waved to the back. Four minutes later, the 'manager' is tugging her blouse down just a little more, and I'm worried that if she sneezes, we'll be meeting both her ladies up close and personal. "Okay," I say. "Do you know what he's talking about with the passcodes and whatnot?"

The woman doesn't even look at me. "Can I just say, Your Majesty, that I am a *huge* fan?" She literally bats her eyelashes. I thought that was a joke. I didn't think any woman actually did it. I've been wrong a lot today, it seems.

Because, blessedly, in addition to flirting criminally, she is completely fine pulling up whatever he needs without any identification. "Here." The woman clacks away on a laptop, and then she swivels it around. "I'm assuming you can login here?"

I watch as Leonid toggles something into a language in which I know not a single letter. "Da." He grins.

The woman giggles.

The thirty-something bank manager *giggles.*

I wonder if she'd giggle the same way if she had just watched —and smelled—him flambé two men. Doubtful. Magic is far less, well, *magical* than I'd been led to believe. It's a lot more messy, scary, and disgusting than the children's stories I've read led me to believe.

"I think my part is done." Leonid swivels the laptop back around.

"Did I mention that I'm just a *huge* fan?" The woman's not even looking at the laptop. "If there is anything I can do for you, Your Majesty, anything at all, please ask."

"I did ask." Leonid's brow furrows.

"Excuse me?" Her eyes fill with hope. "You did?"

He looks pointedly at the laptop. "That's what I need help with right now."

She blushes. "Right. Of course, but anything else, and I'm just as happy to help." She leans toward him, thrusting her jiggling ladies closer.

"Oh, please. Have some dignity," I say. "You're making all women look bad."

The woman glares, sits up straight, and looks down at the laptop. Then she squints. "You want to send this. . ." She looks up. "Where?"

Leonid glances at me. "You'll have to give her your account information now."

"Wait, you're sending it to me?" I frown. "Can't you just, like, put it in a cashier's check?"

"Made out to whom? The local jail?" Leonid rolls his eyes.

"It's going to be transferred over to you, and then you can use it for whatever you choose."

"You can write your information down here." The woman hands me a deposit slip.

I hate how dumb I feel. "Write what, exactly?"

"Do you bank with us?" She's talking to me, but still glancing back at Leonid at odd intervals and shooting him awkward little smiles.

"I do," I say. "That's why I knew this bank location was here."

"Great." Her forced smile's frightening. "Then you know what to write. Account number and routing." She waves her hand.

Leonid leans closer to me, murmuring. "Darling, after we leave here, should we grab something to eat?" His breath tickles my ear.

Darling?

I open my mouth to tell him where he can stick his darling, but he's looking at me intently. Just beyond his face, out of the corner of my eye, I see the woman, her mouth dangling open, watching us.

"Are you two *together?*" She swallows. "Because I heard you were single."

"My sweet Isabel's very private." Leonid catches her eye. "I trust you can keep our secret."

She inhales, sharply, and then she nods.

I hand her the deposit slip, my account number and routing written down.

"This is you?" She frowns. "Isabel Brooks?"

I nod.

She shakes her head slowly, and then she says. "Well, alright."

A moment later, she presses some buttons and I hear a small printer whirring. She whips the paper off and hands it to me. "This shows your current account balance."

I stand up and incline my head. "Thanks for your help."

"Yes, we appreciate it." Leonid drops an arm around my shoulders. "More than you know." His smile doesn't look as forced.

"What's so funny?" I ask, as we're finally walking out of her small office. The bank exit's in sight.

"When we're touching, even through clothing, I can access my powers. All of them." His smile widens. "It's—I've missed it."

"Yes, I imagine that not having the ability to fricassee other humans is a little worrisome."

He pulls my key out of his pocket with his free hand and finally releases me, walking toward the driver's side.

"Wouldn't it be easier if you let me drive?" I ask.

He shakes his head. "No, I find that I quite like chaperoning you around."

"I think you mean chauffeuring."

"Does chauffeuring mean that I'm monitoring the people you choose to trust and help?" He lifts both eyebrows.

"No," I say. "It means you're giving me a ride."

"Since this is your car, and since I'm not just driving you around, I'd like to stick with my original word."

"I don't need a chaperone. It's not eighteen-ninety-eight."

"Thank goodness for that," Leonid says. "I'd barely be born."

What?

"Here." We're in front of the truck, and he has just opened my door.

"I can open my own door." I bump his hand away.

"This isn't done anymore when two people are courting?"

Courting? "What's with the weird comments about what's done now?" I sigh and push past him into the truck. "Everyone else in the country may be in love with you, but I'm not. I'm also starting to think you're really, really weird."

"Let's just say that it's been a long time since I've been on a date. I'm not really sure what people on one do anymore."

I stiffen. "We aren't on a date, Leo. We're headed to jail to help my boyfriend, remember?"

"Leo?" He smiles. "I like that. And I know where we're going. I just take issue with the word *boyfriend*."

"Your issues notwithstanding," I say, "you don't really get a say in my love life."

"Yet." The stupidly hot guy's smiling now. He's *smiling* as he makes jokes about how he and I are dating.

"Stop that right now." I jab a finger at him. "If you make any jokes like that in the prison, I'll—"

He catches my hand in his large one. "What will you do?" His verdant green eyes meet mine. "Tell me. Please. Leo's listening."

"Leo—it's not a special pet name. No one uses the name Leonid here. Leo sounds more natural. And—" I snatch my hand away, but in doing so, my deposit slip thing flutters to the floor of the truck. I reach down and pick it up, grateful for the distraction. He's being really, really intense, and it's freaking me out.

Or maybe what's bothering me most is that my heart's racing.

He's too handsome for me, and I know he was kidding earlier to get that crazy lady to back off, but I almost *liked* when he pretended we were dating, and I have a *boyfriend*.

I'm also not used to people flirting with me, especially very hot, very powerful men doing it. Actually, I'm not sure who would be used to guys like Leonid flirting with them. Maybe a woman on the set of *The Vampire Diaries* or something. I start to stuff the paper in my purse, but something about it catches my eye.

"Wait." I lift the crumpled slip closer to my face. "Why does this say. . ." I blink twice. Then I hold it even closer.

"What?" He leans toward me.

"You transferred *half a million dollars* into my account?"

"A hundred for the bail," he says. "But the rest is for a new car and whatever else we might need. You may have forgotten, but I don't have my wallet."

"Whatever else?" He's a psycho for sure. "What else might we need that would cost *four hundred thousand* dollars?"

"If I've learned anything lately, it's that you often don't know what you need until it's too late. I'm accustomed to a certain quality of life, and I like to be prepared."

CHAPTER 12
Leonid

In my almost thirty years of life, I've encountered quite a few things I dislike. In fact, after spending a few months as the czar of a large country, I might almost say I've become picky. There are very few things I *do* like. Even so, encountering something I truly despise is equally rare. When we walk into the Salt Lake County Metro Jail and complete the paperwork for posting bail, I add something, or rather, some*one*, to that list.

Timothy Heaston.

I was predisposed to dislike him, it's true. His manners on the phone were reprehensible. The way he's tasked Izzy to clean up his messes is deplorable. But when we meet?

I absolutely hate him.

In fact, it feels as if every single part of my body's crying out for his destruction. If I had free access to my powers, I'm not sure I wouldn't have already eliminated him.

Incineration.

Burial alive.

Dry drowning.

Aneurysm that pops.

Suffocation.

Electrocution.

Some combination of the above.

The myriad ways I could destroy him just keep cycling through my brain, but I doubt I could convince Izzy that it wasn't me who did it, so I'm stuck. She was so upset when I rid the world of the other two villainous men who were attacking us that I doubt she'd forgive me for freeing her from him either.

Not yet, anyway.

I was hoping he'd at least be wearing an orange jumpsuit or something when we saw him, but apparently when you post bail, they return the clothes the loser was wearing when he was picked up. He's actually dressed in an ensemble that's virtually identical to mine, which couldn't disgust me more.

"Izzy." Tim's smile's cloying. "You did it. You sold the horse." He shakes his head. "When you said you didn't ask your parents for the money, I was a little peeved. I'll be honest."

Izzy's brow furrows.

"But I never should've doubted you. You pulled through." He opens his arms, inviting her to step in closer for a hug.

Izzy backs up a step, drawing closer to me.

As if he's noticing my presence for the first time, Tim's shoulders straighten, and his smile melts away. "Who the heck are you?"

"Heck?" I frown.

"It's a Utah thing," Izzy says.

I arch one eyebrow. "Like vodka's a Russian thing?"

"Sure," Izzy says. "And Tim, this is Leonid Ivanovich, and he bought the horse. We got the money for your bail from him."

We didn't talk about what we'd tell him, mostly because I didn't care at all what she told him about me or where she got the bail. I'm surprised she's lying about it, but I suppose it makes sense. The horse did technically disappear and I appeared, so what she's saying isn't painfully untrue. We also can't have him wandering around and asking questions about where the stallion went, I suppose.

She's smart. It's one of the things I like about her best. Izzy's eyes widen. "Speaking of, you know that German man, Müller? He said you had a video feed running on the paddock around the clock. Is that true?"

Tim's still glaring at me, but he nods slowly. "I do. I have cameras all over the property."

"Where do the videos go?" Izzy sounds. . .nervous. Then she glances at the cameras in the corner of the room.

Tim smiles. "Don't worry. There's a live stream, but the images aren't recorded. I'd need a lot of space to record the footage from every video camera I installed. It just lets me check on things in real time whenever I want."

Izzy exhales, and I realize she was worried—probably that my transformation had been caught on camera somewhere. That's cute. As if I can't protect myself.

"Well." Tim glances my way. "Thanks for escorting my girl here." He steps toward her and slings an arm over Izzy's shoulders. "I'll take it from here."

An emotion I've never felt before rises up inside of me, a possessive rage that threatens to consume me. He's touching *my* Isabel. If I had free use of my powers, I would incinerate him to ash. Actually, I'd drown him first, then electrocute him, and then I would burn him to a pile of smoking cinder. And then I'd bury his remains so deep and so far that no one would ever find them—his relatives would always wonder where he went.

If they even cared.

But I don't have my powers because he's stolen my Isabel, so I just stand there, fuming, my hands balled into fists at my side.

Izzy ducks out from under his arm and sidles closer to me. "Actually, Tim, I need to talk to you about a few things before we go anywhere."

Tim frowns at her, and then he narrows his eyes, focusing

his gaze on me. "You need to talk to me—with this guy watching?"

Izzy bobs her head at the corner of the waiting room where there's a small table with four chairs. "Can we just chat over there for a moment?"

He drops his voice, reaching for her arm. "Can't we just go home? We can talk all you want there."

She yanks her hand free. "I need to talk to you first."

He glares at me, but he nods and walks reluctantly to the corner. "Fine."

He sits in the chair with its back to the window, squaring off against me. He pulls the chair next to him out, expecting her to take it, but Izzy sits directly across from him, and I swivel the other chair around backward, sitting just behind her and to the side.

"What's going on?" A muscle in Tim's jaw is popping. I'm pretty sure he hates me almost as much as I detest him. Thankfully, I've had a hundred years to perfect my hatred of people and things, and I have many, many more tools than he does to dispatch my enemies.

"While I was on your computer, dealing with trying to sell Drago, I happened to see an email."

His face falls into a deep scowl. "You want to talk to me because you were digging through my email? Don't you think you should at least have the decency to keep quiet about something you found when you were invading my privacy?"

"I wasn't digging through anything," Izzy says. "I was on your computer when an email popped up, and a little notification showed up on the top right side of the screen. I saw my name on it." She shrugs. "Maybe I shouldn't have, but I clicked on it."

Tim stands up. "Heck yes, you shouldn't have. I don't dig through your email."

"Another Utah thing?"

Izzy snorts. "Old habits die hard."

"Not very manly, if he can't even swear," I say. "That's the first thing my British tutor taught me."

"We need to go," Tim says. "Now."

"You, sit." I point. "Until she's done."

Tim's eyes are flashing when he turns toward me, and his lip curls. "No, *you* get out." He tosses his head. "Before I do something very, very stupid in front of cameras that are recording."

"I think it's too late for that," I say. "Maybe if you'd met me sooner, or just tried not to do as many stupid things you could have managed." I shrug. "No way to know."

"Tim." Izzy points at his seat. "Please hear me out."

Tim's nostrils are flaring and his hands are tightly clenched, but he finally sits down again. "Which email that was sent to me did you read without my permission, exactly?"

"It was an email from Dr. Rebecca Hartfield. She was upset with you for asking her to dis-recommend me." Izzy arches one eyebrow. "To USU. For the vet program." She folds her arms. "So, then, I violated your trust more by reading the email *you* had sent to *her*." Her lips are pursed.

Tim leans back in his chair and exhales loudly. "I can't be mad at you for seeing that, because you were doing me a big favor when you saw it. I'm sorry I got upset, and I can explain."

"You can't be *mad at her* for seeing it while she was trying to break an insane stallion, alone, to come up with a huge amount of money for your bail?" I'm trying to suppress my laughter. "How magnanimous of you."

Tim leans back and points at me, his eyes pinning mine at the same time. "I still can't figure out why this guy's even here."

"Without me, you would still be locked up," I say. "Izzy told me about your predicament, and I wired the money over right away."

"You got an amazing horse out of it, so I don't see—"

"I promised him that I'd help him work with the stallion for a week or so," Izzy says. "He's hard to handle, and Drago *trusts* me." She frowns—at *me*. "Now, if you'll just talk to me and ignore Leonid, I promise he'll also refrain from interrupting." She arches an eyebrow and glares at me.

Like *I'm* the problem.

I sigh, but I close my mouth.

"I shouldn't have asked Becca to do that," he says. "But if you were accepted, you would have moved hours away." He sighs. "I just. . ." His shoulders slump. His entire body sags. "I just." He shakes his head. "I'm sorry, but I couldn't bear the thought of losing you, and I—" His voice cracks, and I swear, it looks like he's trying to cry.

She can't possibly be buying this. Only, it looks like she might be softening. "You should've told me that."

"Instead of using your position and authority to manipulate and control her."

Izzy glares.

I throw my hands up. "I'm sorry. Go ahead."

"You made me feel like I wasn't good enough." Izzy sounds so broken in that moment, that leaping across the table and smashing his face into goo doesn't feel like enough. "I thought I was too stupid to be with you. I thought—" She *is* crying. It's not an act. The person she trusted the most betrayed her, and now he's saying he did it *for* her.

I drop a hand on her knee.

And that one point of contact is enough. I already hated Timothy Heaston, but with my hand on Izzy's knee, I can see his soul in his face, and it's dark. It's not the face of a serial killer, not quite, but it's as dark as fouled water, almost as dark as I've seen.

"I am so sorry, Iz." He stands up, arms outstretched, as if he's going to gather her against him and hug her or stroke her hair or something.

Izzy shakes her head and *turns toward me.*

The raging beast inside of me that has wanted to kill

Heaston since the beginning roars. I gather her closer, my arms wrapping around her. "Shh. You were too good for him all along," I whisper in Russian. "Far, far too good for him. You always will be."

"What are you saying?" Tim's fists look ready to try and take me out.

"Nothing you would understand," I say. "Don't worry about it."

"Were the two of you. . ." Tim ducks his head until he's staring at Izzy. "Did something happen while I was in there?" He throws a thumb backward, at the door he just exited. "Did this guy buy the horse because you. . .earned it?"

"Stop suggesting things that you would do," I say. "Izzy's nothing like you." Which I can now visually see. Her face glows like the sun. It's brighter and more brilliant than nearly any other face that I've seen. She's as lovely as he is dark.

And I mean to make sure he never gets near her again.

"Iz, you can't stay mad at me when I was doing it for us. I know it was wrong, and I'm really sorry, but tell me that I can fix it." He drops onto his chair and drags it closer, the metal feet screeching against the tile. "I would leave this practice, or even this state, for you. We can move somewhere close to another vet school. Then you can go to school while I work—I told you the second I got out of here, I'd buy you a ring. I meant it." He stretches his hand across the table. "Come with me. We can go choose one now."

Izzy pulls away from me slowly, like a flower unfolding under the rays of the sun, and she turns back toward him. "Did you do what they're saying, what your partners are saying?" Her voice is small, so small I can barely hear her words. "Did you steal money from the other partners? Did you overcharge clients and recommend surgeries that horses didn't even need?"

It's clear on his face.

He's guilty as sin itself.

"Of course not." Now he's scooting back. I should have expected this. She's accusing him, so he has to get defensive and aggressive in response. "I can't believe that you, of all people, could believe that of me. I thought you loved me."

"I wouldn't have thought you'd email Dr. Hartfield," she says. "I'm beginning to worry that the Tim Heaston I loved. . .isn't you at all. I'm worried I made up some other version of you in my head."

"You've been listening to your friends." Tim's expression is set, angry. "It's that Paige, right? She's always hated me. I think it's because she liked me herself. She's jealous of us—of you."

"Actually, she said you made a pass at her," Izzy says. "I thought she was lying. I thought she was jealous of the time we were spending together, but now?" She stands. "I thought I wasn't good enough when I was with you. I thought I wasn't smart enough, wasn't interesting enough. . .wasn't *enough*. I worried all the time that I'd disappoint you. I'm finally realizing that the only thing that made me an idiot was not seeing you for who you really were."

He leaps to his feet. "If you think I'm a liar, I'm an evil manipulator, then why did you even bail me out?"

"So I could dump you face-to-face, I guess," she says. "Only creeps do things through email, or hadn't you heard?" She turns and starts to walk off.

Tim reaches for her, but I'm not about to let that happen. I step into his space and punch him right in the nose.

He swears loudly, spraying blood all over me, the floor, and his own shirt. He swears again, and then he draws one arm back to take a shot at me.

I bump his arm away from the inside, knocking it wide, and punch him again. If the first hit didn't break his nose, that second one definitely did. That makes me smile.

"Leo!" Izzy's outraged cry reminds me that we're standing in a police station. Plus, she said *Leo*. It makes me smile.

I wave at the camera. "Diplomatic immunity." Then I shrug, spin on my heel, and walk out.

Izzy falls into step beside me on the way out. "Did you use your powers back there?"

I can't help my snort. "Please. I don't need magic to defeat someone like him. I just punched him in the face." I try to suppress my smile and fail. "Twice." I pause, falling behind while she keeps going. "Wait. Are you saying I *can* use them against him? Because, I forgot. . .my wallet. I need to go back in there."

Izzy pivots and glares at me balefully. "No, I'm definitely not saying you can do anything to him."

I trot to catch up with her, but as we reach the truck, I realize I'm covered in blood spatter. "This is unseemly," I say. "I can't be walking around like this. I'm the leader of the noble and powerful country of Russia."

Izzy's eyes widen when she notices the blood on my shirt. "Are you alright?" She grabs my hand.

My heart does a very strange thing. It speeds up. I find myself breathing faster. I want to talk, but I have no idea what to say.

She turns my hand over and frowns. "This one looks fine. Did you punch him with your other hand? I thought you were right-handed." She releases it and reaches for my other hand.

I let her take it. . .and the same thing happens again. Plus, something more happens, something new. A little thrill of excitement runs up my arm and makes my whole body shiver, but not in a bad way.

She looks up at me. "Are you alright? What was that little tremble? Are you sick? Coming down with something?"

I snatch my hand away. "I'm fine. The blood's from that guy." I'm not saying his name. "But I'm glad you're concerned for my well-being and not upset."

"Oh, I'm upset alright." She shakes her head and holds out her hand. "Give me my key and let's get out of here before the police come arrest you."

"Do you know what diplomatic immunity means?" I ask.

She rolls her eyes. "I'm not an idiot, but you have no papers. I know you entered a code at the bank, but you think that's how it works at the local police station?"

"They could watch any news station and see clips of me."

"Speaking of that, why haven't they become alarmed that you're missing?"

"My staff isn't idiotic. We had protocols in place for this."

"You had protocols in place?" She drops her hands to her hips. "Do you often drop off the face of the earth, get stuck as a horse, and almost die? You're frequently *stolen* by twenty-some-thing, recent college grads and *ridden* around a pasture?" Her mouth's twitching. "Really?"

I like it when she smiles, and I don't like it when she's mad. I do sort of like it when she's glaring at me, as long as her eyes are flashing and her mouth is twisting like that.

Which is stupid.

I should not care what this woman thinks. Like she's saying, I have a country to run. I need to focus on getting us unlinked and regaining full use of my magic.

"Let's get you a new car," I say. "Then we can get me some new clothing, and prioritize unlinking ourselves. I do need to be able to use my powers again so I can go back to running half the world."

"Half the world, is it? Because you're executing other dictators so you can take over their countries?" She tilts her head.

"You've been looking me up." I can't help my grin. "Yes, I need to get back to all of that. Executions and world domination, etcetera."

"I can't believe I'm helping Pol Pot."

"Oh please. He ruled for three and a half years, and he killed plenty of good people." I step past her, open the door, and climb into the driver's side. "I'm not going to be nearly that easy to defeat, and I only kill villains—if I then take over their countries, well, it's for their own good."

"Sorry, Stalin. I misspoke."

Now she's really irritating me, but it's in a way no one else ever has.

And I like it.

Maybe too much.

CHAPTER 13

Izzy

Something about Leonid distracts me.

His presence makes me think about his hands, about his wicked smile, and about his bright, terribly green eyes. Then I forget things that matter like...

I smack my forehead. "We can't go buy clothes or whatever else you said. My horses are still at *Tim*'s place."

"Your—oh." Leonid nods. "Your horses and your father's trailer."

"Stepfather," I say. "But, yes. I need to get my horses, and I don't have anywhere else lined up here to take them."

"Do you remember being shocked when I transferred more money than you asked for?" He glances my way, already pulling out on the road back to Tim's place. I'm impressed he remembers how to get there.

As we drive off, I notice Tim jogging out of the jail. He waves at us—presumably wanting a ride. Leonid just smiles serenely as we pass.

"He doesn't have a car here," I say. "Maybe we should let him hitch a ride in the back."

"He can call a friend, if he has any," Leonid says. "Or he can walk. It's not that far."

A week ago, I'd have been frantic at the idea of leaving Tim behind. I'd be worried about how angry he'd be. I'd have been terrified about what might come out of it.

Dumping him is freeing in more ways than one.

"Take some of the money I moved to your account, and find a new place for your horses." He plucks my phone out of the cupholder and extends it toward me. "Isn't that what those are good for?"

"I mean, I guess, but what place is going to take two horses *today*?" I shake my head. "That's not how it works. You make plans. I'll have to leave them at Tim's until I can find—or." How depressing. "I could load them up in Steve's trailer and take them home, I guess."

He takes the phone.

"Hey," I say. "Give that back."

His side eye's irritating. "Then start calling barns with it— start with the nicest one around here—and ask how much they'd charge to take your horses. Actually, call them, and then hand me the phone."

I roll my eyes. "I'm not going to do that." But I know just the barn to call. My friend Breanna keeps her horses there, and it's amazing. Perfect turn out, wonderful care, and the prettiest indoor and outdoor arenas I've seen. I pull up the listing, and I call.

"Hello?" a woman asks.

Before I can say a word, Leonid snatches the phone. "Hello, love."

"Hey," I say. "You just took it. I can talk."

But he ignores me. "I'm in a bit of a bind," he says. "My girlfriend's got the two loveliest horses, and they *cannot* stay another day where she's been boarding them. The grossest guy you've ever met is a groom there, and he's stalking her." His voice drops to barely above a whisper. "I just found out, and I have to keep her safe."

My mouth drops open—I'm sure the woman is responding, but I can't hear what she's saying in response to his ridiculous story.

"I totally understand that it can be hard to move things around, but there must be something you can do. Understand that money is no object here. I'm happy to pay you an extra ten thousand dollars—apiece—to help you find a new home for whatever horses you need to shift."

He smiles, so she must be saying something good.

"Of course I'll have her make a list of what supplements and food they receive." He shrugs and rolls his eyes. "Yes, we'll be there in twenty minutes."

I shake my head. "An hour," I say. "At least."

"Sorry," he says. "I meant an hour."

"It can't be that easy," I say.

He hands me my phone. "I think you'll find that money makes most things exceedingly simple. Life is only hard when you can't afford to pay for things."

Is he right? If so, that's a little sad. "Well, I guess I should say thanks."

"I'm sorry, what?" He turns slightly. "I'm afraid with the noise from the road and the general anger you were just expressing, I couldn't hear you."

I chuckle. "Thank you, Leo. You solved my problem, and I'm not worried anymore."

"You're so very welcome."

The next few hours are strange. I use more than twenty thousand dollars of Leonid's money to find a new home for my horses. The barn owner and trainer of my friend Breanna's place meets us personally, and I'm forced to go along with Leonid's insane story that he's my boyfriend.

"Why yes," he says like it's perfectly normal. "The bloodstains on my shirt are from when I punched that stalker. I'm just afraid that even violence and threats might not be enough to keep him away." He gestures at me. "Look at this stunning creature. What insane person—like that man—could stay away?"

I'm so busy rolling my eyes that I worry they might get stuck up inside my head. But he's not even done. He insists that we drive to a dealership and buy a brand new truck.

"I can't have you driving around in this." He sighs. "To be honest, I wouldn't pick a truck at all, but. . ."

"I have to be able to pull a trailer," I say.

He leans closer. "But the best horses don't need trailers. They can fit in any sports car easily." He runs his hand downward, clearly talking about himself.

And I'm rolling my eyes again. "As far as I know, my other two horses don't transform. Based on what you've turned into, that's a real *blessing*."

"Hey." He's frowning as he hails the salesman who's walking past. It's not the salesperson we've been working with on the new F250. "Don't you have sports cars here, too? Show us the nicest one you have."

The man beams. "That's definitely the Shelby Cobra. We were lucky to get it. It's the only one in the state, and it's a really cool shade of electric blue, with white racing stripes." This guy has clearly been drooling over this car.

Leo's mouth curves upward. "We'll take it."

"You'll *take* it?" The man blinks. "Don't you want to test drive it?"

Leo shakes his head. "You convinced me when you said it was the only one in the state."

"Do you even know what that costs?" I hiss. "I don't need a sports car—I doubt I can afford the insurance. Some of us don't have diplomatic immunity or an entire country's tax revenue to support ourselves."

"That must really stink," Leonid says. "But now you have

me, which is basically the same thing." He turns to the salesman with a half-smile. "I think the women in our lives don't even know what they're missing. It's our job to show them." The salesman's just staring at us, almost like we're speaking Russian. "Go." Leonid shoos him. "Get whatever you need to get that car put in my girlfriend's name."

The second he's gone, I can't help my hiss. "Stop calling me your girlfriend. Have you gone insane? Well, *more* insane?"

Leo shrugs.

"And are you just trying to make me spend every dime you gave me?" I ask. "Because I'll give it all back—we don't have to spend it. And what if my government gets upset and wants me to pay taxes on that money?"

Shoot. Now that I say that, I can see it all unfolding. I'm totally the kind of person who winds up going to jail because of something like this. *Diplomatic* freaking *immunity*. Doesn't help me, does it?

Leonid rolls his eyes, and a moment later, when they bring the final papers for the truck, *he* insists on logging into some system again to wire money for both vehicles, and he puts them in my name. "See? Now I'm not making you use the money I gave you to compensate you for all this hassle, and for the service you're doing to the Russian people, keeping me safe." His grin is irritating.

"No," I say. "I don't want any of this."

He pulls me close. "These expenditures show my people I'm alive and doing fine. It's sending them an important message, without which they will come looking for me. I'm not ready for that yet, because we haven't eliminated this connection between us. But maybe you're ready to announce to the world that you're my girlfriend—because with a beautiful, young, single woman? That's the only story anyone else will believe."

Nope. I definitely don't want to be surrounded by a

hundred overbearing Russians. One's more than enough. I can only imagine what the media would do with a story like this.

When we finally finish, Leo hands me the keys to the cobra. "You drive this one. I'll follow you in the truck with the trailer."

He's right—we'll have to take the trailer with us. We certainly can't leave it here with my old truck.

"I can drive that."

"I bought the cobra for you." He presses the key into my hand, and then he leans closer, his mouth right beside my ear. "Just don't forget to go slowly enough that I can keep up. If you move too far away from me. . ." He snorts, his breath warming my ear. "It would be bad if I totaled your brand new truck."

I shiver. "But it's going to be hard to park that truck and trailer in my complex," I say. "That's why I always left it at Tim's. Maybe you should take the cobra so I can find some place to park the trailer." I can still see him, all focused and careful. The last thing he needs is to try and park my huge trailer in the apartment complex parking lot.

"I'll be fine."

"It's just that, until now, I've—"

"It's fine," he says. "I insist. Just make sure I'm keeping up."

Leonid's definitely one of those people with whom it's easier to just agree. Fighting him would be too much work on something like this.

He follows me in the truck to my apartment complex. He wasn't wrong about the cobra. This little sports car's a *lot* of fun to drive, even going the speed limit and making sure that he's staying close. I'm a little embarrassed as we pull up—I certainly never thought I'd be taking the czar of Russia to see my shabby little apartment. I hover for a moment, but he manages to park the whole thing just fine across five parking spaces on the back row, just in front of the back fence line. Once he's out and moving toward me, I climb out, too.

My next door neighbor's on his way out as I pull up. He

swears loudly when he sees me climbing out of the shiny, new blue sportscar. He runs his hand along one of the white racing stripes. "Nice, Brooks. I guess being with that old-man boyfriend of yours is finally paying off."

"Shut up, Brian," I say.

"She dumped him, anyway," Leonid says.

"You did?" Brian's smiling big. "Good. I hated that guy."

"It seems everyone did," I say.

"He was a dou—" Brian cuts off as Leonid steps up onto the sidewalk next to me. "Wait, who's that?"

"I'm Leonid Ivanovich." He inclines his head half an inch. "But my friends call me Leo."

"I'm the only one who calls you Leo," I say.

Leo smiles. "Precisely."

"You're—" Brian blinks. "Wait, how long ago did you break up with the old guy? Do you *already* have a new boyfriend?"

I roll my eyes and step away from Leonid. I say, "no," at the same time he says, "yes."

Brian snorts. "Geez. A guy can't catch a break around here."

"Nope. A guy sure can't." Leonid waves his hand. "Go about your business, Brian. That is, if you have any." He glares.

Brian wisely pivots and walks off, muttering something I can't quite make out, but it sounded like 'guy's wearing tomato soup on his shirt.' I can't get distracted by any of that, though.

"What was that about?" I ask. "You're not my boyfriend, you know. You can't keep telling everyone that."

"Oh, that makes sense. I suppose you'd rather I tell everyone we meet that we're joined by some kind of magical bond that we can't explain. In fact, maybe one of the people we tell could help us identify the source of our connection."

And I'm back to rolling my eyes again. "You're annoying."

Another neighbor walks past, eyeing the car as he walks.

"Not as annoying as everyone in this place." He glares.

"How many people live here, exactly?" He lowers his voice. "There appear to be people everywhere."

"It's an apartment. They don't have those in Russia?"

"They do," he says. "But most of the people work. They wouldn't all be loitering around." He scowls at the guy, who runs off.

I grab his arm and drag him along, opting to walk up the three flights of stairs instead of taking the perfectly serviceable elevator. He deserves it. Only, when we reach the top, I'm the only one huffing. Leonid seems perfectly fine.

That just puts me in a bad mood.

"I wish I had a shirt for you," I say. "But I don't keep men's shirts here. I'm going to run and change my clothes." I wish I had time for a shower. Hooking and unhooking the trailer and moving two horses was a major chore, and I feel like I still smell like a horse. "Then we can go out and find you some new clothes."

"By all means." He waves his hand. "Take all the time you need." He's walking around my family room, peering at my photos, and I don't like it. I flip the one of me and Tim face down, and then I turn on the television.

"I'm assuming you want to get caught up on the world, having spent the last few days stuck in a paddock." I point at the sofa. "Sit. Watch."

He barely glances at the news. "Sure."

"I may take a shower," I say. "I smell like. . ." It feels rude to tell a horse-shifter that I smell like a horse like it's a bad thing.

"Like a horse?" He's smiling when he turns toward me. "I probably do, too."

"Uh, I just have the one shower."

"I'm fine with sharing if you are." But he doesn't actually take any steps toward me. I'm ninety percent sure he's kidding.

His grin's pretty mischievous, though.

Eighty percent.

"Look, I really did just dump my boyfriend, and I'm sure you're just kidding, and you're the czar of freaking Russia, so I'm not trying to say—"

"I like you, Isabel Brooks." He straightens and turns to face me fully. "I know you barely know me, and I know you just broke up with your loser boyfriend, and I would never dream of pushing you into anything, in spite of what we may be telling people to explain our situation."

I arch one eyebrow.

"At least, I wouldn't push you very much, anyway." He smiles.

My heart skips a beat. Maybe two.

"I have flaws, but dishonesty isn't one of them. When that boy downstairs implied he might want a chance to date you?" He steps toward me. "I wanted to pull his intestines out through his nostrils."

I blink.

"And when your loser ex tried to grab your arm, had I had my powers, I probably would have done even worse to him."

I swallow.

"I'm not the devil." He steps closer. "I destroy villains. It's all I do, really. But many people believe I'm very, very bad, and I *am* extremely powerful." He steps closer again, and he's only inches away from me, his emerald eyes intent on my face. "And probably because of our bond, or maybe because of your dimples, I think of you as mine. I know you're not, but I want you to be." He presses his lips together.

I have no idea what to say to that.

My heart's pounding so loudly that I can hear it in my ears.

I want to grab him and kiss him and then throw him down on my very soft, very close sofa. But that would be *insane*.

"I do have a question for you."

"What?" I have no idea what to do with my hands, so I twist my fingers together in front of my body.

"You could have sold me to that man. You thought I was a horse. You thought I was an unmanageable stallion, and you hadn't seen that email from Tim yet. You still wanted to help him, very much so."

"Right." I twist my fingers even tighter.

"So. . .why didn't you?" His eyes—they look hopeful.

"I—" I look down at my hands. "I'm not sure." I wince. "I mean, I didn't want to falsify the papers. I didn't want to commit a crime for someone who was already in jail. What if I wound up there myself?"

"You were scared, then? That's why you didn't?"

He's being really honest with me. Painfully honest, even. I might think he's saying all this because he's a womanizer, but being realistic, he's gorgeous, he's rich, and he's powerful. He could already have any woman he wants, and being stuck to me isn't really a justification for trying to sleep with me.

Unless he just does this when he's bored.

"You don't have to answer," he says. "It's fine if you'd rather not talk about your reasons."

I force myself to look up. "I didn't want to sell you. Thinking about it made me anxious. I—" I sigh. "I guess that's it. The idea of selling you made me feel sick."

He smiles.

"Maybe it was our connection, or maybe I just liked you. I'm not sure."

"You saved me a few days ago." He's barely speaking above a whisper now.

He's speaking so softly that I take a step closer so I can hear.

"No one has ever saved me before. I've always had to save myself." He reaches out with one finger and touches the edge of my collarbone, and then he runs his finger gently down it toward the base of my throat. This time, he is whispering. "I know we're supposed to be breaking this bond between us, but for some reason, I don't want to."

I can't breathe.

Like, I can't breathe at all.

He lifts his finger, and air rushes into my lungs. It's like, while he's touching me, while he's saying things I have no idea how to process, my body just stops working right. "I—I need to shower."

"Alone, I'm assuming?" His eyebrows lift just a little, his eyes dancing. "Pity."

While I *run* like a scared rabbit back to the bathroom, I hear him laughing in the other room.

CHAPTER 14

Izzy

While I'm showering, I finally have time to think things through. One question keeps bothering me. Why was Leonid at my parents' farm?

That question leads to a whole host of other questions. Why was he stuck in Steve's stallion paddock? Did my parents find him? Was he acting insane because he was really a man? Is that why they locked him up? And what's the connection between my family and Leonid? I feel like if we can figure that out, we might have a shot at breaking the bond that he apparently no longer wants to break.

I shiver again, just thinking of what he said.

And how he said it.

Which is stupid. If I thought Tim was too good for me, the gorgeous, supermodel leader of Russia is *way* too good for me. Plus, what would I do if I wanted to make this work? Move to Russia? I can't even consider that. My entire life's here.

Not to mention, I don't speak a single word of their language.

By the time I'm clean, I feel better, but I've also screwed up my resolve to get some answers. I spend a little too much time getting dressed, and if I put on my brand new, expensive, birthday-present dress that Mom got me from Tecovas, well. I rarely have cause to wear anything nice. It's a deep brownish maroon with tiny stars on it, and it really accentuates my ample bosom and narrow waist. Or at least, that's what Mom said when she bought it.

I haven't worn it yet—I was saving it.

That thought makes me feel kind of stupid for putting it on. It's not like I like really think Leo and I. . . It's just that, if we're going shopping, I should at least look presentable. If someone recognizes him, they'll be sure to take photos of us. I'd rather not have my time with him memorialized as some kind of scrubby country bumpkin following the czar of Russia around.

That's a good reason to look presentable, actually. Instead of ducking out in a rush, I swipe on some eye shadow and mascara, just in case. I almost never wear makeup, but I should look my best for any possible photos. When I finally emerge, Leonid's not watching television at all. He's not even pretending to watch. He's flipping through an old photo album and smiling.

"You're just digging through my stuff now?"

He doesn't even look remotely guilty when he looks up. "Yes, I am."

I scowl. "I can't go through your stuff. Don't you think that's unfair?"

He leaps to his feet gracefully and stalks toward me.

Even with a stained shirt, pants that are too short, and a very used pair of sneakers, he looks like something from a television show. Polished. Smooth. Teeth-grittingly handsome. I realize that he's every bit as beautiful in his human form as he was in horse form.

He tucks the strand of hair that's falling forward across my eyes behind my ear, and he smiles. "What things of mine would you want to look at?"

"I—that's not what I meant."

He drops his hand. "No?"

"I just. . .as I was showering, I realized you seem to know almost everything about my life. Tim, the breakup, my horses, my family, and now you've seen my apartment." I poke a finger at him. "But I know nothing about you."

"I'm the czar of Russia. My life's plastered all over the television." He cocks his head sideways. "I've been in your country for weeks, and cameras follow me everywhere."

"But—that's not—"

He lowers his head so our eyes are almost on level. "Are you saying you want to know *the real* me?"

How does he keep making me so nervous and jumpy? "No. I'm saying I want to know what you were doing at Birch Creek Ranch. Why were you stuck in your horse form at my mom's house?" I nod, proud that I finally got it all out. "What's really going on?" I narrow my eyes in a way that I hope is intimidating.

Leonid straightens, his eyes studying me more carefully. "Good question."

"Are you going to answer it?"

"We'll have a lot of time while we're shopping," he says. "I can start to answer it, anyway."

"Start?" Now I'm annoyed. "I can tell you why I was there in ten seconds. I'd borrowed my stepdad's trailer, and I had to return it."

"But you also wanted to ask them to borrow money so you could bail out your boyfriend," he says. "The reason you didn't return the trailer or ask them for money is that you were distracted by the stallion. But you were distracted so easily, because you didn't want to ask them for money, and you were looking for a chance to get out of it." He shrugs. "Most questions have a more complex answer than the one we give. I'm just telling you that before I answer, I need to lay the groundwork so my answer makes sense."

"Spoken like a politician preparing to perjure himself."

He smiles. "I'm planning *not* to perjure myself. That's what is going to take some time."

"Tell me this." I can't help thinking of his solution to everything—kill people. He's powerful, he has no compunctions eliminating people when they get in his way. I can't forget the diplomatic immunity he's often mentioned either. "Did you harm anyone in my family?"

"No. In fact, when I left, I believe they were all in good health."

"Do you *plan* to harm anyone in my family?"

He tilts his head, like he's saluting me. "Another good question, and also no. I don't have any plans to harm your family in any way."

"Then I suppose you can answer the rest in a long way if you like." I shake my finger at him. "But it's suspicious, and right now, I'm already doubting my judgment. Don't give me a reason to dump you on the side of the road."

"Oh, I don't want you to dump me at all." The way he says it, the way he's looking at me, almost makes me think he's talking about *dumping* dumping me. But that's—I'm beginning to think the czar's just a little flirty. I wonder whether that's why so many women love him. I'm not about to become another bank manager.

So I ignore his innuendo. "We should go, then. You definitely need an upgrade to your wardrobe. It's basically a miracle no one recognized you at the car dealership. If they had, you never could have lived *this* down." I can't help my smirk.

"Fewer Americans than you might think actually watch the world news," he says. "I've gone many places without being recognized."

"That's sadly true," I say.

"Even so, I really need new shoes. If I don't get some soon, I may need new feet."

I chuckle at that, and I grab the cobra key. "If your feet hurt that badly, it's a safety issue. I'm driving."

He, wisely, doesn't argue, but his smile tells me he thought about it.

"You know, we do need to get this connection between us severed." I unlock the car. "I can't just follow you around so you don't pass out."

Leonid climbs in the passenger side while I take the driver's seat. "And I need to be able to use my magic without touching you, but I do like the excuse." He drops his hand over mine.

I snatch it away. "None of that."

He smiles. "Why not? You don't like it?"

"I need room to breathe," I say. "You're already taking over my life. I just got rid of Tim." I realize as I say it that I mean it. If this had happened a week ago, I'd have been inconsolable. Now that he's gone, it's freeing.

I'm not depressed.

I'm not even sad. I hadn't realized how much he hampered my ability to grow, to breathe, to be myself.

"Fine." He shrugs. "I'll respect your space." He whispers, "For now."

I back out of the parking spot and head for the exit, but only then does it occur to me. . .I have no idea where we should go. "What kinds of clothes do you usually wear?"

He shrugs. "Nice ones."

I should have guessed. "Suits?"

"Suits. Slacks. Sweaters."

That reminds me of a place Tim talked about sometimes—Beckett and Robb. It's supposed to be the nicest custom clothing in Utah. I'm not sure whether they sell anything from the rack, but a quick search on my phone shows they aren't *too* far from me. We could at least try it. "I have an idea. I bet it would be perfect for you."

"While you drive, I'll start answering your question."

"Okay."

"But please pay attention to the road."

I can't help glaring at him. "Of course." I roll my eyes.

"I was born in the eighteen hundreds."

"What?" I swerve into the next lane, and the large red SUV next to us honks.

"I told you to focus on the road."

I say a few select words. "You don't look hundreds of years old."

"Very late eighteen hundreds," he says. "And I'm not hundreds of years old. I'm right around a hundred and thirty, but I'm also just right around thirty."

"That makes no sense."

"It's a strange set of circumstances," he says. "Which is why I said it might take some time to explain."

"Well, I'm listening," I say. "Go ahead."

"Of course, when I was born, I had no idea about any of the crazy things that would happen in my life. All I knew was that we were very poor, that I didn't have a mother or any siblings, and that no one really liked my father."

"Why not?"

"My father—I'm not sure what they'd say about him today. At the time, he was all I had. I knew nothing different, so I didn't question it. He told a story to anyone who would listen. I can still recite it verbatim, I heard it so often." Leonid's looking out the window as we drive past the various streets of Salt Lake.

"I'm not sure about things here, but Ivan the Terrible's a ruler most children in Russia have heard of. He was the last great Rurikid ruler. He had three sons with his wife Anastasia. The first son died in infancy. The second son was named Ivan Ivanovich. The third son was Feodor. The records show that the second son, Ivan, was strong, brilliant, fierce, and Ivan the Terrible's choice to replace him on the throne. However, it also shows that after an altercation, Ivan the Terrible struck his son and killed him."

I gasp. "He killed his own son?"

"He was called 'the terrible' for a reason." Leonid shrugs. "It's in all the records, but my dad's story starts here. He says Ivan didn't kill his son Ivan. He says they got into a huge fight, and the son Ivan stormed off. When Ivan the Terrible fell ill, some time later, one of the boyars later spread the story that he wasn't ill. He was quite strong, and in fact had recently been fighting with his own strong, hale son and struck him down."

"That's a terrible story to use to convince people you're not sick."

"It is, but I fear that was more telling of the time they lived in. You were strong, or you were at risk. In any case, not long after, when Ivan the Terrible died, he and his son had not made up, so his sickly, mentally ill son Feodor was made the new czar. When he had no children, the Rurikid line was said to have died out. Only, my father said it didn't. Ivan, who had left Russia, tried to return. He made every effort, but the boyars, desiring to run the country themselves, prevented it."

"If that's true, that's pretty sad."

"Ivan, whom everyone believed to be dead, was instead hiding in Europe. By the time his descendants finally returned, no one believed that they were who they said they were."

"Because how could they prove it?"

"Precisely. My father had an amulet, a scepter, and a crown he claimed were given to Ivan by his father when he was made the heir. My father, generations later, still had them, but he hid them all the time. He would only get them out when he met someone he thought might help him retake his crown. At the time, they were his only proof."

"What did they look like?"

"They each bore the symbol of the Rurikid line, a trident. The same symbol also resembles a three-pointed flame. They all have large, brilliant, blood-red rubies set into them, and I could tell they were valuable."

"What's the point of a three-pronged flame?"

"The three points were to represent the magic in our bloodline, our divine right as the original Rus conquerors of the area, and our ability to claim animal and human dominion." He shrugs. "Also, when Rurik took the throne originally, he did it with two brothers, but he was the only one to survive—the point of the flame."

"This is all pretty weird," I say.

"I thought so too," he says. "And my father didn't even stop there. He would also explain to anyone who would listen that our blood bore the magic of Rurik's line."

"Which I guess it did," I say. "But I doubt that incinerating people made him lots of friends."

"Oh, it was far worse than that," Leo says. "See, he told anyone he deemed important that we could shift into horses and command the elements—earth, air, wind, water, and lightning."

"So he sounded crazy, right up until he turned into a horse, I guess."

"That was the problem," Leonid says. "He couldn't use any magic, and he couldn't turn into a horse. I didn't know anything more about it, then. I only knew that he would tell these stories, and people would laugh, and they would mock us as crazy, and then we'd be run out of another town. Almost as soon as my father found a job, or as soon as we had a place to eat or food on the table, he'd meet new people, and he'd tell his stories, and we'd be run out of town yet again."

"That's horrible."

"I didn't have a very good childhood," Leonid says. "And when I was about ten, he showed the relics to the wrong person, and he was robbed of even those. Frankly, looking back, I was surprised he had them as long as he did. I imagine most people assumed they were fake. But eventually, we found a place to live that was beautiful. He and I both had good jobs—working outside, mostly away from people—and the family didn't seem to mind his ranting. I knew that it was all absurd, and I told them that while he was delusional, he was harmless."

"But you *can* turn into a horse."

"I'll get there."

"Okay." We're almost to Beckett and Robb, but I don't want to stop listening.

"The daughter of the lord we were working for came to me one day, and she asked for a favor."

"Okay." I pull into a parking spot.

"Oh, we're here."

I nod. "Yep. The place I was thinking of is right there."

"I can finish on our way back."

"Fine."

He frowns. "What has you so irritated?"

"I want to know what happens—how did you get from the early nineteen hundreds to now, where you're the czar and you can shift into a horse?"

He smiles. "I have you hooked. It's all going according to plan." He rubs his hands together.

I can't help it. I laugh. "Assuming this is all true, you've at least been watching plenty of modern television," I say. "You mimicked the cartoon villains perfectly."

"In your life, you appear to be surrounded by people who care for you—friends and family. I was not so lucky. It left me plenty of time for catching up on the modern world." Leonid's not someone who feels sorry for himself, clearly, but I sense for the first time an underlying sadness, a vulnerability I never noticed before.

I think he's lonely.

It must have been hard, being poor in that time period, which meant he was truly hungry and sometimes starving. He was ridiculed. His father was correct—as evidenced by the fact that he can shift into a horse—but that almost makes it more tragic. His father wasn't actually crazy, just misunderstood and doggedly determined to stick with what he knew.

Leonid exits the car and looks down at me through the glass. Then he tosses his head.

I follow him into the store I drove him to, but when we get inside, I realize this was a terrible idea. There aren't many articles of clothing here at all. Other than a handful of garments hanging on racks, there's nothing, actually.

"Did you have an appointment today?" The tall, very well-dressed man looks a little confused, like he knows we don't.

"We didn't," Leonid says.

When the man hears his British accent, his eyebrows rise. "Ah. Well, I'm Curtis, and I manage this location. We usually operate on an appointment-only basis, but as I recognize you, I can guess that there might be extenuating circumstances, Your Majesty." He bows his head.

Not only was he recognized, but by the very first person we see.

"I have a need for new clothing." Leonid looks down at his shirt in disgust. "A long sequence of circumstances has led to this, but it seems you understand why I can't go out in public looking this way."

Leonid has a presence. I can't really describe it, but even though his stained, too-small clothes should look ridiculous, they don't, somehow. Clearly the man also sees it.

"Our store makes custom-order suits. We need these sample styles in order to show customers their options and see how standard sizing would work. However, we do sometimes have extras that people. . ." He clears his throat. "Decline to pay the balance on when they arrive."

"Interesting," Leonid says.

"I can also expedite your order, should you like to place one, and have it here in less than a week."

Leonid nods. "I would be happy to take anything you can offer."

An hour and a half later, with a seamstress working furiously in the back to modify a few things, we leave with a trunk full of clothing and another fifty thousand dollars' worth of things on order. "Did you really need that much?" I shake my head. "It won't all fit in my apartment."

He looks transformed. I thought he looked good in Tim's clothing, but seeing him in a dark sweater with light grey slacks? The staff had another shop bring some shoes over, and he looks better than I thought he could. "That's not much of a concern. I'm sure you won't be staying there for very long anyway."

"Why not?" I hardly think I'm about to leave my apartment.

"I'm sure Tim will think to come by soon, if he hasn't already."

"Leo, people don't move after a breakup. They just move *on*."

"Moving on is simpler when you've also moved." He shrugs. "Trust me on this one."

I roll my eyes. "You're crazy."

"Yes, I've heard."

My head snaps to the side. "Oh, I didn't mean—"

He laughs. "I'm not offended. But it is a decent segue into the story." He points down the street at a small stand. "Please tell me there's food close that's nicer than that."

I glance at the sign. It reads, "Hot Dog On A Stick." I can't help laughing. "I'm sure we can find something better."

"If there's a place you really like, let's go there. I'm hungry enough to eat most anything."

"Market Street Grill isn't far," I say, "Do you like seafood?"

"Do they have good seafood here? Isn't this area landlocked?"

"I mean, for this part of the world, it's the best," I say. "They fly fresh seafood in, and I love the crab cakes."

He shrugs. "Sure. Let's go there."

Once we're back in the car, he picks up with the story like we never stopped. "I should go back a bit. One night, when things had gotten particularly bad, I feared Father and I might not live much longer. He was suffering from what I now believe was alcohol poisoning and malnourishment, and I feared he might perish. We had not been able to find reputable jobs in our new town, and on that very night, I saw a woman struggling to carry her drunk companion to a car. Of course I lent a hand. That woman turned out to be the daughter of a local nobleman, hauling her brother to his vehicle. Helping them landed us positions with the Volkonsky family. At the time, I thought of her as our savior."

I hate hearing that. For some reason, I dislike a woman I barely know. She sounds like she was kind—and he sure needed someone to help him, but I still dislike her. I suppress that thought, because it's clearly nuts. "And then?"

"I worked with their animals, mostly. I wasn't great with horses, but I could manage them. I was decent at other animal husbandry. My father obtained a position as their gardener. I later learned to drive a car and became their chauffeur."

"A big step up," I say.

"You have no idea," he says. "After we had been there for almost six months, I had started to gain weight and height, thanks to finally eating well, and my father's sunken cheeks were filling out. I thought nothing in the world had been luckier than the moment I met Katerina."

Okay, yeah, I tried, but I still hate her. I can't help asking, "Was she pretty?"

He blinks. "Does it matter?"

"Doesn't it always?"

"Pretty isn't the right word to describe her." He frowns.

Oh, good.

"Pretty's for women in shops, or perhaps for women who

have worked very hard to look polished. Katerina was beautiful, elegant, and refined."

Okay, now I really hate her.

"Like before, one night, I happened upon her struggling to haul her worthless older brother home after overindulging. Before realizing I was coming to their aid, she muttered something to him, and he nodded. Then, right in front of my eyes, she turned into a horse."

She's gorgeous *and* magical? Ugh. The world sucks.

"That's how I learned that my father might not be entirely insane with his stories. There really were horse shifters in the world."

"You know, if you get online or go to a library, you can find rows and rows of books about wolves shifting into humans and the reverse," I say. "When there really *are* horse shifters, why isn't *that* in any storybook?"

Leonid's smirk is dry. "I'm sure that *is* the reason. How better to make something absurd than to tell stories that are somewhat close, but not quite the truth? Then if anyone does find out, they'll never believe it. They'll assume it's just more fiction."

Weird, but it makes sense, I guess.

"In any case, that same night, when I approached her, Katerina convinced her father to let me and my father in on their family secret. They had been entrusted with a special kind of magic. In addition to shifting into horses, they could manipulate electricity in any number of useful ways."

I pull into a parking space outside of Market Street Grill. "And then you discovered that you could, too?"

Leonid grimaces. "Quite the opposite. In spite of my father's constant claims, neither he nor I could shift into any other forms or use any magic. After he learned what I'd seen, it took me weeks to get him back to functioning shape. During those weeks, I had to complete all of his work and mine. That kind of effort convinced me that pursuing his obsession was fruitless. If our family ever had that kind of power, surely it had long since abandoned us."

"What?" This story sucks. "But somehow, that changed."

He reaches for the door handle. "It did, but let's get into that over some food, shall we?"

"Fine."

After the bread comes, I order my crab and Leonid orders the plank salmon and the swordfish.

"Two entrees, and no lobster?" I ask. "I'm surprised."

He pulls a face. "You know, when I was. . ." He clears his throat and waits for the waiter to walk off. "Back in the early nineteen hundreds, I hear the servants in this area had rules in regards to lobster."

"Rules?" I blink.

"I notice that you didn't order it, either," he says.

"I don't like it," I say. "It's all rubbery and gross. It just tastes like butter, and only because you douse it in butter."

He laughs. "Indeed. Well, from what I've heard, servants in the early nineteen hundreds here in America considered it to be dirty and disgusting. As it was extremely common and cheap, employers would often try and feed it to their workers as often as three or four times a week. They had to institute rules that it would be provided no more often than once a week."

I can hardly believe it.

"But as it happens, in Russia, thanks to Catherine the Great's love for lobster, it was quite expensive. It's not a crustacean that's native to that region, and they had to be imported. I disliked them because as a servant, I watched the wealthy eating it and wasn't personally allowed to even try it."

"Now you could eat as much as you like."

"I could." His lip twitches. "And yet, I find that I have no interest in it, as with many things I thought were so desirable back then."

"What else?" I'm compelled to ask.

"Well, back then, I also fancied that I liked the daughter of the family who had taken us in."

"Katerina." I hate how flat her name sounds. There's no way he didn't notice that I dislike her.

His smile tells me I'm right. "I quickly discovered that while she pretended to like me, she never had eyes for anyone other than Alexei Romanov."

"Wait, *the* Alexei Romanov? From the family that was killed in the Russian Revolution. . ." My eyes widen. "Don't tell me he's from then, too. The one you had an election against? Are you *both* from the early nineteen hundreds? He's the real Alexei Romanov?"

He looks exceedingly annoyed—far more irritated than I looked when I said Katerina. "Alexei beat me back in the nineteen hundreds, but I defeated him earlier this year. The people chose *me* as their new ruler."

"But. . ." I frown. "I still don't understand how—"

Two men approach our table, and they aren't carrying trays of food. When Leonid looks up, he doesn't look worried. He does, however, look irritated.

"How did you find me?" His eyes flash.

Both men bow their heads. "I'm pleased to see you're alive and well." The man turns toward me, bowing his head again. "I'm Boris Yurovsky."

"And I'm Mikhail Kurakin." The other man drops his head toward me as well.

"Why are you bowing to me?" I ask. "I'm not—" I shake my head. "I'm nobody."

Mikhail's eyes widen. "I've never seen His Royal Majesty take a meal with any other person until today."

Take a meal? It's clear that English is not his first language, or probably even his second. "Well, you aren't seeing it today, either. Our food hasn't arrived yet."

As if I prompted it to come, two men emerge with platters full of food.

"It's here now, though," Leonid says. "You two can wait for us outside."

"But what if they're hungry?" I ask.

"I hear there's a hot dog place around the corner." His expression is flat.

I laugh. "Corn dogs," I say. "That was a corn dog place."

Leonid shrugs. "I don't care. You can wait for me outside."

Both men bow and pivot on their heels.

"How many men did you bring?" Leonid asks.

Mikhail pauses, looks over his shoulder, and says, "Only twenty."

And then they're gone.

I have a feeling that life is about to get even stranger for me, because not two minutes later, a half-dozen flashes from the corner of the room alert us to the presence of reporters.

"Well, shoot," I say.

Leonid snorts. "You can say that again."

CHAPTER 15

Izzy

We do manage to eat a pretty nice dinner. I'm shocked that Leonid's able to eat both the salmon and the swordfish.

"You've had me eating hay for days," he says. "There's something to be said for the lean look, but much more of that and I'd move from lean to emaciated." But it's clear from the way his eyes sparkle that he's not actually upset.

Having seen him with his shirt, er, well, *all* his clothes off, I can attest to the fact that he doesn't look like he's starving. He looked. . .just right.

"Why are your cheeks pink?" He glances around. "Don't worry about the cameras. My people will make sure none of the photos we don't approve are used anywhere. And if they are, our hackers are great at shutting things down."

I hope he's kidding, but I'm pretty sure he's not.

He leans across the table and drops his voice. "Isabel Brooks, I swear that you won't be harmed by your association with me. I'd never allow it."

"Do you know why we're linked?"

He shakes his head.

"Do you know anything about what our connection means?"

Again, he shakes his head.

"It's as big a surprise to you as it was to me?"

"It is."

In that moment, I have a choice to make, just as we all make choices all day every day of our lives. I decide to believe him, but it makes me nervous. The last man I chose to believe was lying to me, and now I'm worried he was lying to many others as well.

"Let's go." He stands.

"We can't." I look around for our waiter.

"My people will pay." He waves for me to stand.

"Are you serious? You just wander around, and your *people* eliminate non-approved paparazzi photos and pay your bills?"

"It's the single best thing about being czar," he says. "That, and they clean up all your unpaid parking tickets." It takes me a second, but I realize he's kidding. Leonid's making a joke.

"You're *so* not who I thought you were."

His head bobs back and forth. "I mean, I could neigh loudly in here if it would make you feel better, but I think a lot of people would be confused."

"You're a very strange man." I stand up and follow him out.

On the way out of the restaurant, Mikhail falls into step beside me, and Boris falls in alongside the other side of Leonid.

"Are they, like, your personal guard?" I whisper.

"He doesn't need a guard," Mikhail says. "We're his first and second lieutenants."

"I like them because like me, they don't need guards," Leonid says. "And I trust them."

"You've known them for so long that you trust they'll always support you?"

Leonid snorts. "Not exactly. I can take their power away at any moment, so they never want to make me unhappy."

"That's. . ." Again, it's not what I expected. I want to ask him more about his story, but I don't really have a chance. He wasn't kidding about his people being around—there are at least twenty people in all black gathered in the parking lot, and they surround us like super-fans mobbing a celebrity, only they're all speaking in scattershot Russian I can't make out, and most of them are frowning.

"I'm going to head back to my apartment." I stop walking with them and fish the keys out of my pocket. "I'll give you my cell phone number, though. You can call me tomorrow."

"Wait." Leonid's head snaps backward in my direction. "You have to stay with me."

Or he'll black out. I forgot for a moment. "Right. Well, I guess a few of them can come with sleeping bags or an air mattress or something—"

He shakes his head. "It would be far easier if you would come with us. Is that alright?"

"Where are you going?" I glance at my watch. It's nearly ten o'clock. "I need to sleep soon. I have to work tomorrow."

Leonid's brow furrows. "Work?"

"I was off for a few days, and it's been the weekend, but I have a job at a vet hospital. I'm an aide."

"Okay, well, we can work that out on the way over." Leonid lifts his arm, like he's waving me to come along with him.

"Over where?" I lift my eyebrows.

He smiles. "How about I let you drive?"

Apparently some of his minions understand English, because that sets them off. They're talking in such rapid-fire Russian that it makes me a little nervous.

"They don't really understand," Mikhail says. "While we were gone for a few days, they worked very hard to keep the media from noticing."

"Gone?" I wonder what he means. "Were you gone too?"

"Mikhail and Boris were with me when. . ." Leonid says. "You're trying to jump ahead in the story."

"Always," I say. "But I said I'd wait for your context, and I'm waiting."

"How about a compromise?" Leonid asks. "You let me drive, and we'll meet them at our hotel." He switches to Russian and speaks so fast, I can't even tell how many words he said.

"You have to negotiate with your staff?" For some reason that makes me laugh.

"He's not a monster," Boris grumbles. "No matter what some people think."

"You should have seen how he reacted when I locked him up," I whisper. "He was pretty monstrous, with all his screaming and rearing up and pawing at the ground."

Mikhail actually cracks a smile.

"Did they agree to your terms?" I ask. "Because we do need to go by my place. I have things—things I need."

Leonid arches one eyebrow. "I only pretend to negotiate to make them feel better. I always do whatever I want."

"That's true," Mikhail says. "Which is why they don't want to agree to let you out of their sight."

"I won't be gone long." He points at the black SUVs lined up in a row. "You guys go with them to reassure them, and we'll see you there soon."

His people, to their credit, do listen. I hold up my end and hand Leonid my keys. They are, after all, to a car he just bought me. Once we're inside, I say, "You better pick up the pace on that story. I feel like I have more questions now, not less."

He chuckles. "I'll try."

"Start with the woman."

"Katerina?" His eyebrows rise.

"Don't say her name," I mutter. "Just tell me how disappointing she was."

He starts the engine and pulls up a phone. One of his people must have either found his old one or supplied him with a new one. It's strange, watching a man I know was born in the eighteen hundreds, tapping away on the phone like it's totally normal. Clearly he's had no trouble adjusting to our screen-filled world. He drops the phone in the cupholder. "She was disappointing." He sighs. "She used me to try and convince Alexei Romanov to take a real interest, and it didn't work nearly as well as she'd hoped. One good thing did come out of it for me."

"What?"

He shoots out onto the road going way too fast.

"Hey, crazy man. We have speed limits here." I grab both arm rests.

His smile's diabolical. "Diplomatic—"

"Don't say it," I say. "Just slow down, and keep talking."

Although he does slow down, it's not by much.

"I should've just gotten the truck," I mutter. "Diplomatic immunity won't keep me alive."

"I'll keep you alive." He grunts. "But I almost died back in the nineteen hundreds, and that's what helped me unlock my powers. A sacrifice for someone else, with no gain in it for me."

"What?"

"It's how we gain access to our powers, doing something selfless, and I did it for stupid Alexei Romanov, the man whom Katerina was obsessed with."

"Peachy."

He frowns. "Peachy?"

"Never mind."

"Sadly, the powers I got were worse than useless to me at the time. All I gained after making that sacrifice was the ability to sense whether people were light or dark, and at first, I didn't even understand what it meant. It took years of being around people, of watching them do horrible things and seeing their souls darken, for me to really understand what my new power even was."

"Tell me what you see when you look at me," I say.

He swings the cobra into a parking lot, and I glance up.

That's when I realize that we're already at my apartment complex. "How fast were you driving?"

He shrugs and puts the car in park. "Fast enough." Then he leans closer, drops his hand over mine, and stares into my eyes.

"Hey." I try to pull my hand away.

"My powers only work when I'm touching you," he says softly. "Or did you forget?"

"Right." For some reason my voice comes out all breathy and weird.

He must notice, because he's smirking. "Your face. . ." He's still staring. "It's just the darkest I've ever seen." He drops my hand. "So dark. What exactly have you been up to? Torturing puppies? Kicking old women on their bad hips?"

I roll my eyes.

"Of course it's sparkly and fresh. We wouldn't be here talking if it wasn't." He opens the door. "Let's go get your stuff, Ned Flanders."

"What?" I scramble to follow.

"You don't watch *The Simpsons*?"

"You do?" I swear, this guy keeps surprising me.

"When I woke up, the world had transformed. It took me a long time to catch up, but once I felt like I understood most things, I realized I didn't understand a lot of the references people made. Ever since, I've been trying to watch at least a little of each of the most iconic television shows and movies from the last few decades. No show has run for longer than *The Simpsons*. Did you know it's still being produced today?"

"Yes, thank you, *Rainman*," I say.

"Rainman?" He narrows his eyes as he heads for the stairs.

"Not this time." I grab his wrist. "I almost passed out last time. Let's just take the elevator."

"There's an elevator?" He's scowling as we step inside. "You made me walk just to be mean?"

"I was annoyed with you," I say.

"I'd just bought you *two* cars," he says. "What could you have been annoyed about?"

I actually don't even remember, so I shrug and fold my arms. "You're an irritating person. I'm annoyed with you most of the time."

"That's probably why Katerina didn't fancy me," he says. "But lucky for me, she at least helped me research my powers and the history of Rurik's line in the Romanov libraries. I discovered that my power preceded theirs, and that if they would agree to surrender theirs to me, I could gain all five."

"Surrender?"

"They simply had to agree to grant me access to their powers, and I could use it while returning it to them. Mikhail and Boris did so almost right away."

"So they have been your friends for a long time."

"Friends?" He shrugs. "Not exactly." The doors open. "They gave me the powers in the hope I'd attack the Romanovs for them, and they wouldn't be culpable, and, you know, they wouldn't be killed themselves if it went wrong."

"That's terrible."

He gestures for me to get out before the doors close. "Terrible? No. Opportunists? Always."

I barely make it through before the doors close.

Not that Leonid would have let them close on me. The large doors slam into his arm, but he emerges unscathed. "Unfortunately for them, I wasn't quite as stupid as they'd hoped. Instead of attacking the Romanovs for perceived slights to their families, which has nothing to do with me, I tried to prevail upon the other three families to grant me the powers of wind, earth, and water. They all refused, but I really tried to do things the easy way."

"And then?" I can tell we're close to the answers I need. "What did you do?"

"I tried to force them to surrender their powers," Leonid

says. "It went badly—the harder I tried to pull the powers into myself, the more it hurt. I had quite a bit of energy, thanks to the other two powers I'd mastered, and I pulled far too long. The backlash was. . .unfortunate."

It sounds like it was painful.

"It had several unintended consequences."

"I bet."

"Most importantly, none of the materials I was able to find in the library explained that when Baba Yaga—"

"Who?"

He sighs. "I'm trying to go too fast."

"Let me just grab my stuff."

He plops down on the sofa and starts flipping through my old photo album again. "I'll wait."

It only takes me a minute, but he's already looking at a second photo album when I make it back to the family room. It's from junior high. "Hey." I snatch it out of his hands. "No one gets to see that one."

"Why not?" His bemused expression's a little too pretty. "You were adorable."

"That's about enough of that."

He picks up his phone and waves it at me. "Too late. I already documented all the best ones so I can look at them whenever I like."

I lunge for his phone and fall against him instead.

He drops his phone on the sofa and catches me, his arms wrapping around my waist, his eyes intent on mine. "You're clumsy."

"I am," I agree. "I can't figure out why you like me." Saying he likes me—what am I doing? Heat rushes to my face, and I try to scramble back and away. "Not that you do. I'm just saying, that if you did—"

"I already confessed that I do." His hands tighten around my waist, his head bends slowly over me, and then his mouth closes over mine. I know we're just standing in the middle of my tiny, unimpressive apartment, but it feels *momentous*. It's like the whole world drops away, and I'm tumbling down, down, down into a sea of stars.

His mouth is warm, and his hands are strong, and it's *everything* a kiss should be. My hands press against his chest, and I can't help remembering what he looked like without a sweater. My fingers flex, and he groans against me.

I snap backward. "I—I just broke up with my boyfriend this morning."

He leans forward, his forehead dropping against mine. "It's funny, isn't it?"

"What?" I close my eyes and let my body rest against his.

"People act like *time* is what it takes to recover from something, to heal from it. They judge you for your actions when they take place in shorter than the appointed time, like two weeks or two months or two years is what it will take for you to recover, but time is actually somewhat meaningless."

"What?"

He straightens enough that I can see his face, his beautiful, perfect features, his blonde hair falling down just a little bit over his brow. "I pushed for what I wanted so hard that I shoved myself into hibernation for over a hundred years. That did nothing, by the way. All I gained from that time-out was an appreciation for doing what I want, for taking what I want, while I still can. We don't know how many moments we have, and now that I've met you, I don't want to waste a single one without you knowing that I *do like you*, Isabel Brooks, very much. I like you more than I've ever liked anyone I've known far longer than I've known you. I like you more than I've ever liked any other human being, more than I thought I *could* like any other human being."

"More, even, than the stunning Katerina?" I feel stupid asking, but I can't help myself.

"I didn't expect Katerina would ever do me another favor,

but it appears her name causes you to feel something." He smiles then, his face dropping back toward mine. "But yes, I like you so much more than I ever liked her, that she's nothing to you." Then his smiling lips meet mine again, and this time's not at all like the last.

The last kiss was wonder and awe and worship.

This kiss? It's heat and frenzy and need. His mouth *covers mine.* His hands press me closer, urgently. His mouth's working faster, his breath coming hot and sharp in between kisses, and then his mouth leaves mine, but it doesn't stop *moving.* He's kissing my cheek, my temple, and then he keeps on moving down, trailing kisses down to my jaw, my neck, and then against my collarbone.

I cry out, "Leo," and he still doesn't stop, but he does growl possessively. I half-expect him to say, *Mine.*

What I don't expect is the blaring, clanging sound of cowbells. I freeze, my whole body tightening in alarm. "What's that?"

The way he says the words makes me think they're swear words, but since they're in Russian, I can't be sure. "Our people are waiting for us."

"You mean your people?" I ask.

He snarls. "My people *are* your people now."

I roll my eyes and shove away. "Okay, Fred Flintstone."

"Who?"

"A famous caveman." I pick up my bag. "Me, big man. You mine."

He arches one eyebrow. "You didn't seem to mind that I was a *big man* a moment ago." A cockiness sneaks into his expression. "What was it you just said?" He ducks a little closer. "I think it was my name, you screamed."

"Screamed?" My laughter sounds a little forced. "I just. . .barely mentioned it, is all."

He reaches for me. "Oh, you did? How about—"

I dance away. "No, no, your people are calling. We have to go meet them."

"At a hotel." His eyes are sparkling. "The nicest hotel suite in Salt Lake City."

He drives just as fast on the way, the fingers from his free hand drawing little designs on the top of mine. But when we reach his room, his very nice, very posh hotel suite at The Grand America, easily the nicest hotel in the city, I discover that there was one thing we didn't take into consideration.

The room's *teeming* with his people. They have questions for him—so many questions. He has decisions to make, decisions about lots of governance things that must have piled up while he was masquerading as a horse with me. I try to listen for a while, but it's all in Russian, and I have no idea what's going on, and eventually, I fall asleep on the sofa.

Strong but gentle arms move me at some point, but I swear, all I remember is a murmured word that sounds like, moy you doragoy solnyshka. And then I drift off for good.

CHAPTER 16

Izzy

When I wake up, I'm no longer in the hotel. I don't even think I'm in Utah, though I'm not sure quite where I am.

It's freezing cold, and I'm definitely not dressed for the weather.

I blink and blink, and then I look around. The sun hasn't come up yet, so it must still be the middle of the night. There's a large, beautiful fountain behind me in what appears to be a town square, but there's no water running through it.

Or rather, there would be, perhaps, but the water's frozen.

And then it starts to snow. I shiver violently, and I rub my hands along my arms. How did I get here? Did Leonid bring me to this strange place? I don't understand what's going on.

A little blond boy who must have been sleeping a few feet away sits up then, rubs his eyes, and starts to cry. He can't be more than ten or eleven years old. I stand up and walk toward him, but he doesn't even glance my way.

"Hey, can you tell me where we are? Or what time it is?" I shiver. "It's freezing and I'm definitely not dressed for the weather."

But I notice that he's also not dressed very appropriately. His clothing's tattered, torn, filthy, and. . .not from our time period. But more concerning, the boy acts like he can't even hear me. When he stands, he stares right at me, but his eyes aren't focused, and then, he walks right through my body, like I'm a ghost.

Did I *die*? What's happening?

"Leonid!" It's a man's voice calling—most definitely not Leonid—and I spin around just as fast as he does. If he's here somewhere, surely Leonid will listen to me. Surely he'll be able to sense me, thanks to our connection.

"I'm cold, Papa." The boy's shivering too, and I notice that in addition to the insubstantial and tattered clothing, he's not wearing shoes.

Now that I think about it, I'm not actually too cold myself. It's more like I've been conditioned to be cold when I hear screaming wind, see flurries of snow, and notice moisture puffing out of people's mouths when they speak. My arms have no goosebumps, however, and my hands aren't trembling.

Probably because I'm not really here.

As I start to catch on, I notice other things. No one else is here—no Leonid. No one else I can see at all, other than the boy and the older man.

The clothing the little boy's wearing is trousers, a plain, dirty tunic covering them, and no coat. Unlike me, what I can see of his arms is pebbled with gooseflesh. His feet, his small bare feet, look cold, wet, and ragged. "I want to go. Please, Papa."

"Leonid," the man hisses. "They said they'd meet me here. I promised them."

The boy closes his eyes, and then he turns around. "But Father, they didn't seem to be good men."

"What could you possibly know about good men?" the man asks. "You're not yet eleven."

I realize that they're speaking Russian, but somehow, I understand it. I suppose it's no stranger than anything else I've experienced the last few days. I wonder whether this is some kind of delusional dream or something else. Maybe it's connected to our strange bond.

"They made too many jokes," tiny Leonid says. "They were too jovial to be good men. You shouldn't have brought me here, and you never should have brought that." Leonid points at what looks like a bundle of cloth on the ground. "We could sell that for—"

Without warning, his father advances on him and backhands him across the face. "We would *never* sell these. They're the only evidence of our royal blood. Without these, we'll never claim our rightful place on the throne. Never."

Tiny Leonid already has the vibrant green eyes I love so much. When he rolls them, I laugh out loud. I half-expect him to hear me. He's careful that his father can't see him, which is terribly sad. He didn't mention this when he was telling his story, but his own father was awful to him. "I'm sorry, Father. Forgive me."

"You're too young to understand anything." His father trots back and crouches over the bundle, stroking it with his hand. "Too young, yet. But one day, one day we'll be restored with power and glory." His father's eyes are glowing in a very unhealthy way.

"Not if you keep drinking yourself half to death." Leonid collapses against the fountain, presumably to settle in and wait for the people his father's hoping to meet.

"Did you see Vasily's cloak?" I can't tell whether his father really expects an answer, or whether he's talking to himself. "The gold embroidery alone must be worth. . ." His voice drops until I can't hear it anymore, but he's clearly still mumbling something.

That's when I notice that Leonid's dabbing at his lip with his grimy sleeve. His father split it open, not that he cares. I crouch down in front of small Leo, trying in the moonlight to

make out the features that will one day look like they're practically carved in marble.

He's so young.

So vulnerable.

An awful idea occurs to me. He told me that once, after his
father told them about his signet ring, scepter, and crown, some
men came and *stole* them. Could that be what I'm about to
witness? Is tonight the night his family loses everything? Leonid
said things grew far worse after that, but I don't see how they
could get much worse than they appear to be right now.

Leonid's already barely more than a wraith. His arms are
bony, his face dirty, and he's not wearing shoes. It's far too cold
for him to have to endure any of this. "Oh, Leo," I whisper. "I'm
sorry."

His head snaps up, his eyes widening, almost like he can
hear me.

"Did you. . .can you hear me?" I whisper.

He frowns.

I run a hand down the side of his face. "If you can, hang on,
please. Your life will get harder still, but you're going to become a
very great man one day. A very great, very handsome, and very
powerful man."

He freezes, and his head tilts. Then he blinks.

"I—I'll be waiting for you. Don't give up hope."

He nods.

He *nods* at me. My heart soars—he must've heard me, right?

But then boots come stomping around the corner of a house
on the main road, and four men come into view. The first man's
wearing a very fine cloak with embroidered trim that glints even
in the low light—Vasily, I assume. The other three men appear
to be taking their orders from him.

"Well," Vasily says. "Did you bring it? Or was it all just
another sad, desperate lie?"

Leonid's father springs to his feet. "I brought it. Indeed, I did. I'm most grateful of your help with the audience." He bows his head and holds out his hands, palms up.

The man turns backward toward his three companions, and then he nods. One of them pulls out a club. One of them has strange straps buckled around his hands that look studded with metal, and the last one's holding a knife. They all walk toward Leonid's father.

"Not you," Vasily says. "Sergei, you stay with me unless they need your help."

Leonid's father's face darkens. "I don't understand. You said—"

But then the man with the wrapped hands punches him, and he flies sideways, slamming into the side of the empty fountain, his head rolling around on his neck like some kind of children's bobble-head toy.

He finally stiffens and tries to stand up. "I brought the relics," he says. "They weren't lies—it's all true. I can prove that I'm descended directly from the noble line of Rurik."

"Like any of that matters anymore." Vasily sneers. "As if *anyone* would ever consider you as a worthy replacement for a Romanov."

The man with the club slams it into his side.

Leonid rushes toward his father. "No, please don't hurt him."

Sergei, the man with the knife, lunges for Leonid, and I realize he's about to stab him, a little boy who's already losing everything. Without a second thought, I leap forward, throwing myself between the blade and the boy. It doesn't strike me, of course, but it inexplicably slows, and Sergei grimaces.

The little boy, Leonid, looks right at me, his eyes widening, and then he stumbles to the ground.

"What's going on?" Vasily says. "Take them out and let's go."

Sergei, now towering over Leonid by several feet, sheathes his blade and starts to kick him. He doesn't seem inclined to stop, and all my efforts to drag him away are utterly fruitless.

I'm stuck watching as three men brutalize both Leonid and his father. They don't stop until his father looks dead—lifeless and unmoving—and Leonid has stopped making even the slightest sound. I worry that they might *be* dead. Did my interference somehow make this worse? Was Sergei supposed to stab Leonid? I wish he'd said something about that.

I wish I'd left things alone.

I kneel in front of Leo's tiny, bruised, and broken body, and I try to run my hand over his hair. He can't feel it, or if he can, he can't move or react. A moment later, though, he begins to raggedly wheeze, and then he forces himself to his feet. He stumbles his way over to his father, and he shakes him until he stirs.

"Father," Leonid says. "Don't be upset."

His father grunts. I'm worried that's all he can do.

"I know they stole your relics, but Father, I managed to cut that man's coin purse." He pulls it out from under his dirty tunic. "We have enough for a place to stay and some bread."

He sounds so excited about it that it breaks my heart.

"We sure showed them, Father. You can't mess with a Rurikid and come away unscathed."

My heart, my poor, battered heart can't take much more. Leonid tries again and again to rouse his father, but he can't. He disappears then, and I'm not sure what to do. Do I stay with the father, unable to do a single thing to help? Or should I trail along behind Leonid, wherever he's gone? By the time I decide to try to follow Leonid, he's already disappeared, so I circle back to his father.

Moments later, little Leo appears, a ratty blanket in one hand, and he lays it flat on the ground beside his father. He slowly but carefully rolls his father onto the blanket, and then he gathers up the ends and drags his father out of the town square and underneath a tree just off the closest clearing. "It's okay,

Father," Leonid whispers. "You're hurting now, and you're going to be upset when you finally do wake, but it's all going to be okay." He wraps the blanket around his father, curls up behind him, and closes his eyes. "The world may not love you, and Mother may never have understood. She may have left us, and she may not have believed you. The world may never acknowledge our birthright, but I'll never abandon you, no matter what. I know you need me, and I promise I won't fail you."

I'm crying as I lay beside tiny Leonid, my arms wrapped uselessly around him. He doesn't seem to notice my presence, not this time, but I'll never forget this little glimpse into the life he so nonchalantly described as 'hard.'

If I was wondering whether he was the villain, I have my answer.

He's not.

He's the sympathetic, battered hero—I've witnessed it firsthand.

CHAPTER 17

Leonid

When I was young, lots of women told me that my face was a blessing—a blessing from my mother, I assumed. I don't remember her or what she looked like but I learned as I grew that I didn't resemble my father in the slightest. Everyone just assumed I took after my mother, and I believed they were right.

It brought me no joy—my mother had left us. I didn't want to be like her, but thanks to my face, women noticed me. As I grew older, they made eyes at me. They flirted with me. And then, Katerina Yurovsky pretended to like me in the hopes of making another man, a rich and powerful man, jealous.

It put me in the right place at the right time.

But I also came to realize that having a beautiful face without having power—having a comely appearance without wealth—is more of a curse than anything else. And now that I have power, wealth, and this face? Honestly, it still just makes my life more difficult nearly all of the time. People, mostly men, don't take me seriously. Women are distracted from what I'm telling them, from the point of our interactions. I've considered acquiring a nasty scar down one cheek, or perhaps a burn that covers one side. At least then, people would stop being distracted by something that doesn't matter.

From the moment I won the Russian election, or honestly, possibly even before then, power players have sent women to me hoping to win me over. Other women have come to me of their own will. All of them want something from me, but they're careful to tell me that they're happy to be sent.

Because of my face.

When I refused to ever take the bait, those same men started sending little boys. Cue my retching. The entire world seems to be unable to accept that someone with a beautiful face may, nevertheless, not be romantically inclined. I'm not the kind of person who has ever wanted a partner, a companion, or a soul-mate. I've left my cursed good looks intact only because I believe they helped me win the election.

My face and my body are tools, like any other.

But when I finally wake up after a long night of playing catch-up, I feel someone's fingers stroking my cheek, and I know immediately whose they are.

Isabel Brooks.

For the first time in my life, I *want* those fingers to touch me.

I'm grateful for this stupid, useless face.

Does she like it? Does she enjoy looking at it? And most importantly, if I open my eyes, will she dart away? Or will my mother's infernal face finally prove to be the blessing it was promised to be all along?

I'm too nervous to open my eyes for a long time—a full minute at least. Maybe two. But finally, the fingers freeze, and I realize she must have noticed that my breathing changed or my traitorous eyes moved beneath my lids. Something gave me away, so I go ahead and look at her.

She's staring at me, her large, cornflower blue eyes wide. "I'm —" She snatches her fingers back. "I'm sorry."

I can't help my grin. "Don't ever be sorry around me, love." I shift a little, rolling from my side to my back so I can look at her. "Did you get enough sleep?"

She yawns and stretches, and I follow the line of her graceful arm up and backward. "Yes, but I'm embarrassed that I fell asleep with all these people here." She straightens then, and looks around.

But they're all gone now.

I sent them all away.

A tiny wrinkle furrows her brow. "Where—where did they all go?"

"They have rooms of their own," I whisper. "I told them to find them and stay there."

"You are human, then," she says softly. "You do have to sleep."

I chuckle. "Of course I am. It's my only vulnerability."

She sighs and falls back against the pillows, her eyes closing. "Other than me, I guess."

"Right."

"I—I wasn't—I shouldn't have been hovering like that. I'm sorry. It was rude."

"Rude?" I can't help a bemused smile. I'm not sure I'd call tracing the line of my cheek rude, but I don't know what I would call it instead. I want to ask her whether she likes my face, but I'm afraid she might say no.

"Did you finish all your stuff?" She yawns again. "Are you free again?"

This time, I find myself yawning back. "Everything urgent has been handled. Once you take a job like mine, you never really finish. There are always new problems that crop up, and there's always more to decide."

"Why are you here—in the United States, I mean?" She rolls onto her side, stuffing a pillow underneath her head.

"There was a weapon being prepared here, to turn on me." I watch her carefully, waiting for a reaction. One call from her mother or stepfather, and she might already know. I've been wondering when that might happen. They might be the architects of our connection. For all I know, Izzy's also in on it, but I don't think so. She was far too shocked when I shifted. "I came to disarm it."

"And did you?" She narrows her eyes. "Are you safe, now?"

I shake my head slowly. "I—I didn't disarm it. But the people who were creating it, they took a misstep. Instead of firing on me, they powered me up."

"How?"

"Context," I say. "I'll get there, but I have more to tell you first."

"Last night." She closes her mouth and frowns.

"Last night?" I like where this is going. "I almost slept on the couch, but after everyone left, you looked so. . .peaceful. I don't often pass peaceful nights, and I couldn't quite resist the draw of sleeping beside you. I hope you're not upset."

"That you slept here?" She sits up and pulls the blankets up under her armpits. "I guess I should be." She frowns. "You could have slept on the sofa instead."

"I didn't bond us," I say. "It's not my fault we're stuck together. And I haven't done anything horrible since we met."

"I'd call incinerating two men pretty horrible." She shakes her head as if to clear the image. "And they were trying to harm us, but. . ."

"But what?"

"Maybe it's because you were sleeping so close." Her brow furrows again.

"What's because of that?"

"I had a dream last night," she says. "A really strange dream."

I can't help my smile. "Was I wearing clothes in this strange dream?"

She slams me with a pillow. "Stop."

I shrug. "I guess we didn't have the same dream."

Her gasp is so cute.

"Tell me about yours." I sit up and fold my arms. "I'll be good."

She blinks. "You're—you're not wearing." She clears her throat and turns away. "You're not wearing a shirt. Are you wearing. . ." She coughs.

"I'm wearing pants," I say. "And I had a shirt on last night, but I get hot when I sleep. Sometimes I yank things off."

"But not your pants, right?" She clears her throat and hops out of bed, still wearing the flowy dress she had on yesterday, and hunts around until she finds my pale blue t-shirt, discarded in a heap on the floor. She chucks it at my head. "Here. Put that back on."

I'm laughing, but I pull it on dutifully, and then I pat the bed. "Sit, and speak."

"I think we should go out into the mountains where no one else is around that we can hurt, and we should check out what we can do—what you can do." She nods. "We can talk about all of this out there. Away from. . ." She's glaring at the bed like it might bite her.

Like *I* might bite her.

She's probably not wrong to be wary. I am a little ferocious when there's something I want, and the more time I spend around her, the more I *want*. "Fine." I climb out of the soft, fluffy blankets and straighten, stretching. "I'm going to shower. You're welcome to do the same."

She blushes bright pink. "I'm not—I know I was touching your face, but it wasn't that kind of dream."

"It's a suite." I point. "There are two showers."

"Oh." Her laugh's so awkward it's adorable. "Right. Okay."

It takes her longer to get ready than it takes me, probably because of the whirring of the blow dryer. When she comes out, her hair looks fluffy and perfect, falling in little layers around her face. "Sorry," she says. "I'm not the fastest."

"I'm not in a big rush." Except I do want to hear about her dream. "Let's go." I grab the keys.

"What's that?" she asks. "Those aren't mine." She's holding her purse, staring intently at my Mercedes keys.

"Ah, well, now that I've been discovered, I have duties and people making demands. But I also have all my toys back, including my SL 63." I can't help my smile. "It has a bit more horsepower than your little cobra without all the accompanying growl, but you insisted on a truck from that dealership, so my options were limited."

She swallows and nods. "Fine."

"I have a meeting later with the governor of Utah," I say. "Apparently there's no way around it, now that we've been seen in this city, but we have a few hours before then."

She barely speaks while we walk to the elevator, and she doesn't bother pressing the button for the first floor. She pressed it on the way up yesterday, smiling like a little kid when it lit up for the penthouse.

"Are you alright?" I don't mean to stare, but I can't help worrying that she's looking at the floor. It's not like her.

"I'm—I'm fine."

"So you're clearly not fine," I say. "No one who's actually doing well says they're *fine*."

Her eyes snap up. "That's not true. It's exactly what I am— fine."

I inhale slowly, and don't say another word. I give her a minute to process whatever weird thing she dreamed about. But once we reach my car and she's safely ensconced in the passenger seat, I say, "Tell me."

"What?"

"Tell me whatever weird thing you dreamed so I can reassure you that it's not real."

She frowns.

"My dad used to have dreams," I say as I follow the map

toward Emigration Canyon. "He'd dream that we'd been betrayed, or he'd dream that he was finally crowned, or he'd dream that he'd buried some treasure in a strange place. The only way he could let go of his anger or his fear or his hope was to speak the dream out loud. Sometimes we even had to travel to whatever place he'd imagined and try digging around." It was actually one of his more harmless delusions. I found it sort of endearing, most of the time.

"It's not like that," she snaps. "Or. . ." She slumps in the seat. "Who knows? Maybe it is."

I like driving toward the mountains. They're much steeper here than back home, but with mountains visible in most directions, it's easy to orient where you are. Following a path here is predictable. It's reliable. And as the path to the mountains passes outside of the city, I breathe a little easier. Mountains, like most land masses, are honest. You know where they are and what their limitations will be.

"Last night, in my dream, I was like a ghost, watching you and your father."

"What?" I can't help my smirk. "Isabel, he died a very long time ago."

"Yes, he probably did," she says. "But he was very alive in my dream." She leans her face against the cool glass of the window. "It was the night Vasily and Sergei and two other men came and stole your father's relics."

"What?" I look at her, confused now. "Did I mention their names?"

She shakes her head. "No, you didn't. In fact, there were a lot of things about that night you failed to mention."

"But—"

"I saw them, Leonid, and I saw you. You didn't say this either, but I watched them beat you badly. Your father looked dead by the time they were done, but you proudly told him that you stole a coin pouch, and then you wrapped your dad with a blanket, and you dragged him into the woods all by yourself."

My hands tighten on the wheel. She—she couldn't have seen it. It's. . .crazy. But is the idea of her seeing my past any weirder than the way in which we're already connected?

What bothers me is that I don't understand what's going on or who's behind it. In my life, I've learned that when something inexplicable happens, there is an explanation—you just don't have it yet.

"I think we need to try to figure out exactly what's going on," she says. "And why it's happening."

"I wonder whether it's related to my mastery of all five powers. I was knocked out. . .I'm not sure for how long. When I woke up, I was stuck as a horse, and you showed up moments later."

"Did my parents stick you in that pasture?" Her eyes are intent on mine.

"No," I say. "Some people had come to talk to your family friend, a woman named Amanda Saddler. They were distant relatives of hers from Latvia. I followed them, because they were from the two lines I hadn't yet acquired powers for—wind and earth."

"Did you kill them?" She doesn't look away when she asks, which is progress.

"I did not," I say. "In fact, I healed your family friend Amanda Saddler, though I doubt anyone there credits me for doing it. Her heart was actively failing, but I swear I had nothing to do with that either."

Her face looks terribly pained. "Is she alright?"

"She was better when I left than when I arrived." I can't help my frown. "She was bright-faced—I wouldn't have harmed her. I told you I only kill villains."

She doesn't speak as I drive up, up, up, winding a path into the mountains, but once I find a small clearing and park, she follows me out of the car and down the path. Ours is the only car in the parking lot, and I wonder how long it will be before my team follows us out here.

"At least there's no one else to overhear or interfere," I say. "Yet."

"Because it's freezing," she mutters. "I should've brought a heavier coat."

I reach for her hand. "That's easy to fix." I've had the fire magic for so long, I can do most anything with it—including warming the area around us—without much thought.

She arches one eyebrow and pins me with a look.

"I have to be touching you or this won't work, but have a little faith."

As the air warms, she gasps.

"See?" I don't release her. "I think this may be the key to understanding what this is and how it works. I can show you what my magic does, and you can tell me what you feel when I use it." And if it draws her to me a little bit, like my stupid face, well, I won't hate that either.

"I guess." She looks around. "It's not like there's anyone to see us. I guess that was the point."

"Exactly," I say. "Let's start with fire. As I already showed you, I can heat things up." I pick up one hand, palm up. "I can burn most anything, without a spark, and without a power source. I guess *I'm* the power source."

When she smiles, I can't help smiling back. "Don't burn yourself up, please." She squeezes my hand.

"I'll try," I say. "But how about that sagebrush?" I point, and it bursts into flames, catching the small scrub next to it on fire as well. "It behaves as all fire does, but thankfully, I can also suppress the flames—putting it out." I demonstrate.

Her eyes widen and she nods. "That's pretty cool."

"Thanks." I point. "Or, if I didn't want to just snuff it out, another element, water, would be able to stop it. The difference between fire, a destructive power, and water, a life-giving power, is that I need to draw water from the surrounding environment. Luckily, there's almost always water somewhere close. I can sense it in the air, the ground, and any standing water nearby."

She tugs on my hand. "And as we're walking along, as long as you're touching me, you can feel it all around us? How far out?"

"I'm not sure," I say, "but close to a mile. Maybe more."

"That's amazing." She looks like she means it.

"Water's the best one, I think. You can do the most with it. I can heal people's injuries, like Amanda Saddler's, or a broken leg, or a gaping wound, or even cancer. I can make it rain where that's needed, pulling from the ocean or a nearby lake. I can attack with water, and I can kill if I have to, removing water from people's bodies. It's the most versatile element."

Her face is scrunched up now. "Kill?" She shudders.

Instead of letting her dwell on that, I press on. "The other power I've had for a long time is the manipulation of currents. All humans have electrical currents, as do the more obvious things, like electric lines and cellular phones. Like the fire, I don't have to pull from a power source—I can make one." I pick up the same free hand and pop a small crackle up and out before it absorbs back inside my body. "It can be a little uncomfortable to learn, but once you do." I shrug.

"That feels like fire—a mostly offensive power."

"Maybe," I say. "But if there was a power surge or a lightning strike, I could simply absorb and ground the power, preventing it from harming anyone. It has plenty of practical uses as well, and when combined with fire and water. . ." I shrug. "Like all the other elements, it has the potential for both good and bad."

"None of the other magic users can combine powers?"

"Aleksandr, Grigoriy, Alexei, Boris, and Mikhail. They're the men who came forward with me from around the time of the Russian Revolution. As far as I know, only the five of them and Katerina were pulled through, and none of them can." I feel a little guilty leaving Gustav out, but I haven't explained why it was important that he not be allowed to threaten me yet. I'll get to it, once I'm sure she'll understand.

"Boris and Mikhail—as in, the two men I just met?"

"They're the men who surrendered their magic to me before I tried to force it—Boris is Katerina's older brother. When I met him, he was a complete mess. He's come a long way since she had to haul him around, drunk all the time."

"But they—can they still use the elements?"

"When I allow them to, yes."

Except I'm not sure what happens with Gustav added to the mix. His control's similar to mine—that's the big unknown. His impact's my big vulnerability, other than Izzy.

"And the other elements are?"

"I just acquired earth and wind," I say. "You can fly with wind, once you learn how. I've never even tried."

"Fly?" Her eyes light up. "I've always wished I could fly."

"The last thing I'm doing is trying it with you for the first time." I pull on wind and it picks up all around us, whipping through her hair, and shoving it into her eyes. "See?" I shake my head. "It's too dangerous at the beginning."

"Well, you can't use it without me." She tugs her hand away. "So I'm not sure what choice you have."

I step closer. "I think you'll have to let me try some smaller things and work my way up at the very least."

Her breath hitches, and I smile.

She isn't running, and that's progress. I close the space between us, my hand cupping her cheek. "Like this." I drop a kiss on the side of her mouth, my finger stroking the smooth skin of her cheek. "Or this," I whisper, pressing a kiss lower, right on her soft, full lips.

She softens, tipping her head up toward me.

The beast inside of me unfurls, growling *mine.*

"You must have kissed a lot of women," she whispers. "Every girl we meet stares at you."

I freeze, my hand still curled around her face, my fingertips brushing the edges of her hair. "No, actually. None."

"None?" She pulls back, her arched brow and incredulous eyes focused on me. "I don't believe you."

I release her face and step back. "You should. I never lie."

"Never?" She snorts. "I don't believe that, either. You're like the wind—tempestuous and uncontrollable. You must have women chasing you from every continent."

"I can't be caught," I say. "I've never been caught." I step alongside her, one hand encircling her wrist. "At least, not until now." I whip my free hand around in a circle and snag a pinecone in loops of air, swirling it up, up, up in front of us, and then freezing it mid-air. "You say 'mid-air.'" I chuckle. "I'd never thought about that English phrase before now, but it's apropos for what I do. This is literally hovering amid bands of air."

"What's the last element?" she asks. "What can you do with earth?" She's not meeting my eye, and I can't tell whether she's embarrassed that we kissed, or upset at her reaction, or avoiding me because she disliked it. Interpreting her feelings is more disconcerting than trying to master two new powers.

"Earth," I say, casting about for knowledge on something I don't yet have. I gained these powers and then was knocked out immediately. "It's a power that allows you to grow things. It's mastery over dirt, rocks, and the elements, including. . ." I smile, and I reach out and around with my senses. I feel quartz—plenty of quartz. That's boring. Feldspar, I think? There are a few garnets here and there. But then I sense it, something valuable. Something precious.

An emerald.

I tug, and it barely budges.

I tug again.

"Are you alright, Leo?" Izzy's waving her free hand in front of my face. "You sort of froze, there."

"I've never used earth, but I've heard there's a trick you can do to pull rocks you want toward yourself." I sigh. "It's harder to do than I thought it would be."

She smiles. "Poor Leonid, struggling with something super-human. That must be terrible for you."

I scowl. "I'm not struggling, I just. . ." I dig deep, and I pull hard, and then I take that power and magic and might, and I yank as hard as I can on the little piece of emerald I feel, deep, deep down below us.

The ground splits open in front of me, and I shove Izzy backward to keep her from tumbling into the crevasse. There's a massive groaning in the earth, and a small, blue rock shoots out of the crack, landing at my feet.

"Got it." I lean over and pick it up, frowning. "Well, shoot. This isn't green. It's not an emerald at all."

"It's a blue beryl, you idiot," a woman's voice says.

I spin around, finally spotting her, perched on the edge of a tree limb twenty paces behind us. "Who—or what—are you?"

"What on earth was that insane stunt?" She drops to her feet and stalks toward us. Her hair's blue, her pants look like studded leather, and she has a glinting, sparkling stone stud in her nose. "Are you *that* desperate to unleash the end of the world?"

"The—what?" I ask.

"You don't even know who I am." She shakes her head. "Ridiculous."

"You must be Baba Yaga's contemporary here," I say. "Squannit, right?"

Her entire face contorts. "She knows that's my least favorite name. She uses it just to irritate me. Squannit, like squatting?"

I glance at Izzy, who looks even more confused than I do. "What are you—are *you* the end of the world?" Izzy steps toward me, reaching for my hand.

"Don't even think about it," Squannit-who-hates-that-name says. "Not a speck more magic out of you, or he'll wake up for sure."

"Who will wake up?" Izzy beats me to the question.

Squannit-who-hates-that-name growls. "I swear, it's like she taught you nothing. Xolotl. Ta'xet. Whatever name she uses for the Lord of Mictlan. The death God of the Aztecs." She throws her hands up in the air. "Do you two really know nothing at all?"

Izzy shakes her head.

"Baba Yaga told me she has three sisters, and she said their names were Squannit, Boohag, and Chedipe," I say. "But that was a very long time ago."

"Oh, won't Tituba be angry if she knows Baba Yaga's been calling her Boohag again." She actually smiles. "I'm Lechuza, and there are four of us, but your mother left out the most important part. We're only half of the balance of the circle of life on earth. Our powers help restore and heal and strengthen all living things."

"Half?" Izzy's now standing right beside me, and she slides her hand into mine, twining our fingers together.

"You know, the balance that Yamauba's responsible for—the one you call Baba Yaga—was destroyed when she shared her magic with a human man." She snorts. "The balance that keeps living things growing and yearning was just shattered thanks to her actions."

"Okay," I say. "But what's the other half, the non-living and growing side?"

"At least you're asking the right thing, finally. Ding, ding, give the baby boy a prize."

Izzy glances at me with the exact expression of baffled confusion I must share.

"You and your stupid little war here almost woke up the local horseman."

Izzy wants to ask. I want to ask, but we both wait. The questions seem to annoy her.

"Tell me you've heard of the four horsemen of the apocalypse." She lifts both eyebrows. "Do you just wander around using magic, ignoring every single legend we left to explain the truths of the world?"

"I guess we do," I say. "I thought that was all make-believe."

She casts her eyes upward and shakes her head. "Oh, it's all real, and you two are a hair's breadth away from waking the horseman of death who's been sleeping right here, under these confounded mountains." She points at the crack. "This right here?" She clenches her fist. "Pure idiocy."

"I'm sorry," I say. "I had no idea—"

"That's clear." She sighs. "You were about to undo the damage control I was doing when I linked the two of you in the first place."

"Linked us?" I suppose Izzy couldn't help herself that time.

"You didn't know you were linked?" She frowns. "It was so easy to connect the two of you because you were already a soul match."

CHAPTER 18

Izzy

My dad died fourteen years ago.

He was a great dad. He loved me, he loved my siblings, and he adored our mother. His death wrecked our family, like a bowling ball barreling down the alley to knock all the pins in different directions. My brother Ethan completely changed his mind on the kind of future he wanted. My mom became obsessed with resurrecting her career and earning enough money to take his place. She almost turned into a robot—she scheduled everything to the minute, like if she could be everywhere and do everything, we might not notice that he was missing.

But we did notice.

Losing Dad felt like a bullet had punched a hole in our hearts, the blood just draining and draining and draining.

For our entire family, really.

Mom's the heart of our family, but Dad held her heart together, and after he died. . .I guess my analogies sort of don't hold up, because it sure felt like her heart was turning to stone. If you had told me a dozen years ago that my dad was Mom's soulmate, that he was her only perfect match in all the world, I might have believed it. Mom certainly acted like that was true after he was gone.

But then we moved from Houston to the middle of nowhere, and Mom met Steve.

He wasn't anything like our dad.

I mean, sure, they were both men, but where Dad was polished and well-spoken and sophisticated, Steve wore dirty cowboy boots and lugged two forty-pound grain bags—one over each shoulder—half a mile to the barn without a thought. To do the same task, Dad would have found a dolly and carefully stacked them and slowly wheeled it out, all the while ensuring nothing could scuff his shoes.

Actually, Dad never would have moved grain bags in the first place.

Mom was very happy with Dad. She was prim, polished, and well-educated. Everyone always called them a power couple. But she was happy in a completely different way with Steve. She was relaxed, and she laughed louder. Her eyes lit up brighter, somehow.

Sometimes I wonder whether she loves Steve *more*, which would be kind of crappy since he's not really my dad. Or maybe it's good, since he's here with her now. I don't know, really, because when she was with Dad, I was pretty small. I didn't know any different. Maybe she was just as happy in a different way. But ever since she met Steve, and I could tell she was happy with him, I guess I haven't really believed in soulmates.

The whole idea's kind of ridiculous to me.

One person in all the world who's your perfect match? Somehow the fabric of who and what you are just meshes with theirs in a way it can't with anyone else on earth? I've seen my mom's happiness and joy and life fit well with two very different men in two very different places, so that must all be nonsense.

I just don't buy it.

"A soul match?" I snort. "Please."

"You don't even know what it means," Lechuza says.

"The idea that there's one person who's just perfectly suited to make you happy?" I arch an eyebrow. "Only one person in the world who can complete you? I know that doesn't exist."

"You're right." Lechuza strolls closer very slowly. "That nonsensical thing you just said doesn't exist. A soul match isn't that. It's something very different."

"We're listening," Leonid says.

"Sit." Lechuza points at a log. "You two sit there, fold your hands on your laps, and close your mouths." She wanders closer, peers over the edge of the crevasse that Leonid opened up when he was fishing that blue rock out of the earth. "Sit!"

Her shout shocks me into compliance, and I drop to my bum. Leonid's right beside me, but instead of folding his hands on his lap, he takes mine in his.

"See?" She shakes her head. "Even now, you reach for one another."

"He can't access his powers without touching me," I say. "I'm like a handgun he feels better while cradling."

Lechuza rolls her eyes. "Nice analogy. You're *so* American. But a soul match isn't one person in an entire universe. It's, maybe, one in ten million. There are plenty of people in the earth's current population that might be a very, very snug fit with your personality. People you complement in every way that matters."

"But he was born in the eighteen hundreds," I say. "So—"

Lechuza's eyes spark. "Yes, and you little idiot, if you expand the search parameters to include past, present, and future, there would be thousands of matches. Now shut up, and listen."

I close my mouth, but I don't like her tone.

"*You* are an abomination." She jabs a finger at Leonid. "Humans shouldn't be using our powers at all, and we ought to have roasted Yamauba for what she did."

"Why didn't you?" Leonid asks. "If it was so wrong for her to share her powers with a human."

Lechuza laughs. "Share? You think she *shared* them, like you'd hand someone half an ice-cream sandwich?" She lowers her head. "She slept with a human—the great and handsome Rurik—and then she made children with him. And then, that human, that arrogant, powerful, stupid, perverse human, he cheated on her." She looks ready to burn something down. "Baba Yaga or Yamauba or whatever name she's chosen lately, got just what she deserved. A broken heart."

"So that's why you didn't punish her?"

The pep in Lechuza's step dissipates some. "Well, not exactly."

"You did it too." I can tell by her expression. "You couldn't really fault her, because you. . ." I clear my throat. "You were also guilty."

"I certainly never slept with a human." She spits. Then she focuses again on the crevasse. "I'm going to clean this up. Give me a moment." She tilts her head, sets her feet, and spreads her arms wide. Then she heaves, and the ground trembles slightly, and the two sides of the mountain groan and rejoin. She wipes her brow. "Idiot human, using ten times as much power as he needed."

"I'm new to using earth," Leonid says.

"You split that mountain with a combination of your other powers." She snorts. "If it wasn't so clumsy, I'd actually be impressed. I tried to slap a governor on you, and you went ahead and accepted the shackles, leaning into the bond."

"What *is* the bond, exactly?" I ask.

"You show up here, stomping around with your poorly aligned energy in my part of the world." Lechuza shakes her head. "He was bound to notice the signature was wrong, and I knew it would wake him up. I went to confront you—to kick you out—but I could sense her." She points at me. "Your stupid great-great-great-whatever grandmother would surely have shown up to defend you if I evicted you." She tsks. "Just as stupid now as she was back then. I didn't want to fight her, so when I saw you there, just bumbling around, I took my chance."

"To do what, exactly?" I ask. "So what if our souls align? Bonding someone to their soulmate stops them from being able to use magic?"

Lechuza laughs. "You idiots know so little that all your questions are wrong."

"I wonder whose fault it is when the children are ignorant," Leonid says.

"I can see why she likes you." Lechuza spits. On the ground. Like some kind of. . .redneck. "Soul matches aren't one-in-the-universe, but they're rare. Things don't just happen. Isabel Brooks came by the exact location where you were at that moment, when I was also present and looking for a way to mute you for a reason. So when I realized you were a soul match, I pushed a little harder." She beams. "But the soul match wasn't what allowed the bond to exist." She walks around me, searching my face or body for something. "No, I could bond him to you because of who and what *you are,* Isabel."

"What is she?" Leonid's eyes light up. "Is she like me?"

Lechuza laughs. "The mold was broken when you were born, beautiful boy. No, she's something very different." She crouches down in front of us, and this time, she whispers. "My mistake wasn't in loving a human. It was in loving a devil."

I blink.

"While Baba Yaga was fooling around with Rurik, she begged me for a favor. She asked me to distract her horseman, Thanatos. Or you may have heard him called by the name Hades. At first, I thought I'd fail in coming to her aid. But then, the more time I spent pursuing him, trying to distract him. . . He and I. . ." She stands. "Let's just say we were something like a soul match." But her smile's *very* smug.

"What does that have to do with me?" I ask.

"You're my great-great-great whatever." She shrugs. "Thanatos' dark energy and my light energy combined to make children who could not work magic—no mess to clean up—but were nevertheless created by equal parts light and dark. That's why Baba Yaga and our other sisters couldn't get mad at me. But you do carry within you the dark and light magic from both sides, and I pulled loose just enough of a thread of it to tether this one to you." She blows a kiss to Leonid. "You're welcome."

"Why would you do that, though?" Leonid asks.

"To keep you from waking up the pain in my mountain, Xolotl. Or weren't you listening at all?" She gestures at Leonid, but looks at me. "So he's gorgeous, but sadly as dumb as a bag of rocks, huh?"

I laugh.

"Now that I've explained *everything*, linked both of the bumbling idiots who were spraying magic all over, and cleaned up your mess, I'm leaving. I have things to do. Don't make any more messes for me to clean up. I have my own things to take care of. Got it?" She pivots.

"Wait," I ask. "How can we break the bond?"

She pauses, looking over her shoulder. "Now who's the dumb one?" She shrugs. "You're soul matches whom I've joined magically, tying his light to your dark." She shakes her head. "You don't break it—joined till death."

Then between one breath and another, she's just *gone*.

CHAPTER 19

Izzy

Not even married, and already bound until death do we part.

"This is jacked," I say. "I barely even know you."

Leonid stands. "Do you?"

I frown. "What does that mean?"

"You barely know me?" He arches one eyebrow. "You've seen me naked."

"Well, but, I mean." I hate how flustered I am.

"You've *ridden* me," he says. "And I liked it."

"Are you making jokes right now?" I ask. "We came up here, in large part, to try and figure out how to break this strange bond—you can only use your powers when you're *touching* me —and she said we can't break it." My eyes widen. "Unless you kill me." All the fight goes out of me. "You're going to kill me, aren't you?"

"If I had to be stuck to someone. . ." Leonid laughs. "At least I won't be bored ever again."

"Were you bored a lot? It's boring, running Russia?"

"It was," he says. "I was bored almost all the time before I met you."

"You have to be at least a little distressed," I say. "You didn't choose me. I didn't choose you. That insane lady, witch, thing, just. . ." I hold up my hands and smoosh them together. "She just smashed us together, and bam. Now we're stuck forever."

"I would thank her if she just came back." Leonid pivots and nearly runs right into me. He grabs my hands. "Tell me you're really upset that we're bonded."

"There are no good sides to this," I say. "You lost power and control, not to mention freedom. Yes, I'm upset."

"Well, I'm not." He tilts his head. "That's a strange feeling for me, believe it or not, but I'm not upset. Not even a little bit. I meant it earlier when I said I almost didn't want to break the bond."

I roll my eyes. "Alright, so you're just trying to keep me happy so I won't try and sneak off and knock you out."

"No, that's not it." He shakes his head. "I'm actually grateful of the excuse to keep you near. And if someone threatens you, I'll burn them and their entire family to the ground to keep you safe." He leans closer. "And I won't even feel guilty about it."

"Burning the world down is *bad*, Leonid," I say. "Please tell me you know that."

He shrugs. "The world's overrated, honestly. I've seen most of it, and none of it impressed me."

"But a cowgirl from backwoods Utah did?" I arch an eyebrow. "I know when someone's blowing smoke."

He frowns. "Blowing what?"

"Let's just get back down the mountain," I say. "You have that governor thing."

"Shift me, and I'll give you a ride," he says.

I freeze. "Why would you do that?"

He shrugs. "You liked me better as a horse, I think."

"But you have a governor thing."

"Which is why you'll change me back when we get to the

bottom of this trail. It'll spare you the hike, and we can find out whether I can still use my magic when I'm in my horse form, as long as you're touching me."

"If it's for research," I say, "I guess it's fine."

He hands me the blue rock.

"You kept that?"

"Should I have thrown it away? I ripped a mountain apart to get it for you, and it got us the answers we wanted, even if it wasn't in the way we planned."

"Is blue beryl valuable?"

He shrugs. "How should I know?"

It's valuable to me now, not that I'd admit that to him. I stick it in my pocket, and I drop a hand on his arm. "I—I want you to turn into a horse."

It's apparently that simple, though it may be less about the words and more about shaping my desire to change him. There's a jolt, and then a weird kind of ear-popping sensation, and he blurs into Drago. He's not right that I like the horse version of him better. . .or at least not exactly. As a horse, everything with him felt so uncomplicated. As a horse, there weren't stories and magic and history. As a horse, he was a little maniacal, sure, but he wasn't burning things down or reducing humans to ash.

I was just a girl, stealing a horse to bail out her criminal boyfriend.

"So maybe my life wasn't quite so perfect before, either." I huff.

Drago whinnies, like he agrees.

I realize the other advantage to this form is that he can't

really make any snide or disturbing comments. I think part of my objection to his human form is that he says a lot of things I shouldn't really agree with, but somehow, I often do. As a horse, he's so much less complicated. When he drops his shoulder, I know it's time to climb onto his back. He's so dang tall that it's still hard, even with a lowered front end, but I manage to scramble on very inelegantly. It helps to know that he won't spook at a bird whistling and kill me. "I do miss having a bridle," I say. "I know I'm basically a passenger, but I'm used to having a bit to take hold of when a horse misbehaves."

He snorts, and I know he's laughing.

"Next time, I'm bringing one."

He trots off, then, like the scree under his feet doesn't bother him at all. Shifter-horses must have amazing feet.

That thought leads to others, questions he can't answer this way at all. "Hey, can you colic? Like, if I didn't shift you back, and you ate, like, a hamburger, would your stomach get all tied up? Or do you have a different digestive tract than a typical horse?"

He keeps trotting.

"What about paper bags? Do they sometimes suddenly scare you? Are they, like, bigger or billowy-er now that you have horse eyeballs?"

He slows down, whips his head around, and blows a bunch of air at my leg.

"Fine, fewer questions while you can't answer." I think that's why I was asking them all. I can ask whatever I want, and he can't stop me. "Do you think you just like me. . .and I just like you. . .because of the bond or maybe the soul thing and not really because we just *do*?"

He freezes, sliding a foot or so on the debris underfoot, and then he swivels his neck around again and tosses his head.

And neighs.

Loudly.

"I'm not turning you now. Get me down the mountain first."

He throws his head again.

"Why do you think I asked you all that? You can't tell me anything, so it's a safe question."

He throws his head straight out toward me, and he screams.

"Whoa." Two hikers duck around the bend ahead of us. "They have horses on these trails?" The one with a knit cap on waves.

The other one, a tallish man, peers at us. "You don't ride with a saddle?"

"It's a trust exercise," I say. "I'm training him to be a good horse."

"How's it going?" knit cap says. "I think I'd be scared to do that."

I shrug. "He's a stallion, and he's not very well behaved. I'm thinking of having him gelded, but whenever I say that, he screams even louder."

Drago screams then, and I can't help laughing. "See?"

"I had no idea horses were so smart," tallish man says. "That's amazing."

"This one's a little unique," I say. "He kind of tries to kill everyone but me."

They shift over and give us a wide berth. Almost as soon as they're past, Drago poops.

"Really?" I ask. "You are such a teenage boy, deep down."

He snorts.

"We're almost down the mountain. Let's just go." But with hikers coming now, I realize that he might need to shift back soonish. For some reason, it only occurs to me then that his clothes are missing. He didn't take them off when he shifted, and they didn't rip or tear or anything.

They just. . .disappeared.

What's going to happen when he shifts back?

Shoot.

"Umm." I slide off his back and head for a little copse of pine trees. "Follow me, you naughty stallion." I toss my head this time.

Thankfully, he listens. Chalk one up as a win for the trust exercise.

"We don't have clothes," I hiss. "I hope you have a plan for this." I wince. "Because those hikers showed up, and now I'm worried there might be more of them."

He whinnies loudly.

"Yeah, I was wondering that, too." I touch his shoulder, close my eyes, and say, "I want you to be a man now." Same ear-popping feeling. Same whoosh, and then I slowly open my eyes.

He's naked. Totally and completely naked. Again.

And his smile is *smug*.

"Why are you smiling? This is a disaster."

He shrugs. "Embarrassment is for people who don't look good."

"You can be arrested for being naked in public here," I hiss. "There's no 'he's hot' exception!"

"Diplomatic," he says slowly, his voice low, "immunity."

"Oh, my, gosh." I stomp down the trail ahead of him and nearly run into someone. As I back up, casting around for Leonid, I realize it's Boris.

He sighs. "I brought him clothes—they're in the car. I'll get them."

"How did they know where you were?"

Leonid's strolling down the hill behind me, not even wincing from the rocks under his feet. And I can't deny—he *does* look good. Ugh. "I left my cell phone in the car. When I don't answer it, and when it stops moving, they usually show up wherever I am. It's very annoying."

"Well, in this case, it's handy. Because you need to get some clothes on!"

"You asked me a question, you know," he says. "And you didn't let me answer. That was rude." He's walking toward me, making eye contact, just chatting, like he's not *hanging brain.*

"We can just talk about it later." I cover my eyes with one hand, but I can't help stealing just a little peek. I mean, he's not wrong about. . . Okay, I think the soul bond's wrecked my normal decency.

"It's not the bond," Leonid says. "The way I feel about you —it might be the soul thing, but it's not the string that crazy witch tied between us. I like you because you're bright. You're innocent, even though you're not dumb. You're fiery, and you're generous, and you're considerate. I like all those things about you—but mostly, I don't feel alone when you're nearby for the first time in my entire life."

I forget my other concerns, and I stare only at his face. "But that could be from the connection." I blink. "Right?" Because I feel it too, whatever it is, the strange belief that he's just what I need. That he's like me, and that I can trust him.

"Here, boss." Boris tosses a bag at him.

Leonid's movements are always so graceful. He catches the bag, nods at me, and turns to dress.

I shouldn't, but I can't help watching him.

I look away the second he turns around, but his chuckling follows me the last two dozen steps to the car. I'm not sure how he knew I was watching, but he's onto me.

"Are you ready to meet the governor?" I have no idea how Boris keeps a straight face.

"Of course," Leonid says.

"Will the girl be coming?" Boris side-eyes me.

"The 'girl' will always be coming, but you won't go anywhere else if you ever call her 'the girl' again," Leonid says. "Isabel Brooks, or maybe later, Isabel Iv—"

I cover his mouth with my hand, and he licks me.

He *licks* my palm.

And then he winks. "Fine, you can keep your name."

I swear, he's cracked.

What does it say about me, that *this* is my soul match? Even thinking that sends a sort of a shiver up my spine. "I—I don't hate it either," I whisper. "Maybe she was right about the soul thing."

Leonid's smiling when we reach the other members of his staff. They're all gathered near two dark SUVs, and they're all wearing suits. I glance down at my blue sweater and dark jeans. "I'm going to wait in the car," I say. "I'm definitely not dressed for a meeting with the governor."

Leonid rolls his eyes. "You're just fine. You're the czar of Russia's date."

Date.

I'm his date. . .and his soul match. It's a really weird thing to say out loud, but for some reason, I don't hate it.

I mean, with Tim, everyone hated him. I tried not to care, but it made me question my judgment. And then, it turns out I was wrong. He was bad. . .for me, and also, just in general. But in this case, my judgment doesn't matter, right? I mean, one of the four witches of the world who provide strength to all living things said we're a match.

He's too good-looking for me, he's too rich for me, he's too well-educated for me, and he's definitely too powerful for me, but I'm his *soul* match, so it's fine.

I'm actually surprised that when we reach the Utah State Capitol building, no one questions what I'm wearing. I'm standing in a sea of suits, wearing jeans and a sweater, and no one bats an eye. They do clip a microphone to my lapel, and the makeup lady keeps brushing things on my face last minute, but when the recording starts rolling, everyone's smiling, including Leonid.

"You've been here, in the United States, now for several weeks," the governor says. "And in every formal, official interview, visit, or chat, you've been alone." He smiles. "And yet, here today, you're sitting next to a very pretty blonde woman."

Leonid reaches out and takes my hand.

The governor's smile broadens. "Tell me, who is this?"

My horse-shifter soul match presses a kiss to my hand. "This is my girlfriend, Isabel Brooks. I'm head over heels, and I'm not embarrassed to say that."

The governor and his wife both clap. His wife, Betty, squeals. "This is so exciting."

"And how did the two of you meet?" Governor Kuykendall asks.

"It was accidental." Leonid leans forward and drops his voice. "But if we're being totally honest, I think we could call it fate. I was in a bit of a bind, and this lady totally saved me." He's looking right at me, his brilliantly green eyes shining.

"The two of you are quite the pair," Betty says. "Do you think you'll be spending more time in Utah now, thanks to her?"

Leonid shrugs. "I have a lot of work to do in Russia, and I've probably stayed here too long already, but I will just say that even though I haven't known Isabel for very long, I can't imagine not having her by my side." He winks, and I know it's a joke about how he passes out if I'm not near, but it also feels like he means it.

"Can we expect a visit to Tiffany's?" Betty asks. "Or is it still too soon?"

"Tiffany's?" Leonid asks. "Russia's famous for its garnets, emeralds, alexandrite, and diamonds. I doubt I'd have much need to purchase a little blue box."

"No?" Betty asks.

Leonid smiles. "The gems I choose for this woman won't fit in a small box."

She roars at that one. "But Isabel's so petite. How will she lug that around on her finger?"

"She's stronger than she looks," Leonid says.

"And I'm five eleven," I say. "I don't think anyone, even Leo, has ever referred to me as petite."

"Does she call you Leo?" the governor's wife asks. "That's so cute."

"But no one else should try it, for the record," Leonid says. "Only she calls me that."

The interview moves along to other matters—foreign trade, his priorities at home, and his thoughts on tariffs and import taxes—and I can't help thinking about what might happen to *me* if I don't somehow break this bond. He's the czar, and he's ruling Russia. He needs me with him, but I don't want to leave my family, not even for him.

I paste on a smile, but my mind's whirring.

Once we're finally done, I walk arm-in-arm with him until we're finally leaving the capitol building through the back door. I can't help breathing a big sigh of relief that the whole ordeal's finally over, but this is an everyday occurrence for him. It must be terribly exhausting, and I can see why he might feel lonely. It was all so surface-level.

"Sir," Mikhail says, "There are some people here to see—"

Leonid shakes his head. "I'm not seeing anyone else today. That was more than enough for my first day back. Isabel and I have things to discuss."

"They're not here to see you," Mikhail says. "Isabel's *parents* are here to see *her.*"

"They're here?" I ask. "In Salt Lake City?"

Mikhail nods.

Leonid swears under his breath. "Izzy, there's something I've been meaning to tell you."

"Izzy." Mom shoves past one of Leonid's people and jogs in

my direction. "Isabel Brooks, I forbid you to spend another second with that tyrannical despot."

"It's not like that," I say. "You're watching the wrong news channels. Come meet him, and—"

"He threatened us, held us captive in our own home, and almost let Mandy die," Mom says. "Don't say another word to defend him. I know Leonid Ivanovich better than I wish, and I *forbid* you to talk to him for another single second."

CHAPTER 20

Leonid

For quite some time now, I've been able to burn, electrocute, or drown anyone who disagreed with me. If someone defied me, they didn't do it for long.

I've executed thieves, sexual predators, and murderers.

The world's a safer place due to my violence, and no one can get in my way. Anyone who does, I immediately dispatch. If they're not evil, I simply detain them until they can't interfere. But in this case, I feel like flinging Isabel's mother into a nearby tree, or wrapping her in bands of air and stuffing a gag in her mouth would be taken the wrong way.

Which means I'm stuck staring at her while she accuses me.

Unfortunately, everything she's saying happens to be true. I did detain her family, and I threatened to harm them, and I was using Amanda Saddler's weakness to spur Gustav to action. She's not even wrong to call me a despot or tyrant. I've been a villain for most of my life.

I thought my own father was a lunatic spouting seditious nonsense, and it took me years, but I finally quieted him and found him a place to hide, essentially. Then after I discovered he *wasn't* just insane, I didn't try to heal his broken mind. No, instead, I worried about myself, convincing Boris and Mikhail to surrender their powers to me. When the others wouldn't follow suit, instead of walking away, I tried to forcibly take their abilities. That threw us all into some kind of stasis, and then I literally threatened Alexei into offering me his control of water.

All because I wanted the power of our bloodline I'd been denied.

It wasn't until the past few days that I realized. . .I'd been searching for the wrong thing. I thought if I was powerful enough, I could eliminate all the bad in the world. I thought I could make things safer not only for me, but also for all the other powerless, unloved souls who were despised by the world. I used that excuse to justify all kinds of actions. . .that shouldn't have been excused at all.

I realize that I was wrong, but it's too late to change the past.

I thought power could solve all my problems, but really, more than anything else, my biggest problem was that I was lonely.

There are some things in the world you can't describe or understand until you've experienced them. Salt. Pain. Heat. Pleasure. Cold. Hunger. Until you've felt these things, experienced or endured them for yourself, good luck understanding what they mean. In my entire life, with my manic father, with my limited set of acquaintances and enemies, I had never felt anything *other* than lonely.

For a brief moment, I fancied Katerina was a friend, but I discovered quickly that to her, I was just another tool.

Until I met Izzy.

Her smile was just for me.

Her words were kind, caring, and considerate, even after she discovered that I wasn't the poor, beleaguered stallion meant for slaughter that she originally believed me to be. The way she looked at me after witnessing my beating in that dream—it wasn't sympathy.

It was empathy.

The difference, I realize, is that she doesn't feel sorry for me. She hurts *with* me.

But the look in her eyes now?

It's revulsion. It's fear.

She detests me, and that hurts more than anything else ever has, redefining pain for me. My soul-match, the end to my loneliness, wishes she was nowhere near me. She appears to wish that she'd never met me. For the first time in my life, no amount of power can vanquish my foes, because I am my own foe. If I try to force myself into her life, I'll only firm up the things her family is saying. I'll convince her that they're right—I'm irredeemable.

So I say nothing.

I do nothing.

It rankles in a way nothing has before.

"The thing is," Izzy says in a small voice, "I'm kind of bonded to him."

"You—what?" Her mother frowns. "What does that mean?"

Izzy looks around, taking in my people, scanning the gathering audience of people we don't even know. The parking lot behind the capitol building isn't exactly the best place to be having this conversation.

"You may hate him," Izzy whispers, "and you may even be right, but we can't talk about this right now. Come with us back to—"

"You come with us." Steve steps forward, beckoning Izzy to follow him.

The beast inside of me swells, demanding that I protect what's mine. But she's only mine because she's chosen me. She's only mine because she doesn't detest me. If I harm her stepfather, she'll run for sure. It's hard, and it's painful, but I suppress the beast, and I merely say, "Izzy."

Her head turns toward me, and her eyes are pained. She knows if she goes with them. . .whatever link Squannit forged, it'll snap. One or both of us may die. "I swear I won't harm any of you," I say. "If you'll just follow us back to my hotel, you'll be in no danger whatsoever and we can discuss all of this."

"You can't believe a word he says," Abigail says. "He's insane."

Izzy shakes her head. "I can explain some things, but I think in this case, we can believe him." She ducks her head a little. "You were right about Tim, though. He—we broke up."

"I thought he was about the worst man I could imagine you being with," Steve says. "But I guess I was wrong." He's glaring at me, and I can't blame him.

"Just come with us, and you'll understand more," Izzy says. "But I have to ride in the car with him."

"She has to ride with him?" Abigail frowns. "Do you think it's like with Gustav and Gabe?"

"What about them?" I ask.

"They can't be far apart," Abigail says slowly. "Or it causes both of them pain. Does that sound. . .familiar?"

"That Lechuza." Izzy closes her eyes and shakes her head. "It sounds like I wasn't the only person she used."

If Izzy was the descendant of Lechuza and Thanatos, her brother would be as well. Could she have bound Gustav to Gabe? If I wasn't so upset right now, I might even laugh. No wonder I haven't heard anything from him. He couldn't find me, but even if he could, there's not much he can do, either. He's stuck like me, but to an overzealous *teenage boy*. If I weren't in the middle of the worst meet-the-parents ever, I might feel sorry for him.

"We aren't meeting you at your hotel," Abigail says. "The only place we'll consider is neutral ground." She folds her arms.

"Fine," I say. "Tell us where."

"And we're supposed to believe that you'll come?" Steve's frowning.

"I'm many things," I say, "but I'm sure that Katerina and Alexei will begrudgingly confirm that a liar isn't one of them."

They murmur for a moment, and then Abigail nods. "Fine. You can meet us at Limekiln—in fact, you can drive over with us." She drops a hand on Steve's arm. "We'll follow along behind them the entire way."

He glares, but then he sighs. "Fine."

I direct my people to head back to the hotel, which they aren't pleased about. Boris and Mikhail especially are upset, but they do listen. I don't like it either, but I know how to keep my people in line. I'm pretty sure Abigail and Steve aren't planning on showing up without an entourage. In fact, I'm quite sure I'm walking into an ambush—they're just changing the location.

Izzy doesn't say a word as we walk to the car and when I climb in—she doesn't even ask to drive or hassle me for doing it myself. "You alright?"

She turns toward me slowly. "I—I've dated a loser for years. Everyone disliked him, and I was the only one too stupid to see it."

This isn't starting off very well.

"Now, one day after we break up, I'm kind of dating you."

"Well, it's easier to explain that we're dating than to say we're soul-bonded, but—"

"You just told the world we were," she says, but she doesn't sound angry. She sounds. . .tired.

"I know." I squeeze the wheel. "I'm sorry about that."

"It's fine." She's staring at her hands. "It's—I didn't stop you from saying it. In fact, I felt fine with it during that interview, and I wasn't upset when Lechuza came to see us. But if I've learned anything in the past week, it's that *clearly* I have bad judgment."

"Your judgment—"

She shakes her head. "You don't get to disagree, because you hated Tim, too."

She's right about my feelings on Tim. "But I don't think your admiration for him, or your defense of him once you'd decided to like him, was a flaw. You defend what's yours. That's admirable."

"You know what's more admirable? Knowing when someone's bad and not letting them take advantage of me and others I love."

I can't argue with her about that. I don't want to argue with her at all, but I have a feeling this meeting's about to go really, really badly. Normally, I'd be making a backup plan, and then a diabolical contingency plan to follow behind the backup plan.

But any plan I make in this case would possibly harm her family.

Which would only make her hate me more.

Boris and Mikhail were probably right. There's no way for me to win today. For years, I've been fine with doing the hard things. I've been okay with eliminating the bad guys in ways others didn't approve of in order to make a safer place here on earth. I've never cared whether people approved of my methods, or whether they thought I was worthy of the powers I've been given. But today, for the first time, I really hate being a villain.

Limekiln, as it turns out, is on the side of the mountain, just a tiny hike right outside of the city. It's a twelve-minute drive from the capitol building, and then a quarter-mile hike. It's just far enough away that we might not blow up Salt Lake if our argument goes badly. It feels like a fight's imminent, and I don't have powers unless I'm touching Izzy, so I'm guessing I'm going to march in there and take a real beating.

I wonder whether I can still choke down on the other people's powers. . .including Gustav's. I haven't tried since waking, but I've been a little distracted. I reach for Izzy's hand to see, but she yanks it away. I guess I won't *be* trying anytime soon, which is pretty unfortunate. It could save us all from a bloodbath.

"Why are they so sure that you're a bad guy?" Izzy turns toward me—I can feel her eyes on the side of my face.

I keep staring at the road—I don't want to scare her off. "I am a bad guy," I say. "Or at least, by their reckoning, I am."

"Tell me what they'll say."

"I kidnapped a woman, thinking she was Kristiana, and then I found out she was someone else. I held her, threatening to kill her to try and find out where the woman I wanted was being held."

"Why?"

"In the process of kidnapping her, I killed a dozen men. Bad men. Men who were sent to kill the woman I took. Men who worked for a terrible man, doing dark and depraved things, but I still roasted them into sooty little piles of ash in the street." I risk one glance her way.

She swallows and blinks. "Okay." Her mouth's compressed tightly. "And did you—what did you do with the woman you took?"

"She escaped," I say. "She was a friend of the woman I was looking for—the woman who had the ability to nullify my powers."

Izzy frowns. "So you were threatening them and seeking the other woman. . .to do what?"

"To kill her," I admit. "I'm not sure whether I would have done it—it would've depended on how her face looked."

"Her face—whether it was dark or light, you mean?"

I nod.

"And have you met her now?"

"Yes."

"And how did she look?" Her tone's hard. "Did you try to kill her?"

"I wanted her dead," I say. "But I was conflicted. Her face was dark around the edges—she'd done some questionable things. But it was mostly bright, as was her brother's. He was actually the bigger threat."

"Is that why you didn't kill them?"

I shake my head. "I didn't kill them because they tricked me —they gave me the earth and wind powers I wanted, and doing so knocked me out. It was too much magic to assimilate all at once. Then I woke up, stuck as a horse, and the rest you know."

She closes her eyes and presses her fingers on the bridge of her nose.

"If you have a headache, I can heal that," I offer.

"No, thanks."

"You can't deal with violence and clean up ugliness without getting a little dirty yourself," I say.

Her eyes fly to mine. "You can't kill people who are *a little bad.*"

"Why not?" I ask. "Aren't I better at deciding that than anyone else, thanks to my powers?"

She flinches. "You can't do it, because that's my only defense for you. When my mother and Steve and the others say you're too dark to be saved, when they tell me you need to be destroyed, when they say you're a bad man I should abandon, I will tell them that people can be redeemed. But if you go around killing people who are bad, then that means you don't think it's true. It means people *can't* be redeemed."

Shoot. I'm undermining my own argument without realizing it.

"You can't see your own face, can you?"

"With a mirror," I say.

"I mean the light and the darkness."

I swallow. "No."

"But this other guy, he could see your countenance, right?"

I nod slowly. "Probably."

"And if yours is dark? If your face is more dark than light, should you be killed?"

I sigh. "Yes, by my own ethics, I suppose I should be."

"I don't agree." She reaches for my hand. "I don't agree that we should be killing *anyone* who's still light. I think we should be trying to save them." She threads her fingers through mine.

She thinks I can be saved.

She thinks I'm worth the effort.

I hate it, I *hate* doing it, but I don't have much choice. While she's placing her trust in me, I reach out and feel the powers gathering around me—all of their abilities have been reset now, thanks to my regained ability with wind and earth.

So I switch them all off, including the one that shines the brightest.

The one that can manage all the powers, just like me, Gustav, his light winks out just like the others. With one squeeze, I eliminate the risk to me, to Izzy, and to my position here. When I park and exit my car, at least I do it knowing that no one will have any magic except for me.

I'm pretty sure that I have a dark face, though. If I'm being honest, that's always what I've been afraid of, but I hoped that eliminating all the darkness around me might redeem me somehow.

If I'm lucky, Gustav won't be able to see it.

But I'll still know the truth.

Izzy's many things—beautiful, bright, hopeful, and pure. But one thing she's not is right about me. Sometimes optimism's misplaced, and this is almost certainly one of those times.

CHAPTER 21

Izzy

I was in the ER on the day my father was diagnosed with cancer.

The ER doc came back with a very sad expression on his already serious face. Mom looked worried. Dad held her hand. After they told us he'd need to see an oncologist for further information, Dad searched up his kind of cancer online. The internet prognosis was bad—he probably wouldn't live more than a year.

I wasn't there when they saw the oncologist, but Mom told us what he said. He told Dad that he had to choose.

There was an aggressive treatment option. It wasn't very successful in curing the cancer. Less than one percent of cases survived five years from the diagnosis. But Dad would probably live a little longer with a 'full court press,' as they called it. He'd likely live more than a year, maybe even six months more, but whatever time he had would be spent in the hospital.

Mom and Dad were optimists.

Cancer pulls optimists out by their roots and leaves them to die. That's what it did to my parents, or really to my entire family. We had to watch as the poison they gave Dad killed him every bit as fast as it killed the cancer cells.

He wilted.

Right in front of us.

In the end, he didn't die at home with his family. He didn't have some good days and some bad. All his days were bad, and he survived less than a year, all of those days spent lying in a hospital bed in terrible pain.

It made me hate all the people who were on social media or commercials claiming they had beaten cancer. Every time one of them said how *strong* they were, it felt like they were saying my dad *wasn't*. When they talked about how their families supported them, and without their love and unfailing strength, they wouldn't have been able to keep going, it felt like we failed our dad.

In the end, I only knew one thing for sure. When the doctors told us to choose between coming home and spending as much good time with Dad as we got or fighting the cancer to try and get more time with him?

We chose wrong.

I'm not a big fan of life versus quality of life choices.

But it frustrates me when people say that some things are 'life and death,' implying that's a hard decision to make. When something's black or white, of *course* you pick white. Life or death? You always pick life, idiot. It's life or *quality of life* decisions that are hard, and now I'm facing that very kind of choice.

I can feel it.

I always know when stuff like that's coming my way. It's like something's hanging in the air. A weight. It warns me when hard choices approach. The air's terribly heavy right now, as I walk beside Leonid toward the stupid limekiln ruins—so heavy that I feel like I could almost cut it with a knife.

Mom and Steve are walking up ahead of me, hand-in-hand as well, and Mom keeps glancing back at Leo's and my joined hands and glaring, like my support for Leonid is an affront to my love for her. It hurts, honestly. But Leonid needs me, at least, right now he does. I can feel it. I may not be able to see his face, and I don't know how bright or dark it is.

And my judgment has been really bad lately.

I know that, too.

I'm sure my whole family's been talking about it. It's not a lovely feeling, knowing that everyone you love thinks you're a moron. I can't argue with them, either. They were right. When I think back on my time with Tim—I can't believe it took me so long to see how selfish and dishonest he was. I think I stuck around for so long because leaving him meant giving up on myself.

And even now, I'm not sure he couldn't be saved by someone. The right person. I've just lost interest in being the one to do it.

That's the bummer about optimists. We're the happy ones, always hoping, always wishing, but we're also let down more than anyone else in the world. Your bubble can't be popped if it's not floating, and each time it is, it hurts.

"We're almost there." Abigail stops, releases Steve's hand, and turns around. "We said we'd talk."

Leonid looks around, squeezing my hand. "I can sense the others. We may as well walk all the way to where they're waiting for us."

The others? I look around, unsure whom he means. "There's no one else," I say. "They'd have said."

Mom looks at the ground.

Steve grunts.

"They're all right up there, around the bend." Leonid sounds utterly calm.

"I thought you told Boris and Mikhail not to come." I frown.

"I did." He tosses his head at Steve. "They made no such promises."

"You didn't ask," Steve says.

"I didn't ask." Leonid tugs on my hand, and then he starts walking again.

"Who is it?" I seem to be the only one who doesn't know. "Who's up there?" I stomp. "Is it Aunt Helen?"

"Perhaps she's with them too," Leonid says. "But those whom I can feel are the people I've mentioned before. Aleksandr, Kristiana, Gustav, Grigoriy, Alexei, and Katerina."

Stupid Katerina? Ugh. I guess I'll find out just how pretty she is. Which is *not* the point. "Why are they all here?"

"To destroy me." But Leo's smiling.

"Why aren't you worried?" I ask. "You should be nervous."

"He's not nervous." A man steps out from behind the edge of the massive stone kiln up ahead. "Because he's rescinded our ability to use our magic."

Gabe hops out from beside the man. "Hey, Iz. I can't believe you knew about all this too! Mom said I couldn't tell you, but I really wanted to call anyway."

"We were trying to keep you safe," Mom says. "Clearly that didn't pan out."

As we approach the limekiln, a large stone facade with small arched doors in the front, all of them barred over, I see quite a few people. Gabe's the only one I know, other than Mom and Steve.

"Who's who?" I whisper.

"The blonde who's small and crazy looking is Adriana." Leo points. "The other small blonde's Kristiana, who's Gustav's sister. The third, taller blonde—not much diversity in Russia— is Katerina."

"Their names are confusingly similar, too," I say. "If the same person had named them all, say, an author of a book series, I'd say she was a total idiot."

"No kidding," Leonid says. "The big bulky man, that's Grigoriy, and his wife? Girlfriend?" He snorts. "I can't keep up, but she's the one brunette, the one who looks like she may have eaten once in her lifetime." He points again. "Grigoriy normally has wind magic, when I choose to allow it. The tall dark-haired man's Aleksandr, Kristiana's husband, who usually has earth powers. The slim blonde man is with the tiny, crazy woman, and his name's Alexei Romanov. Water powers."

"I recognize his face from the news," I say. "Vaguely."

"You should let go of his hand and come over here," Gabe says. "Red Rover, Red Rover, send Izzy over." He smiles.

Does he really think this is all just some kind of game? Of course he does. Gabe thinks everything's a game. And with their faces—they all look like they could walk right off the set of a movie. I might think this was all fun too, if I were his age.

"He has a pretty face, so it's confusing, but Iz, trust me. He's the bad guy," Gabe says. "He threatened Mom and Dad before, and he almost killed Mandy." He nods. "Honest."

"Are you tied to him?" Mom asks.

It makes me rethink what Lechuza said. . . That she 'linked both of the bumbling idiots who were spraying magic all over.' I thought she meant me and Leonid, but I can't spray magic. I didn't have any. Did she mean. . .Gustav? I'm pretty sure she linked him to Gabe, but I want more info. "Tell me about Gabe and Gustav."

"You took Leonid," Mom says, clearly ignoring my demand. "On the day I called, Oliver was right. He'd seen you—you were talking to the stallion who was set to be killed, and you stole that horse to save him from being killed. Am I right?"

More or less. I could explain that I stole him to *sell* him for my criminal boyfriend, but I feel like leaving that out doesn't hurt anyone, so I just nod.

"You discovered he wasn't really a horse, and then he was kind to you, and he listened to how we'd all disapproved of Tim, and then. . ." Mom shrugs. "Then what? He convinced you that he needed your help?"

"He was a horse for quite some time," I say. "And the second we reached Tim's place, he tried to run away. But when he did, he passed out."

"See, they're tied too," Gabe says. "Sounds just like me, except, like, probably more running away for them. I wonder what Tim thought. I wish I'd been there to see his face when Leonid turned into a man." He's smiling—of course he is. It's all a game.

"It was several days before I turned him back into a human," I say. "And Tim was in jail during all that time."

"Jail?" Mom's eyes widen. "Why was—"

Steve wraps an arm around her shoulders. "Focus."

"Right," Mom says. "Okay, so you're stuck. You're somehow linked to Leonid, but we have a plan to get you unstuck."

"You—what is it?" Leonid asks. "Because we understand a bit about the connection, and we were told it's not something that's breakable."

"We know who will know." Katerina looks smug. "We found the spell you used to summon Baba Yaga before."

"That's not a good idea," Leonid says. "The person who linked us was another witch, the one who monitors this area, geographically speaking, and she's not happy that we're here. In fact, she made it sound like any additional magic used in this area would be a very bad thing."

"Convenient," Katerina says. "You always have all the answers, but this time, we're all going to hear them together."

"But that spell might summon Lechuza," I say. "I doubt she'll be happy to see us again either."

"Who?" Mom asks.

"Wait, is he telling the truth?" Katerina asks. "You saw it too?"

I nod. "She came to talk to both of us—she wasn't happy

that Leonid was using his magic. She told us I was supposed to be a governor, of sorts, keeping him from using any magic at all, thanks to my dark-magic-half."

"Why?" Steve asks. "Why does she care? Is your usage pulling on her magic since we're here?"

I shrug. "She didn't say, but she's worried about us waking up a horseman—some kind of death-bringing-balancer."

"Ridiculous," Aleksandr says. "If that existed, we'd have heard of them before."

"Yes," Kris says. "Because Baba Yaga's been so clear with us." She looks a little nervous.

Aleks frowns.

"I'm doing it," Katerina says. "Gustav can't use his powers unless he's touching Gabe, and—"

"Actually." Gustav clears his throat. "My powers are gone right now."

"Yours are too? I knew ours were, but. . ." Katerina freezes, and then her eyes swivel toward Leonid. "You did that too, I assume?"

Leonid shrugs.

"What?" I ask. "What's going on with them losing their powers?"

"When they gave me their powers," Leonid says, "they knew I might be able to block them all from using them."

"When we failed to contain you, we knew it was a risk," Katerina says. "But Baba Yaga's the one who told us to stop you, so we're calling her to help finish what we started." She hurls something at the ground, and Gustav pulls out a blow torch.

Of course.

They'd be prepared for Leonid to take their powers. Contingency plans are just smart. Now Katerina's chanting something, and then the stuff on the ground kind of half-explodes. Katerina and Gustav leap back.

All around us, thunderbolts strike.

The earth groans, almost like it did before, when Lechuza came to yell at us. Then there's a strange moaning sound, like the pounding of sledgehammers against the foundation of a large building, and then a clap of thunder again, but this time without the lightning.

I blink.

And I cover my ears.

Not that it matters. The voice is booming inside my brain. "How dare you call me here of all places?"

I crouch down, releasing Leonid's hand. He wraps himself around me, his arms making me feel both stronger and braver. "It's fine," he murmurs into my ear. "You're going to be just fine."

Redeemable. See? What kind of villain protects the girl? Unless the girl's his only way to access his magic, I guess. Then, pretty much a hundred percent of them would.

Gah. See? Bad judgment.

When I finally poke my head around Leonid's shoulder, I see her. From the voice, I expect a fearsome warrior the size of a mountain. I *don't* expect a tall, svelte woman in a very stylish ski-suit. She's scowling something fierce, though. "Was it you?" She's glaring at Leonid.

He shakes his head. "Not this time."

"Who?" She swivels, and then she stops, glaring at Katerina. "It must have been you, then." She scowls. "What do you want?"

"We have questions," Katerina says.

"Do I look like a wiki page?" She grows precipitously in size —the woman I assume is Baba Yaga becomes larger, taller, and brighter. "You can't simply summon me whenever you want, especially to someone else's demesne."

"About that," I say. "We saw Lechuza, and she wasn't very happy."

Baba Yaga freezes. "You saw her?" She grimaces.

And shrinks.

"She doesn't like being called Squannit, either," Leonid says. "Just FYI."

Baba Yaga rolls her eyes. "Does she think I chose the name *Baba Yaga*? What a stupid name. We don't get to choose the names that stick, but there's power in a name spoken by a hundred thousand tongues."

"We called you because we're now connected," Katerina says. "Gustav's connected to this boy." She points at Gabe. "And Leonid's connected to her." She points at me. "They can't use their powers without touching."

"And if we move too far away from each other," I say, "Leonid passes out."

Baba Yaga steps toward me slowly, her eyes studying me. "You're different." She glances around the group, pausing and studying Abigail and Gabe in the same way. "You're born of magic."

"So Lechuza told us," I say. "She said we were the children of a witch and a horseman."

Baba Yaga's eyes widen. "She spoke of their union?"

I nod. "She tied us, according to her, to keep Leo from waking the horseman by using magic here. I guess Xolotl is near here, and close to waking."

Baba Yaba trembles. "He's. . .close to waking?" She inhales, her eyes wide.

"So she said," I say. "But I'm not sure—"

"You mustn't use magic here," she snaps. "You must all come home immediately."

"Who are the horsemen?" Katerina asks.

"Yeah," Kristiana says. "I want to know the answer to that one, too."

"We have the magic of life." Baba Yaga's whispering, like even her words might wake him if they're too loud. "We help all things to grow, strive, and thrive. But they're the balance to our life—they bring death and destruction. Floods, fires, calamities, and plagues all come from them.”

“And when they wake?” I ask.

“All of that happens while they’re sleeping,” Baba Yaga says. “Their magic spawns it from their dreams. But when they wake. . .” She trembles. “War. Bloodshed. Destruction. They rebalance a world that’s thriving into. . .” She shivers. “Balance isn’t kind.”

That sounds horrible.

“People can’t truly appreciate life without death,” Baba Yaga says. “It’s why children flourish after war. It’s why new growth redoubles after a fire.”

“Okay, but about these links,” Katerina says. “Can you undo the connection? Because Gabe’s not from here, and if we’re going back to Russia—”

“I can’t undo it,” Baba Yaga says. “I didn’t forge it, and it was only possible because of who he is at his core.” She frowns. “If you want to sever the link, you’ll have to forcibly separate them.”

“But they’ll both survive?” Katerina asks. “If we do that. . .”

Baba Yaga shrugs. “How should I know?” She glances back and forth. “I must go. Even my presence could wake him up if he’s not slumbering soundly.”

“But before we go, she said we’re soul matches.” I step backward, putting some space between me and Leonid. “Lechuza said she matched me with Leonid because our souls fit.”

Baba Yaga’s eyes widen, and she follows me, her eyes going out of focus, like she’s looking at something else, something I can’t see. “A soul match is a beautiful thing.”

“Is that—” I don’t want to ask with all these people listening. With Leonid listening. “Is that,” my voice drops to a whisper, “is the soul thing the reason I like him? Is it the reason I want to save him?”

Baba Yaga smiles this time, and she walks toward me. Once she reaches me, she drops one hand to the side of my face. She’s whispering, too. “You know, I’ve met only one soul match in my very long, very lonely life." She sighs. "Rurik—he loved me, I believe. Not the same way I loved him. I have no idea whether it was from our soul bond, but we cared for each other. Still, we made choices. We were who we were. I can't tell you what part of you loves him for that, or what part loves him for the connection, or what part of him cares about you or how much."

"I don't love him," I say.

"Lying won't do you any good." She cackles. "At least, it never helped me."

"Would you try to break the bond?" I ask.

"I'm not even sure you can," she whispers. "Not without it killing you both, but if you can break it. . .and he's your soul match." She shakes her head. "With his magic, he'll be the only one who can heal you from the wound it causes. Can you trust him to do that, when it causes more pain and more weakness to him?"

I don't know what I can trust anymore, but with this thing in the way, with this *soul* thing, how can I ever know whether my judgment's impaired? How can I know whether he can be saved or whether he's even worth saving?

"You need faith," she says softly. "Anyone can be saved, but they have to choose to change themselves. You can only give them the chance."

"What about Gabe and Gustav?" I ask. "They aren't soul-bonded, right?"

She shakes her head. "No, she bonded them simply to contain Gustav."

"So can they separate?"

Baba Yaga sighs. "I've never tried to bond anyone that way, because I was the one who gave them this power to begin with." She frowns. "I think if you two can separate, their split should be much simpler. Yours would involve separation of both the soul bond she never should have forced and the separation of

Leonid's power to you, which makes it almost impossible for him to access his magic."

If we stay bonded, but I don't let him use his magic. . .that's the safer bet. It would ruin my life, but it might help many, many others. But I can't help thinking that he's changed, and he deserves the chance to prove it to everyone. He deserves the chance at real love, and we can only have that if we show we're free from this bond. But then, isn't that the greatest lie women tell themselves about men? That they've changed them? Am I just lying to myself? What's Leonid really like?

"I want to see his face," I say. "Can you show it to me?"

She doesn't bother asking what I mean—Baba Yaga must understand. If Leonid got his powers from her, she must be able to see the light and dark as well.

"I can hear your thoughts, girl," Baba Yaga says. "I can feel your heart, and yes, I can see your face. And I'll show you his. Once. But like our souls, the light in our faces is always changing. Seeing it once —I'm not sure it will give you what you want. But for his sake, for my child's child's child, I'll do it, and then I must leave." She presses one hand to my cheek. "A forbidden daughter." She steps back. "And a forbidden son." She tosses her head, and I follow her gaze.

Leonid and the others are standing several paces away, all of them watching us, and all of them confused.

"They can't understand us," Baba Yaga says. "I'm not powerful here, but I can manage this small feat at least." She smiles. "But look at his beautiful face. He looks just like his many greats grandsire, Rurik." She sighs.

Leonid's face truly is glorious.

It's sharp angles and bright colors and a strong, commanding air. He was born to rule. He was made to be worshipped. He's staring right at me. His face is as light and beautiful as I've ever seen, but it's ringed in dark, twisting cords of what almost look like barbed wire.

"His heart's good, and it's true," Baba Yaga says. "But he's lost sight of what he's doing. He needs a touchstone, someone clear and clean." She sighs. "I didn't promise you this, but. . ." She holds up a mirror, and I see myself.

I'm bright.

I'm light.

Not a speck of darkness.

None at all.

"You're too good for him," Baba Yaga says. "You're too good for all of us." I see it then, the pulsing, twisting, bright flashes underneath. "You can see it, girl, can't you? The divine inside of there? Only with darkness can the light become this strong. It comes from your long-ago parentage. You have magic inside of you, magic that's contained because it's equally light and dark. You're in perfect balance." She snorts. "No wonder he likes you."

I can't believe that. I'm nothing special. I'm *normal*. Stupid, even. Gullible. When I turn to look at Leonid again, I feel very unworthy.

"Never mistake hope and optimism for stupidity, girl. My child doesn't think it is. Keep shining for him, so he won't lose his way. Darkness is coming, and the world will need you to survive it. I think he'll be smart enough to give whatever it takes of himself to keep you safe after you break the bond, but that's a risk you'll have to weigh."

"What?" I spin around to ask her what that means, but she's gone.

"What did she say?" Leonid rushes to my side. "Can she unlink us?"

I frown. "You all heard her. She said we can forcibly separate, but there's no way of knowing whether we'll survive." I think about telling him all the stuff she said about him giving of himself, about the pain if he tries to save me, but. . .I can't. I can't ask that of him. It sounds like he's likely to survive it, and I'm the one at biggest risk.

He'll refuse to try if I tell him that.

Leonid shakes his head. "No, I didn't hear that. Katerina asked if we could survive, and then she walked to your side, and the two of you spoke, but none of us could hear a thing you said."

"What?" I look around, but Mom's nodding. They all are.

"She said. . ." I blink.

And just like that day, so many years ago, I have a choice to make. I should leave here with Gabe and Gustav and Leonid and never look back. Baba Yaga and Lechuza are worried about the fate of the world. They're worried about what this horseman may do when awoken.

Maybe I'm selfish, but I'm only worried about one thing.

Life doesn't matter if the quality of life is terrible. If breaking the bond destroys Leonid and his magic, we can't awaken the beast. The world won't be harmed by us. But how can I make any choices while I'm stuck with the one someone else made for me? How can I know what power I have to save Leonid or what magic he may have to change unless we're free to choose for ourselves?

"She said if Leonid and I forcibly separate, the bond will break."

"But will you survive it?" Mom asks.

"Leonid and I will try it first," I say. "And if we survive, then Gabe should make it, too. He's not soul-bonded. They're just linked thanks to Gabe's parentage."

It's a risk, but I'd rather die than not truly live.

CHAPTER 22

Leonid

I've killed thousands.

In fact, I've killed so many people that I've lost count of the exact number. But there's only one person I truly cared about who died because of me. His death hurt more than all the others.

"I'll stay here," I say. "I'll never use my magic again."

Izzy turns toward me slowly. "Why?"

"You don't even have to see me," I say. "I can follow you around quietly, or, you know. . ." I throw my hands up in the air. "I don't know, but I can figure this out."

"It's not because I despise you." Izzy presses a hand to my cheek. "It's because I *don't* despise you that I need to find out."

"You should despise him," Abby says. "Why don't you?"

Izzy turns around. "You don't know him—none of you do. This bond has allowed me to see things you can't understand. I can relate to him in a way no one else ever has." She glares at Aleksandr and at Katerina. "You all betrayed him as much and as often as he betrayed you, and shame on you for it."

Abby shakes her head. "But, sweetheart, he was going to kill

Mandy, and he was demanding that Gustav and Kristiana also die when—"

"You don't know what he would have done. You just don't. He's never killed someone who wasn't dark—he's only killed villains. He healed Mandy instead of hurting her. I don't think he'd have been able to do any of those bad things, but even if he would have back then, he wouldn't do them now. He's changed in his time with me." She squares her shoulders. "I've seen his face—Baba Yaga showed it to me. She told me that my job is to help guide him in a way no one else ever has. I've seen all the light in his soul, only bounded by dark on the edges from decisions he thought he had to make. I believe in him, and I know that no one cares what I believe. Thanks to Tim, no one trusts my judgment, but I *have* to trust it. I have to, because that's just who I am. I won't hate myself for making a mistake, not anymore. Not when the stakes are so high and I know I'm right."

"Let's say we do believe you," Abby says. "Let's say you're right about Leonid—it's still too dangerous for you to try to break the bond."

"Gabe's bound to Gustav by nothing more than a magical twist tie," Izzy says. "For all we know, if Leonid restores Gustav's magic now, that connection might already be dissolved."

I hadn't even considered that. Could it have been that simple to sever their bond? If Lechuza only put it in place to prevent Gustav from using his magic, and I removed his ability to reach his magic...

"But before we look into all of that," Izzy says, "Leonid and I are going to see whether we can break this bond between us. Then you won't have to wonder whether I really love him. . ." She swallows.

"Love him?" Steve asks. "You barely know him. You met *days* ago."

"Is it time, then, that determines how much you care for someone?" Izzy asks, echoing my words. "Did you love my mother because you spent enough time with her? It's like a tree growing slowly, your love for her? And if so, how much time would I need to convince you? A month? Two? Six? A year?"

Steve frowns.

"Or, was loving her a choice you made, over and over? Did you find her attractive from the start, and then you served her, and the more you helped her, the more you did for her, and the more choices you made to put her first, the more that love grew?"

Abigail's frowning, too.

"Leonid wasn't raised like I was. He didn't have a happy home. He didn't have parents who loved him—not even one." Her eyes are flashing as she dares them all to argue.

I hate this. Why's she telling all of them about my parents. . .unless. Is she telling them this. . .because she *wants* to be with me? Is she trying to get them on our side?

"And these people right here, the ones you trust and admire?" Izzy rounds on Gustav and Katerina and the others. She jabs her finger at Katerina. "She used him. They all did, to some extent. He had lost everything, and they gained from his family losing power, and they didn't care."

"I hardly think," Aleksandr says, "that his woes—"

"You *didn't think* about it. And you didn't care about him, even though he was like you." Izzy shakes her head. "Ignoring bad things is just as bad as doing them, or at least it's close."

"But he *took* what he wanted," Kristiana says. "He always took it."

"When no one will give you anything, what choice do you have?" Izzy asks. "In spite of not being given a loving home or model parents to follow, Leonid's grown strong. He's had his own, slightly off-center moral code that he's stuck with for all this time."

"Off-center is right," Aleks mutters.

"But now he has me by his side to guide him," Izzy says, but she's not talking to the Russians anymore. She's talking to her mom. "I know you hated Tim, and you were right about that. I wasn't sure about myself or much of anything, especially with him beside me, telling me I was small and that he was great. In fact, I think I knew you were right about him, so I stayed away from you."

"That hurt us more than anything," Abby says.

"I don't want to live or love like that anymore," Izzy says. "But if we don't break this bond, I'll have to go to Russia with Leonid forever, just to stay alive. I'll have to leave all of you again. I want to break this connection so I can be one thousand percent sure that my judgment and my decisions are based on what *I* want. That they're based on what *I* know. So you think it's a risk. You all do." Only, she's looking at me now.

"I think it's a risk we shouldn't take," I say. Because if something happens to her. . . She's right that I need her to guide me. I'm not sure what I'll do without her.

"You think we shouldn't do this, but that's just exactly why we have to do it. I need to find out whether I really love you, or whether I'm just bonded to you." Izzy shrugs. "I think I love you, but I need to *know*." She points at her mother. "They need me to know beyond a doubt."

This time, when she steps toward me, when her hand extends to me, I curl into her touch. The whispered words feel almost pulled from me. "It's too dangerous." I can't risk her. She's the only thing I have. She's all I care about.

"What are you worried about?" She smiles. "You've already survived lots of times when people thought you wouldn't, right?"

She doesn't know the half of it, but I grit my teeth, because it's different now. We're not talking about my survival, but hers. "I can't risk you." My voice cracks on the next words. "I can't."

"Leo, I can't ask my brother to stay bound to Gustav either, and I'd rather risk my life than his."

"I wouldn't," I say.

She rolls her eyes.

"Besides," I say. "I can check right now whether—"

She shakes her head. "I have to know—for me."

"Why don't we try it first, me and Gustav?" Gabe frowns. "If the whole. . ." He karate chops his left palm with his right hand. "Leonid taking the power didn't already kill our connection, then we can try separating. Then if we're fine after, then you will be too. Right?"

Izzy shakes her head, and I know what she's thinking. Even if they can separate, it might mean nothing for us. I doubt Gustav and Gabe are soul matches, judging by how Katerina's practically crawling into Gustav's arms.

"It has to be us," Izzy says. "I have to know."

I want to argue with her, but I can't think how.

Abigail's brow is furrowed. "Before we try this, I'll go get Whitney, Nathan, Ethan, and—"

The ground beneath our feet rumbles, and the earth shakes.

"There's no time for that." Izzy sighs. "We need to do this now." She crosses the dozen feet separating her from her mom and hugs her. "I love you, and I'm sorry about before, but I need you to trust me now." I can barely hear her next words. "Because if you don't, I'm not sure I'm strong enough to trust myself."

Her mother doesn't let go, not for a very long time. When she finally does, they're both crying.

"Tell them I love them, if I. . .If I can't. . ."

"Stop," Abigail says. "You're going to be fine."

Izzy nods. "I think we are, Mom, because he's a good person, and good things happen to good people, right?"

Her mother sighs. "I wish that were true. I wish I believed he was good."

Izzy's head tilts. "You haven't seen it yet, but he's done a lot of hard things and a lot of good things. He's also saved my life a few times, and he hated Tim on sight. You have that in common at least."

Abby's half-smiling through her tears, now. "Fine. If you say so, I'll believe you, because I can't lose you again. Not like we did with Tim."

"Then how do we do this?" I ask. "I still think it's a bad idea, but if you insist." I shrug, because I can't fight her. I don't think I'll ever be able to fight her.

"I'll walk away," Izzy says, "since I doubt you'd be capable."

I did collapse on the ground the one time I tried to leave.

"I'll pick Izzy up and keep moving if she falls," Steve says. "But how far should we go?"

Izzy shrugs. "I imagine you'll know."

"Keep us apart, though," I say. "If you just bring us right back together, it won't accomplish anything." Why am I telling them how to do this successfully? I should keep my mouth shut.

But it might hurt Izzy more if we do it wrong. At the end of the day, that's the one thing I can't withstand.

While Izzy and her parents begin to walk away, Katerina strolls over. "What are you up to?" she asks in Russian.

"What do you mean?"

She frowns. "White knight doesn't look good on you. It's. . ." She snorts. "Frankly, it's both disconcerting and ridiculous."

"Noted."

"You can't really care about that girl."

"Why?" I turn to face her. "Because I didn't curl up and die when you didn't care for me?"

"You never cared for me either," she says.

"It's a good thing," I say. "If I had, you'd have shattered me."

She rolls her eyes.

"She's not like you," I say. "She's not like any of you."

"Gustav grabbed Gabe's arm when you first arrived, and he saw her then. He says she shines." Katerina doesn't look very pleased when she admits it. I'm surprised his powers worked well enough for him to see that, but perhaps it's because I only took his access to the elements.

"She does," I say. "But it's not just her soul. It's her mind. Her fearlessness. Her willingness to sacrifice. She's brave, brilliant, and kind. It's a rare combination."

"You don't deserve her at all," Katerina says.

I can't argue, but I realize that she's distracting me. She came over to talk, at least in part, so I wouldn't obsess over Isabel moving farther and farther away.

"What do you think will happen—" But before I can even finish the question, I black out.

At first, just like the other times, nothing happens. An absence of sensation or consciousness. But then pain blossoms, starting in my head, right behind my forehead, where I can usually feel all my magic. It's like a strike of lightning has burned its way through to my brain, and it radiates outward from there.

Sharp, repeating strikes come faster, harder, and more intensely as they roll through me. I would scream if I had a voice. I would arch and bow if I had a back. But I'm nothing—just darkness, misery, and throbbing pain.

Until I wonder what's happening to Izzy.

I've struggled with pain for the better part of my life. When I was young, I was beaten often by my own father. Then I was nearly killed on several occasions by men who hated or mocked him. Later, I was broken half-to-death by those who stole from us. And finally, I was beaten, attacked, and battered by a plethora of enemies. Many of them are standing beside me now, as I convulse on the ground, more than likely.

But the thought of her pain being *anything* like this allows me to step away from it. Once I'm outside of the suffering, once I stop fretting about it, I can sense what's happening to my soul —and then I can follow that link to *hers*.

Her bright, shining, pulsating avalanche of light, beauty, and peace.

She's *writhing.*

Her soul, where it's bound to mine, is unraveling. Bits of light and magic are fraying and exploding and then dissipating until they're *gone.*

Even without a voice, without a body, I cry out then, misery ricocheting away and outward, and I follow the threads back to myself, where I can finally sense it. . .my own magic. My own soul. My central being. I dig deep, and I tunnel out all my own power, and I shove it down the line, healing the shards of Izzy as they unravel, undoing myself to try and keep her intact.

There's a giant explosion of light and power and energy, and then nothing but the deepest darkest black I could never have imagined.

CHAPTER 23

Izzy

It's happening again, just like before.

I'm awake, and I'm not awake. I have a body, and I don't. When I glance down at the split-rail fence in front of me, I can tell it's substantial. But when I press my hand against it, my hand slides right through.

I'm here.

And I'm not here.

I can't tell whether I'm a ghost or this is a dream, but either way, it's not my life.

Leo's far easier to spot this time. He's whistling, his shining face utterly breathtaking. He's walking in a jaunty manner I could never imagine he might walk, bouncing just a little with each step, his feet kicking up puffs of dust. He's also dressed in fine clothing, albeit not very modern. Even with the dust, you can tell that his black boots were quite shiny before. His pants, dark and finely made, are somewhat voluminous. His tunic's finely woven.

"Father," he calls as he rounds the bend where the road meets the path to the rough-hewn wooden building behind me. "Father, it's me."

It must be the summer, because it's not cold.

It's actually very, very hot.

But everywhere I look, there's nothing but clouds of dust. No crops grow, and no grass either. In fact, even the trees that line the road sport no more than a few brown, bedraggled leaves. There's clearly been a drought.

A bad one.

"Father!" Leonid's beaming, as if he's not worried in the slightest about the lack of greenery. "I'm back. Did you hear me?" He sighs, wiping the dust from his face with a piece of cloth, and mutters, "You can't be working that hard. What would you even plow?" He chuckles then, like it's a joke.

He walks right past me without pausing, and I trot alongside him as he goes into the wooden building. But before I can go more than a few steps, he turns around and ducks back out.

"If you're not here. . ." He scratches his head.

"Leonid?" A woman with dark grey hair waves from across the yard.

"Natalia," he says. "Have you seen my father?"

Again, they're speaking Russian, and somehow, I understand it.

Her face falls. "He's. . ." She points. "He's ill."

Leonid moves faster then, his steps not jaunty at all. "What's wrong?" He rushes toward her with an urgent stride that pains me. "What happened?"

She shrugs. "Everyone's ill—there's no food. Not anywhere. At the grand house, they killed the horses even, but they didn't give any of that meager meat to us."

"They killed—" Leonid clenches his hands into fists. "That can't be. Surely it's not that bad."

"The family's not in town. They went to St. Petersburg," she says. "It was the steward who ordered the horses be slaughtered."

"Where is he—my father, I mean?"

Natalia's head tilts and she clucks. "If he's yet alive, he's in

Zoya's old hut. When she died, her daughter took in all those who were suffering."

He takes off at a ground-eating pace. I worry I won't be able to keep up, but apparently in this dream-memory, I'm as fast as a racehorse, and as tireless as a robot. When Leonid finally stops running, I can barely make myself follow. I'm sure he feels the same way, but I don't want to see what's inside.

He ducks into a small, earthen-walled hut. The roof thatch isn't in very good shape, and it smells like moldy puke. I wish these non-dreams didn't come with quite such authentic smells. No one has bothered to clear out waste or clean this place in quite some time, and the smell of sickness makes even the more normal, disgusting smells more pungent.

As I follow him inside, I realize it's worse than I feared.

There are three cots in the hut, and side-to-side, they nearly span its width. On the far right side, there's a man with crazy, tufty white hair. He's moaning, at least. His arm keeps thrashing around, and he's calling for something. I'm not sure what.

The bed between's ominously empty of all but soiled rags.

But the cot on the far left has a man lying on it, and that's the one Leonid approaches. He drops to one knee, and I crouch to peer over his shoulder. The man on this bed looks *terrible*, with sores opened up on nearly every part of him that's visible. "No." Leonid shakes his head. "Father, I came with good news. You were right—we're Rurikid, and I've unlocked the magic inside of us."

His father turns his head, but his eyes are rheumy. If I had to guess, I'd say he can barely see at all. When he smiles, it looks more like a grimace. The two teeth that remain in his mouth don't look great, and the smell as I draw closer leaves me gagging.

He smells like rotten meat.

Unworried about all of that, apparently, Leonid clasps his hand. "Father, I can set fires, I can make lightning, and. . ." He drags a breath in slowly. "I—I can't help you at all. Neither of those powers have a healing element."

His father shakes his head and tries to move his hand, but it looks like a struggle.

"I was busy learning, and I didn't make sure you were alright."

"Leh—" His dad chokes. "Lehnid. . ." He shakes his head. "Proud."

A tear rolls down Leonid's face. "If they won't give me their powers, if they won't share the water with these people who are dying, if they won't heal the world, I'll *make them.*"

His father's eyes close, and he drags in a breath, but it sounds like it could be his last. It looks like any day could be his last. Leonid presses a kiss to his father's miserable forehead, and then he stands. When he leaves his father, he looks terribly resolved.

He walks slowly, almost like he's in a trance, until he reaches the empty wooden building. He stands there, looking around. "No water anywhere," he mutters. "Except. . ." He ducks around the building and trots toward a circular stone structure behind it.

As he climbs up on the top of the stones, the wind whips through his hair. "You said I can't," he calls out in Russian. "You said I mustn't force your powers, but they're not yours. They're *mine,* and I won't abuse them, not like they do. I know what it's like to need. I know what it's like to want. I watch the people they ignore, and I deserve the power to fix this, to care for them." He spreads his hands wide.

The wind screams past.

He's standing on a well, I realize. A water well. He grabs the rope and begins hauling it up. Once it hits the top, he plonks the bucket down on the side of the stone circle.

"Here I am," he calls. "I'm Rurik's child, and I can sense the power inside of me, but it's blocked, much as this stone blocks the water and also keeps it safe."

I wonder who he's talking to?

Maybe Baba Yaga?

Himself?

He grabs the bucket, and he holds it up in the air. The wind whips past again and again, pulling on his hair and his face. The stones beneath his feet hold him up, but it honestly looks almost like something else is holding him aloft. He throws the water up in the air, and at the same time, lifts both hands. A bolt of lightning strikes one, and an explosion of flame engulfs the other.

And then I feel it—a great, sucking vortex sensation.

Leonid's eyes shine like the sun, and his arms tremble, and the wind howls, and the ground beneath us shakes, and then the earth underneath his feet splits open in a long, terrifying line, and Leonid falls forward into the gap.

After he disappears, I expect to blink out.

But I don't. I just keep staring at the gaping hole in the earth, a hole Leonid created, trying to claw the powers he desperately desired from the earth itself.

Just when I'm about to sit down and bawl, a large, terrifying grey horse clops his way out of the crack in the earth. Smoke streams from its flared nostrils. Every hoof strike causes the ground to tremble. When his head turns my direction, his eyes are flames. He snorts, and smoke billows toward me.

My child.

I scream, and he must hear me, even in this wraith form, because he laughs and laughs and laughs.

The sound scares me more than anything else ever has.

CHAPTER 24

Leonid

When I wake up, I realize I must be in hell.

Surely heaven would be prettier than this, right? But as I look around, memories start to trickle back, and as I turn my aching neck, I see the limekiln, each of the walled-off entry points chock full of trash.

So I'm not in hell.

Just another place humans have treated like a landfill for no reason.

"He's awake." Katerina.

I groan as I shove myself into a seated position. "I didn't die."

"More's the pity," Alexei mutters.

I rub my hands across my face and blink repeatedly. My head's pounding, and I don't feel very strong, but. . . the bond to Izzy is gone. I can't sense her, but I can sense something else.

My magic. It's still intact.

And, perhaps more telling, I no longer need physical contact with her to use it. I straighten. "Is she—did Izzy—"

"I like this." Grigoriy chuckles. "Now you're acting almost

as nervous and effeminate as you always looked." He kicks a rock that rolls right up and nails me in the knee.

Without even thinking, I flick the fingers of my right hand and fling it right back at him. He can't block with wind, so it strikes his shoulder. Hard. He cries out like a little girl.

That makes me smile.

"Maybe don't call him effeminate," Mirdza says. "I like you to be able to walk and talk."

"Where's Izzy?" I ask again, more forcefully this time.

"Do you even care anymore?" Katerina asks. "Her parents said she wasn't doing great, but then, *bam*, all of a sudden she was fine. She woke up. She talked to them, for a while actually, saying all kinds of disgusting things about how great you were, but then. . ." She sighs. "She came to look at you. She touched your face, and then she got pale. She slumped a little. She was clearly tired. She laid down in their car and just. . .went to sleep."

"Not until after Gabe and I separated successfully," Gustav says. "It wasn't fun, but it seemed way less horrible than what you just went through. I guess we should count that as a win."

"He did spasm and writhe a lot," Katerina says, "but not nearly as much as you did."

"But now?" I ask. "Where's Izzy now?"

"Once Gabe woke up and started talking, she totally passed out." Katerina shrugs.

"You said that already."

"Yeah, well, she looked like she might sleep for a while, so they just. . ." Katerina points. "They left with her and Gabe both asleep in the back of the car."

They left?

I shake my head. "She wouldn't leave me."

"Effeminate *and* stupid," Adriana mutters. "Apparently the key to Leonid's intelligence was his evilness." She snickers. "She was sleeping, idiot. She didn't leave—they left you with her in tow. Then once they got a mile away, they called Kris. You weren't convulsing again, so they decided their job was done."

Their job of disconnecting us. Right. I struggle to my feet.

Aleksandr offers me his hand.

I'd rather cut mine off than take it. I stand up and shove past him, not even bothering to glare. "You know, if I wanted someone more powerful than I was to return my magic to me, I might not insult them from the second they wake." I shrug. "But what do I know? I'm just an effeminate moron."

By the time I reach my car, they're all scrambling along behind me in a very satisfying way.

Kristiana shoves Aleksandr. "—told you that you shouldn't have let them—"

Adriana's poking Alexei's side. "—save people when you can't even fill a glass with water. A shotglass."

I can't help a chuckle. "None of you are supposed to be using your magic at all. Weren't you listening? Use your immense wealth, that I haven't taken from you thanks to my unappreciated largesse, and get on a plane back to Russia, stat."

Gustav clears his throat. "But if you could just—"

"No." I shake my head. "Once you've landed, send me a text message and let me know you're no longer at risk of waking anything horrible here. Apologize, from the heart, and I'll consider letting you play with your toys again."

Kristiana opens her mouth, but Aleks slaps a hand over it. "We'll book some flights."

"But you should remember that Izzy won't like you if you're mean to us," Gustav says. "No one that shiny could like a villain."

I hate that he's right, because being a hero's a real *drag*. "Just go."

They're heading for their SUVs when I realize that I'm not sure where Izzy's parents were headed with her. Probably Birch

Creek, but who knows? I could waste a lot of time looking when these people probably already know the answer. "Wait."

"Yes?" Gustav turns, a half-smile telling me they were waiting for this.

"Where did Izzy go with her parents?"

Kristiana drops her hands on her hips. "Shouldn't you head back to your hotel and wait for her to come to you, like a good boy?"

I can't help my snarl. "A *good* boy?" I snort. "There's a difference between a reformed villain and a 'good boy.'"

She glares. "And you want the information that we have. So what are you offering for it, *good boy*?"

I roll my eyes, and then I flip all their powers back online. "You already know that I can turn them off again just as fast. Now tell me where she went."

"Her parents were taking her home. They left half an hour ago."

Shoot.

I jam directions back to Birch Creek Ranch into my GPS, and I hit the gas. I haven't gone very far—traffic in Salt Lake's so infuriating that I'm contemplating using wind to just *shove* a few dozen cars off the road—when my phone rings.

"Hello?"

"Hey." Katerina clears her throat. "Not everyone wanted me to call you." Her voice drops to barely a hiss. "But Steve called us, and apparently Izzy woke up and insisted they let her out. She made them drive her back to her car so she could go to her old apartment to pick up her stuff."

"She went back for stuff?" I sigh. "Thanks for telling me."

Now I'm stuck making the same horrible time going the other way, but eventually I work past the rush hour congestion, and I make a bit of incremental progress. As I'm driving, I think about what I can possibly say to her. Sure, I no longer *need* her with me to live, but I still want to be with her all the time. That should count for something, right?

Or maybe I should make my good behavior contingent on her spending time with me.

No, that's too villainous.

Good boys wouldn't do that. Gah, I hate being a *good* boy.

"Oooh, I have an idea." And now I'm talking to myself, like a villain in a bad movie. I'm monologuing, and not even to the good guys. "I'll tell her that I have a lot of magic that I *could* use for good or bad, and that I need her to help me to know what's good." I nod. "That's a good idea. She'll like that."

But when I reach her apartment, and I see her cobra parked just outside, I'm not relieved.

Not at all.

Because there's a big truck parked next to it, a big, green truck. It's a truck I've seen before—parked at Timothy Heaston's house. I'm practically fuming when I reach the elevator, which has two small people who look like teenagers waiting on its arrival.

I take the stairs three at a time, and then I stare at her front door.

326C.

Should I give her space? What would a good boy do? I think about how Tim reached out to try and grab her arm and force her to listen, and I stop dithering. I grab the doorknob, and I channel a tiny bit of fire and earth inside, and the lock pops.

I yank it open.

The scene I was expecting doesn't materialize. They're not in the family room, locked into some kind of physical altercation. I walk down the hall, the voices growing loud enough that I stop to listen.

"—thought you'd be the kind of woman who would fold at the first difficulty." There's a thwack sound.

"I didn't," Izzy says. "In fact, I got you out of jail, though I probably should have left you in there. You didn't care that I had no money, that I had no way to get you out, and you wanted me to beg my parents—"

"Don't act like it would have been hard. All you had to do was ask Mommy and Daddy, and they'd have given you the money. Your pride was—"

"My pride?" She's shouting now. "I barely had any pride left, thanks to you. And you know what?" I hear her stomp. "As soon as I got back here today, a moment before you arrived, I reported your interference to the school board. I should've done it before, but I didn't want to hurt Rebecca. Today, though, I took screenshots of the email you sent to her, and I sent them over. She was doing what she thought was right. You were just trying to control me, so I figure they'll sort that out."

"You—you did what? I had no idea you were that selfish, or that painfully stupid."

"I'm just embarrassed it took me so long to do something about it," she says.

And then I hear a crack—a sound I'd know anywhere.

I round the doorway as he's reaching back to strike her again. I whip him backward with bands of air, and then I release him. He falls forward on his hands and knees.

I smile.

"You struck her." I glance back, and fury floods my entire body.

Izzy's on the ground, a bruise already spreading across her cheek. Her lip's bleeding, and there's a small cut under her left eye. She shoves up to her feet, shaking her head. "Leo, no."

"No, *what*?" I'm so angry that my hand's shaking where I've balled it into a fist at my side. "I won't even use magic." I toss my head. "I can destroy him with my bare hands, just like last time, but this time, there's no camera recording it."

Tim's back on his feet. "What was that?" He's scowling. "What kind of sick, weird technology do you have, weirdo?"

Before I can say another word, he comes after me. I'm smiling when I clock him hard on his jaw. He stumbles backward, swearing under his breath. "I will end you, Ruski."

I laugh. It's going to be very, very fun tearing him apart.

"Leo, please," Izzy says.

I turn around, my whole body aching to attack. "But he's dark. Really, really dark."

She shakes her head.

"He's—you know he is. You said you turned him over to the board."

"You were listening in." She sighs. "Now that I've done that, we'll wait and see what they do."

"What if they don't do anything?"

He swings at me again, a slow, lumbering blow that's easy to dodge. I dance around and slam him in his ribs.

"Fine. I won't kill him. I'll just beat him up really bad." I lift my eyebrows. "Surely that's fine."

She shakes her head again. "Leo."

The disapproval in her face has me gnashing my teeth.

He tries to grab me then, with his meaty arms. I let him, gritting my teeth while he pulls one hand back and clocks me in the jaw.

"There." He's still trying to clobber me, but I dance away. "He got *me*. Now I can retaliate, right?" I dance a step or two, and then slam him good.

This time, the big idiot collapses to the ground, groaning.

It's so unsatisfying to beat up a wiener like this.

"I can drag him outside," I say. "I'll use air, so no one can track me, and then I can take care of him out in the mountains."

"Leonid."

"Before you say I'd be breaking the law. . ." I pause.

"If you say diplomatic immunity," she says.

"Then what?" I arch one eyebrow. "Marry me, and you'd have diplomatic immunity too. You could *help*."

She scowls. "Leo, drag him outside and dump him on the sidewalk, and then leave him alone."

I straighten. "I'm the czar of Russia, and I have the power to gut thousands. Maybe millions." I jab my finger at the waste of space on the ground. "This one hurt you." I want him to suffer. I want to *make* him suffer. "I told you I'd burn the world down for you."

She steps closer, and she turns her head up. "But will you spare the world for me?"

It's harder.

Burning the world comes naturally to me.

Sparing it?

Ugh.

"He deserves it," I say, aware that I'm whining now like a petulant child.

She goes up on her tiptoes and presses a kiss to my mouth. Her lips are soft, and her arms wrap around my neck, pulling me down toward her. I fall against her, consuming her in a way I never have before. She's everything I need. Light to my dark, balm to my fury, calm to my rage. All my bottled-up, shaky desire to decimate slowly, surely ebbs away.

"That was sneaky," I whisper against her mouth.

She smiles, and then she winces.

I forgot about her lip.

I reach out with just a ribbon of water and a touch of air, and the bruising on her face, the cut on her lip, and the tiny laceration under her eye *disappear.*

"I would do anything for you," I say. "Even. . ." I huff. "Even this, I guess."

"You promise?" She stares into my eyes.

And I nod. "Even this."

"What about the next one?" she asks.

I groan. "Are you talking about your neighbor? Because if that idiot hit on you too, then—"

She laughs, pressing a hand to my chest. "I meant, the next time a small, dark person like him does something stupid. Will you let me help you know what to do?"

I step back, finding it hard to separate myself from her hand. "When I was a horse, you wanted to break me, right?" I narrow my eyes at her. "You wanted me to do anything you asked, using your feet, your hands, and a metal bit to force me if I balked."

She frowns.

"You wanted me—Leonid Ivanovich, ruler of the largest country in the world—to submit completely to you."

"I'm not saying—"

I press a finger to her mouth. Her beautiful, perfect mouth. "Just a nod would be fine."

She's half-smiling as she nods. "I guess," she mumbles against my finger.

I drop my hand, and I duck so my face is right in front of hers. "It almost killed me when you broke our bond." I press a small kiss to the side of her mouth. "I liked that bond. I wanted an excuse to have you around."

"I had to know," she says. "I had to know whether I really liked you, or whether I was just stuck with you by fate or the universe or some kind of magic."

I freeze. "And?"

"When I was out, I dreamed of you. I saw what was probably your worst pain. And when I woke up, all I could think about was you."

Shoot. Should I not have kissed her? Should I have given her more space? Did I rush over here and mess this up?

"I love you, Leonid Ivanovich. Maybe it's because our souls are like puzzle pieces, formed a hundred years and a billion miles apart."

"I mean, it's probably more like five thousand miles," I say.

She flicks my chest.

I laugh.

"I love you because you listen to me. I'm not sure why you do, and I'm still not sure why you like me." When she tilts her head, she's so painfully beautiful, I could cry. "But my soul, shredded and battered though it is, still longs for yours." She wraps her arms around me, and then she presses her mouth to mine. Then, with her lips touching mine, she whispers, "I think I'll love you forever, you poor little broken Russian prince."

When she kisses me this time, I forget where we are. I forget my own name. I forget what I was worried about, and what I wanted to do, and I forget everything but how much I love this woman, and how I would do literally anything for her, including sparing the whole undeserving world on her whim.

Until someone groans from the corner, and says a very ugly swear word. "What am I looking at right now?"

In my love-inspired haze, I forgot about stupid Timothy Heaston.

"Can I kill him now?" I mutter.

"Sure," Izzy says.

I leap toward him, eager to do it before she changes her mind.

But she shouts, "*Leo*, I was kidding."

I can't stop before I kick him, at least. Hard. And then I lift him with air, and I drag him down three flights of stairs, and then I drop him in the bed of his own pickup truck, which, in a stroke of luck, still has a muck tub full of horse manure. I can't help my smile as I upend the tub. . .dumping a juicy pile of my well-aged horse crap over his head.

I brush my hands off, even though I didn't have to touch him, and I spin on my heel.

"Are you quite done?" Izzy's watching me, one eyebrow raised.

"You can take the evil out of the villain, but you can't take the villain out of the. . ." I pause. "You know what I mean."

She laughs. "He really should have dumped that already."

"From now on, though," I say. "I'll do much better at listening."

"Somehow I doubt it." She sighs. "But a girl can dream."

Another truck pulls up then, a big grey one. The doors open right away, and Steve and Abigail both climb out.

"I forgot to mention," Izzy says. "When I told Mom that I wasn't giving you up, she said she has conditions."

"Conditions?" I blink.

"You have to come home and meet us all," Steve says. "Amends will have to be made."

"I didn't actually harm anyone," I say. "Maybe you can keep that in mind."

Izzy winces. "I did text my Aunt Helen."

"Helen?" I vaguely remember her. She was irritating.

"She's had some reparations to make before," Izzy says. "She recommends Lucchese boots."

For. . .kicking? "For. . .what?"

Abigail laughs. "You have a lot to learn, but I think you're showing a little bit of promise. More than that guy, anyway." Abigail's eyes widen as she glances in the back of the truck bed. "Although, this is a good first start."

"We have a little common ground, it seems," I say.

"The Brooks women are a little hard to love," Steve says. "But they're worth the effort. Only really strong men can handle it. After watching you today, you might one day become one of them."

CHAPTER 25

Izzy

At least Mom and Dad let us drive back to Birch Creek together.

I drop my hand over Leonid's and I lace our fingers together—for no reason other than I want to touch him. "My family's a lot," I say. "I'm sorry in advance for the misery you're going to endure."

"I'm sorry I wasn't the nicest to them the last time I was there." He winces. "I—I had some things to learn, I suppose."

"You aren't the first person who's made a mistake."

"Once I win your family over," he says, "where will we go?" He sounds almost nervous.

"Are you asking whether I'm going to insist on living in Utah?" I lift both eyebrows.

"I'm—I just—"

I squeeze his hand. "You're the *czar* of Russia. Of course I don't plan to keep you here."

He exhales loudly. "Really?"

"Do you have vet schools there?"

He cringes a little. "I mean, we do, but they're all in Russian."

"It may be a while before I'm ready for that," I admit. "And I'll want to come back and visit my family often."

"That's not a surprise."

"Will you be fine with that?"

"I'll come with you," he says. "Every time. And of course, I'd be happy to bring them to Russia as well." He smiles at me, and my heart melts a little. It's still pretty surreal that someone who looks like him, someone who basically runs Russia, loves *me*.

"And I want to bring my horses." I bite my lip. "Is that crazy? Maybe it would be too hard on them. Maybe I should leave them here with Steve."

"I'm not going to lie," he says. "I kind of figured I'd be the only horse you rode from now on." But his eyes are sparkling, and I can tell he's teasing me.

"I'm pretty sure that they have skijoring in Russia," I say. "And if they don't, I know what sport we're going to have to introduce. I can invite my friend Paige to help us get it going."

"Back at the turn of the twentieth century, the Romanovs loved tennis. It became the most popular sport in the country. I bet we can make Russia the home of skijoring."

I can't help my smile. "You do have to be very careful, though. No more magic at all until we're in Russia again."

He nods. "Agreed." Then he bites his lip.

"What?"

"While we were breaking the bond, I saw your soul."

I blink.

"It's—I think I could restore our soul-bond. I mean, not the same as what Lechuza did. I don't think it would cause us to have to be close or keep me from using my magic. But I think I could kind of knit our souls back together if you wanted."

I pull my hand away. "You haven't even proposed yet." I scowl. "You think I want to join *souls* with you?"

He splutters.

"I'm kidding," I say. "But by way of warning, if you propose to me right now, I think my dad might shoot you."

"You usually call him Steve."

I shrug. "I mean, sometimes I do. Sometimes I call him Dad. It's complicated." I think about the whole soul thing. "It's not, like, soul-bond complicated, but it's confusing, anyway. Sometimes calling him 'dad' feels right. Sometimes it feels like I'm betraying my real father, and so then I say Steve."

"Does he care?"

"He's never said a word about it if he does. He's a pretty good guy—I think he knows that I love him, and that I'm sad he exists, and that I'm grateful my mom has him. Life's like that. You have to take the good and the bad and be grateful for what you have."

He keeps staring straight ahead, into my dad's taillights.

"I think I don't want our souls to be woven together," I say. "I mean, it sounds romantic, but at the end of the day, I like the idea of you choosing me over and over. That's actually why I chose to break the bond. I wanted to make sure you're picking to be with me, and I'm making the conscious choice to be with you." I can't help my smirk. "Is that stupid?" I sigh. "Maybe it is."

"Not at all," he says. "And I'll do that—happily. As long as you'll allow it."

"There's something I didn't mention." I sigh. "I mean, I'm not sure what happened, or whether there *is* something to mention, but I have a question first."

"Okay." He raises his eyebrows and glances my way.

"It was a long time ago, I know, but back when your dad lost your relics, and those men beat you. . ."

"What?"

I shake my head. "Never mind."

"Say it."

"When that happened, do you remember anything weird

happening? Because when I saw the whole thing, I'm not sure if it was a dream, or a. . .I don't know what it was."

"Did I see anything?" He frowns. "What would I have. . ." He freezes. "Like a woman's face?" His hands tighten on the wheel so much that his knuckles go white. "Right when the man, Sergei, was going to stab me, I saw an angel stop him, an angel who saved my life." He exhales. "I told my dad about it later, and he said I hallucinated."

I'm not sure what it means, but. . . "It was me. I lunged at the man with the knife. I couldn't allow you to be stabbed, you know, and it didn't stop him. I couldn't touch anything. But it slowed him, and you fell out of the way."

"You *were* there, then," he says. "I wonder what it means."

"Well, on that note." I can't help cringing a little. "After we broke the bond, I was dreaming again, and. . ." I sigh.

He grabs my hand again, lacing his fingers through mine and squeezing. "I never saw that angel again, at least, not until the day you drove onto the Brooks ranch and saved me. Should I have? Did I forget something else?"

I tighten my fingers. "No, but I saw something else. I was there, the day you tried to take the powers from Aleksandr, Grigoriy, and Alexei. I understand why you did it. Your dad. . ." I shake my head. "I'm so sorry you had to watch that."

"I think he had scurvy," he says. "I've researched it, and it was a simple disease, so easy to cure with the right nutrition, but the nobles just didn't care. Alexei and his father and the others, they only cared about their own. They only cared about saving the right people, not all the people."

"Not to discount your pain and all that," I say. "But I watched as you kind of cracked a hole in the ground and got sucked into it."

"That went very badly," Leonid says. "When I woke up, a hundred years and change later, I still had no extra powers, and the world had completely transformed."

"Yeah, I know," I say. "But after you went down that well, something else came out of the crevice in the ground you cracked." I wince. "Something big, something horse-shaped, and something very angry. It had eyes like fire, and it called me, '*my child.*'"

"My child?" Leonid turns around fully to stare at me. "Are you serious?"

"It was pretty freaky," I say. "So when I woke up, I told my parents it was fine if they drove me to my apartment. I figured I could find you once I'd had time to think it over. But then you found me, and. . ."

"You knew you were half-witch and half-monster," Leonid says. "Lechuza said as much."

"I mean, not half," I say. "A billion generations back or whatever, my ancestor was half and half. I'm like, mostly human, now."

He shrugs. "I'm not sure how it works, but I'm going to guess that was Lechuza's horseman boyfriend."

"Probably."

"Freaky."

"And it makes me worry about what happens when the horseman here wakes up."

"So maybe we don't stick around for a super long time here," Leonid says. "I'll make amends to your family, and then we'll head back to Russia."

I smack his arm. "Now you're just looking for a way to cut the suffering short."

His chagrined face tells me that's at least partially true.

But when we finally arrive, we don't get the welcome I'm expecting. Everyone's there, and everyone's scowling, but when I get out of the passenger side of the Mercedes sports car, I look up at Mom and Steve's porch, and I see an enormous sign taped to the trim.

WELCOME BACK TO THE BEST VILLAIN SINCE MEGAMIND.

"I wanted it to say Maleficent," Whitney says. "But Gabe was a big baby about it."

"Maleficent's a girl," Gabe says.

"And Megamind's *blue*," Whitney says. "Like that's not worse."

"But," Gabe says. "Megamind gets the girl." He's beaming then, and he does little gun fingers at Leonid. "Welcome to the family, king horse guy!"

"Can I get a ride?" Whitney asks. "Or, like, is it *only Izzy* who gets to ride you?"

"I think you have to say yes," I whisper. "Pony rides might be better than Lucchese boots."

"Hey," Aunt Helen says. "I heard that."

"I want to see you set something on fire," Gabe says. "And then put it out with water. And then lift something up with air, and then—"

"Did you not get the memo about him not using magic?" I ask. "We're not supposed to be doing things, *no* things at all."

Gabe rolls his eyes. "Oh, come on. A little bit's fine, right?"

Leonid chuckles. "We'll see."

"I know what that means," Gabe says. "It means *no*." He's still grumping as we go inside. "Now we have to eat Whitney's sucky cooking *and* we don't get any magic."

"I do have some good news," Leonid says.

I can't wait to hear what this is.

"Before she agreed to return to Russia with me, I bought your sister not one, but *two* new vehicles." He smiles. "I thought Gabe might want the brand new truck I bought her."

His eyes widen and his mouth makes a big round o.

"And I thought Whitney might want the sports car I bought her."

"It's a Shelby Cobra," I say. "It's blue with white racing stripes."

"What?" Gabe swears loudly. "Why does *she* get the race car and I get stuck with the crappy old truck?"

Leonid frowns. "I thought you'd want the truck, since Steve—"

Gabe rolls his eyes. "I have a beat up old truck already. I want the car."

"I'd prefer the brand new truck," Whitney says. "Maybe we can trade?"

Leonid throws his hands up in the air. "I should have known I had no clue."

"He's one step closer to getting it," Steve says.

Everyone laughs.

"What about me and Ethan?" My youngest brother, Nathan, asks. "What do we get?"

Leonid's brow furrows. "What do you want?"

"I want to come to Russia." Nathan nods. "I like the idea of telling people what to do, and saying, 'you have to listen. My sister's married to the czar.'"

Mom freezes, clearly uncomfortable about the *marry* bit.

Leonid doesn't even blink. "Do you speak Russian?"

Nathan frowns. "No."

"You learn Russian, and you're welcome to come visit and order people around."

"But you have to get married *there*, right?" Nathan's still scowling. "I mean, if you don't, won't your people get mad? I would, if the president didn't get married here. Not *here* here, like in Birch Creek, but like, in America. Mom gets weird about buying things that aren't made in America."

Leonid laughs, and then he pulls out his phone. He taps on the screen, and he taps his foot.

"What's going on?" I ask.

Finally, my cobra comes roaring around the corner.

"Whoa," Gabe says. "I really hope that's my car."

Leonid smiles. "Mikhail finally caught up."

But when he climbs out of the car, he's holding a small box. He hands it to Leonid, who drops to one knee.

"The jeweler was *not* very fast," Leonid says. "Even though I know all of this has been a whirlwind." The wind whips through my hair then, and I can't help wondering whether it's him causing it.

"I know your family isn't sure about me, and I know that you may not be either, but—"

I grab his shoulders, and I pull him up, and then I kiss him right on the lips.

Gabe may cheer the loudest, but he's not the only one cheering.

"I love you," I say. "And I worried, for a bit, that my family might not accept my judgment, what with the speed of all this, and with the way I liked Tim the loser." I can't help grimacing. "But I don't just like you. I don't just adore you. I *love* you, and I trust you to change into someone even better with me at your side."

"So you'll marry me?" He's grinning.

Uncle Eddy and Uncle Will, Great Uncle Tommy, and Ethan all whoop. Then everyone else cheers.

"I will," I say. "And as Nathan pointed out, it'll probably have to be in Russia."

"You might want to take a look over my ticker one more time," Mandy says. "I hear it's a long trip. And while we're at it, Tommy could use a tune-up as well. He's been limping."

Leonid slides a ring on my finger then, a ring that's far too big, and somehow shrinks down as he's putting it on. It's a white gold band, but set in the center, there's one of the brightest, sparkliest blue rocks I've ever seen.

"It turns out blue beryl *is* a valuable stone," Leonid says. "I told Mikhail to get this one made into something spectacular, so the rock that split open the mountain can be the one you carry around with you." He leans closer, pressing his mouth to my ear. "If you don't like this one, though, I can crack open a dozen more mountains."

"Maybe we keep all the mountains intact," I say. "And if I want something different, we can just *buy* it."

"Do you want something else?" he asks.

I look down at the ring, which sparkles like blue fire.

"It exactly matches your eyes," he says. "But if you hate it. . ."

"I love it," I say. "Almost as much as I love you."

Gabe groans. "It's a good thing I'm getting a car out of this, because I'm already maxed out on my limit of corny crap for the day."

"Speaking of our new cars," Whitney says. "When do you think you'll be heading back to Salt Lake City to fly home?"

"What?" I roll my eyes. "Already trying to get rid of me?"

"A few days at least," Leonid says. "I don't want to rush her."

"If you could give me a ride back when you go, that would be great." Whitney points at a beat-up old yellow truck parked around the side of the house. "And it's good timing. My old truck kind of died, and I have a competition in Salt Lake at the end of the week."

"Siblings," I say. "Perennial mooches."

As we walk inside to eat, Leonid whispers in my ear, "But I never had any, and I kind of like it that you're sort of a package deal."

CHAPTER 26

Whitney

November hurricanes are rare, but they *do* sometimes happen. In fact, Hurricane Whitney hit Houston on the very weekend I was born. Mom was at the hospital when it lost power, and then they evacuated us. Mom was huffing and measuring the time between contractions while driving out of town.

She gave birth to me in the back of our family Tahoe on the side of the road. Dad caught me—he said he'd never been more terrified.

Mom said she should've known I'd have a tempestuous personality. Maybe she did. She named me Whitney after the hurricane, after all. So while the rest of my family has always been all sunshine and rainbows and happiness, I've always gravitated toward storm clouds, lightning, and gale-force winds.

Even so, my mom and stepdad were shocked when I told them I was getting a handgun. They were even *more* surprised when I told them I wanted a rifle. And when I started winning competitions—sharp-shooting, shotguns, and handguns—no one really understood it. At least when I ride and shoot from horseback, they get that. Sort of.

But no one understood when I said I was graduating with a Political Science degree—specializing in peace and conflict. I have no idea what I'm going to do with it, and they *really* don't get that. The Archer-Brooks family is nothing if not practical.

"I guess you can always come back here and help me with the horses," Steve had said.

"You could go to law school with that," Mom said. "It's a good foundation for law and order."

"Or you could help us run the retreat," Aunt Helen said. "All your attack training might help the visitors sleep easier."

I'm sick of people patronizing me.

Even though I know they're not the problem. They all fit in beautifully with one another. They all belong. I'm the odd one. I'm the square in a family full of circles.

I'm all sharp edges and snarling irritation amidst a sea of "I'm sorries," and "oh, let me help yous."

I'm the pea under the royal mattress.

I make everyone uncomfortable. But riding in the car with Leonid? I feel like he might actually get me. "Thanks for the ride," I say.

"And the brand new truck," Izzy hisses.

I suppress my smile. She's *so* much like our mom without even realizing it. "Yeah, that, too. A new truck will be awesome, you know, for the not-breaking down thing. But also, that awesome toolbox in the back's going to be perfect for all my guns."

"Good grief," Izzy says. "I'm so happy to know that the box I had custom made for saddles is going to be filled instead with weapons."

Yep. Exactly no one gets me.

When my old yellow truck backfires, again, Izzy grumbles.

"I know it's not the most comfortable way to ride back to Salt Lake," I say.

"But you wouldn't have fit in the back of the Mercedes," Leonid says.

"And neither would all of my stuff," Izzy says.

"Which we could have sent back with my people," Leonid says. "Along with the boxes and boxes of things you're worried you won't be able to buy in Russia, like peanut butter and Nutella."

"It's a miracle your people got this old bucket to run at all," I say, "especially with all the errands Izzy kept sending them on."

"I like having people," Izzy says. "So sue me."

"Diplomatic immunity," Leonid says.

Izzy smiles.

"As for the truck, we Russians are pretty good at getting old, crappy cars to run," Leonid says. "Russia's doing much better now, but for years, almost all our cars were crappy. We either had to keep them running or walk." He's a good sport about things, though I suppose laughing at yourself is sort of an age-old comedy schtick.

"I still can't believe you found a guy like this attractive, Izzy," I say. But really, I'm covering up my jealousy. After she spent two years dating the world's biggest loser, I haven't found myself jealous of Izzy much at all.

Until recently.

Her new fiancé's gorgeous, rich, strong, powerful, *magical*, and he looks at her like she's made of stardust or something. I'm happy for her, but it feels like someone like him might have actually understood me. It's a waste to put someone broody and powerful and half-evil, to hear the others talk, with Miss Sunshine and Yellow Daisies.

"Why are you so sour?" Izzy asks.

I consider telling her it's because I think she's a bad fit for her boyfriend and she should hand him over to me, but I'm pretty sure they'd both think that joke was being made in bad form. "No reason."

"When should we get married?" Izzy asks.

I roll my eyes.

"How about the winter?" Leonid says. "All that white—whatever colors you choose will really stand out."

Izzy blinks. "Is that some kind of joke? I would freeze, and so would all my family and friends."

"Fire, remember?" He holds up his hand, and the entire car heats up ten degrees. "We'll all stay warm."

Must be nice.

"No magic," Izzy snaps.

He sighs.

"Okay, how about the colors?" Izzy's flipping through a bridal magazine, which I thought hadn't existed for a decade or more. I can't help wondering how on earth she got one of those in sleepy little Manila, Utah. "This is nice—ooh, wait. We could do Christmas colors. Red, white, green, and gold."

"So we'd get married. . .in five weeks?" he asks.

"That's way too soon," she says.

"So. . .a year?" He looks sick.

"How about powder blue and white," I say. "Do a winter queen theme." I can't help my smile. "You could wear black, and everyone else could look like fairies."

"Black?" Izzy looks horrified. "Is it my wedding or a funeral?" She's frowning.

Until she looks back at me.

"Okay, you got me." She laughs.

I don't tell her I wasn't kidding, but I can't help thinking of how great the crown would look in all black, with large onyx stones. I'd want a scepter with daggers and glinting black stones, too. It would be *sick,* especially in the snow.

After another hour and a half of Izzy asking questions, and then being horrified at my answers, I sink into a quiet funk. I decide to go over my meditation techniques in the back.

"Hey, are you melting the snow?" Izzy sounds like some kind of schoolteacher, I swear. "We said no magic!"

"It's not my fault," Leonid says. "You wanted to stay longer, and then that blizzard hit."

Utah weather in the fall is seriously whack.

"It was so pretty, and kind of cozy, being stuck at home with all that snow falling." Izzy's looking at him with that disturbingly dreamy look in her eyes.

"Yeah, Dad and Mom thought it was *super* cozy," I say. "I remember them walking past my room about one hundred times that night, making sure Izzy was still in there."

Leonid's eyes were burning in a very inappropriate way, and I'm wishing I hadn't been stuck in that room. Being her chaperone when she's already engaged was. . .awkward.

"Alright," I say. "Let's talk about what decisions you two disgusting lovebirds made."

"February wedding," Izzy says. "Valentine's Day. Pink and red colors that'll be super vibrant in front of the backdrop of snow."

Puke.

"And all my bridesmaids will wear the same dress, but the shade will shift just a hair for each."

"I'm not a bridesmaid though, right?" I ask. "Because I do *not* want to wear pink."

Izzy rolls her eyes. "Of course not. I'll give you blood red."

"I'll accept it."

All around us I notice the snow that mounded up in big, fluffy piles is melting. Rapidly. "Hey, how hot is it?"

"Freak blizzard," Izzy says. "And now it's. . .almost seventy degrees? That's so weird."

"I heard there was flooding from something like this in Saratoga Springs last year," I say. "Snowmelt in big chunks was floating down the mountains."

"It's going to be fine," Leonid says. "I'm here, remember?"

"You're a normal guy right now," Izzy says. "And the closer we get to Salt Lake City, the more normal you're going to be."

He salutes.

It makes me laugh.

There's a lot of water running onto the roads, most of it with floating ice chunks, but so far, it's all good. We're almost to our exit, where we'll leave I-80, when a semi truck comes barreling down the steep incline in the road much faster than it should. The Runaway Truck Ramp signs aren't inspiring confidence, honestly, but clearly this is already a dangerous spot for them.

Leonid's smart, giving the stupid truck plenty of space, but another driver isn't. The tiny sports car darts between the semi and us, flying past, spraying snow-melt up and over our windshield. Leonid honks, which is appropriate. Either the honk, or snowmelt, or something else entirely throws the semi truck off, because he slides out of his lane and into ours. Only, with all the melting snow-slush, his swerve turns into a slide, and the truck collides with us, shoving us off the road entirely.

It's our bad luck that we're approaching Parley's Canyon, and other than a small guard rail, there's nothing to keep us from barreling off to our deaths.

Leonid snaps to attention, bracing our battered old truck with what I assume are bands of air, and then shoving us back onto the road. Up ahead, the semi's still struggling, knocking another truck and two cars over the edge. He glances at Izzy, who's paler than an albino snowflake, and she nods. "Just do it."

He uses his left hand to guide all the cars back into place on the road without a word, and then he melts the snow chunks along the road ahead and flicks the water all off the road in a whoosh.

I don't think it's an accident that the rest of our drive's clear and dry, but that's an awful lot of magic for someone who's supposed to be playing it safe. All of us hold our breaths—barely speaking—for the last few miles of our drive. When Leonid drops me off at my new truck and helps me unload all the guns into the tool box, he seems relieved.

"Looks like we didn't destroy the world yet," he whispers. "Now, you be safe until you come out for that Valentine's Day wedding. Got it?"

I nod.

"Thanks for not being a hater."

I hug him.

He grunts. He doesn't hug me back, but he doesn't incinerate me, either. I feel like it's a good first step towards making him a Brooks-Archer. "Take care of Izzy while I'm not around to do it."

"I'll sure try."

Then I watch, a little sadly, as he and Izzy climb into a big, black SUV and drive away. Izzy's face is pressed to the glass until the very last moment, and then she sticks out her tongue. I'm smiling as my sister drives away—headed very far away indeed.

I have three hours before my competition, and since Izzy gave me her key—she's paid up on her apartment for four more months, apparently—I decide to take a little nap before I compete. I'm one of those people who goes hard and rests hard, too. A nap always helps me focus.

When I wake up, I realize I've overslept. That's hardly a shock to me, since I sleep in about once a week. I snatch my bag, brush my teeth, and slide into my boots. I'm going over my mind-calming exercises as I open my new truck and climb in.

"Hey," a guy says. "Who are you?"

I startle. "Uh, I'm Whitney. "Who are you?"

"Theo," he says. "I live next to your apartment." He points. "You must be Izzy's sister."

I frown.

"Izzy's single little sister, right?" He shrugs. "I saw you visit, like September maybe?"

"Oh." I nod. "Yeah—early October. I came for a school thing and stayed for a Halloween party."

"Black cat," he says.

And now it's getting a little creepy. "Alright, well, I've got some bullets to fire." I pull my gun out of my holster and show it to him. "You into guns?"

He blinks. "Uh, no, not really."

I can't help my smile as he walks away. Failed the litmus test. I doubt Leonid would have run from a gun. Most all the other guys I meet do.

A few minutes later, I'm surround by guys who like guns. You'd think I could find my perfect match here, but I've discovered that my skill makes it even less likely. Most of the men I compete against resent the fact that I'm a better shot than they are. It's funny—guys think they'll love the idea of a girl who can shoot. And they do, right up until I shoot a perfect circle around their one lopsided, off-center shot. Not many guys like to be shown up in the activity that makes them feel manly.

So I keep beating them all and going home by myself.

Every guy I meet's either not manly enough, or too 'manly' to handle being shown up by a girl.

Today's a little different, though. In the middle of my third round, there's a massive earthquake. I glance at my watch and realize my sister's plane's already in the air. It's probably for the best. Another huge earthquake would have her freaking out for sure. I'm not sure I buy that there's some kind of horrible death-monster lurking in the mountain, but they all sure seem worried about the prospect.

After watching Leonid wrap cars in air—I'll take their word for it.

The competition takes a hiatus, and they're making calls, and people are frantically rushing around when there's another quake. This one's much larger, and it's *loud*.

People all around me start screaming, and then the mountain behind our targets rips open with a horrible screeching wail. Everyone loses their ever-loving minds. That's very, very bad when they're all holding guns. In spite of what we've been taught, at least two people fire a shot off—at what, I'm not sure.

"Knock it off," I say as loudly as I can. "Everyone should have their safety on."

Only, in that very moment, there's another grinding sound, the loudest yet, and then a crack like Thor struck the mountain with a hammer the size of an elephant. And then a large, long, dark crack opens up in the earth and starts running right toward us.

People are screaming even louder now, and most of them are racing for their cars. Because that makes sense. Trap yourself in a small, metal box while we're running for our lives.

And that's when a massive black horse leaps through the opening in the side of the mountain and lands on his spread hooves, his mane and tail billowing out around him, smoke pouring from his flared nostrils, and flames burning where his eyes should be.

It's the most beautiful horse I have ever seen.

I pick up my phone, and I call Izzy. It goes right to voicemail, so I leave her a message. "You're never going to believe this, but I'm standing right in front of Xolotl." I chuckle. "He's the most magnificent beast I've ever seen, and I *want* him."

I try to snap a photo, but my phone starts to melt in my hands. I drop it, unsure whether the message went through. I realize that I may be about to die. The woman next to me has begun screaming like a banshee, and then her head bursts into flame.

I pick up my gun, click the safety off, and then unload all eight bullets into the black horse, just in case. It doesn't appear to have any effect at all, until he rears back, throws his head forward, and screams at me. I figure this is probably when I die, so I cock my arm back as far as I can, and I chuck my Ruger right at his head.

It spins, end over end over end, but my aim's not as good with throwing as it is with shooting, and it winds up smacking him in the chest instead.

"Well, shoot," I say. "That's just going to piss you off, isn't it?"

He throws his head again, his mane rippling beside him, and then he takes off at a dead run. I'm sure he's going to run me over, but instead, he swerves, and I realize he's going to run right past me. Only, there's a crack following along behind him like a freight train, preparing to swallow me whole.

So when he passes me, I flip sideways, brace my arms on his withers, and leap onto his back. "If you're going this way anyway, be a doll and give me a ride."

He screams, but he doesn't buck me off.

Good enough.

Only as he runs, I notice something. Houses on either side of us catch fire. People run from them screaming, but he doesn't slow or stop. He just keeps galloping. He's headed for town, and that seems like a very bad place for the fire-starting misery beast to go. I decide to do something else that I'm sure is very stupid, and instead of clinging on for dear life, I use my legs to try and guide him to the side, and back toward the mountains where no people live.

It works. He swings wide, and pretty soon, we're not headed for town. We set fewer and fewer homes on fire, and I'm a little proud of myself for sparing all those people this miserable death. Plus, you know, property damage averted is always a good thing. Higher taxes on everyone and all that.

But mostly the death thing.

And then, abruptly, he stops. He swings his big old head around, and he neighs, right in my face, smoke surrounding me.

I cough. "Dude, someone needs to teach you some manners.

That's just rude, and also you need some *massive* breath mints. Or maybe, like, a toilet bowl cake. Those are minty."

He shakes then, and it forces me right off his back. I land pretty hard on my butt on the ground.

"Yep, you're a grade A jerk. I was trying to *help* with the mint suggestion."

In a strange sort of flickering avalanche of lights and sparks and blackness, the horse changes into the tallest and the most terrifying man I have ever seen. Eyes black as night. Ebony hair flowing over his shoulders, and teeth so white they're nearly blinding. "You."

"Hey." I shake my head and snort. "You learned a word. Nice work."

"*You* are *mine*."

"Yours?" I shake my head. "Nope. I'm mine. You are yours. But that was three words. Pretty good job for a newborn baby who throws fiery tantrums."

He scowls.

"You are mine, human. You will help me restore the balance."

Oh, shoot. He knows lots of words, which means all of mine probably didn't make him less cranky.

He turns and starts to walk, his massive black boots tromping on the ground ahead. "Come."

I try to turn and sneak the other way, but it's like something's tying me to him. I find myself tripping along behind him, stumbling and bumbling, and nevertheless walking as fast as I can to try and catch up.

Even with as beautiful as he is? I *hate* this guy.

I hate him a lot.

And I have a feeling we're just getting started.

***

I hope you loved My Trojan Horse Majesty! (Leave me a review if you did! It helps us so much when you do that, anywhere and everywhere. Tell your friends, tell your family, tell your Goodreads enemies. LOL!)

And if you loved it, you might be happy that the FINAL BOOK is now up on preorder. You can pre-grab My Death Horse Overlord right now. I'm hoping to get it out much sooner than that. It's already outlined, and in case you can't tell, Whitney is pushy. She doesn't like waiting! She's actually modeled after my own Amethyst Whitney Baker, my third daughter.

And if you like the Birch Creek Crew, you can read more of them under my B. E. Baker pen name, and you can save by grabbing a series bundle on my website (where you can also sign up for my newsletter!) at www.BridgetEBakerWrites.com

THANKS FOR SUPPORTING ME!! <3 (Almost all proceeds go to pay for MY eight horses and MY five kids! LOL!)

Acknowledgments

THANK YOU to my readers. Without you guys, this would NOT be possible, writing horse shifter romance that everyone told me NO ONE wanted.

And a huge thanks to my girls, for loving horses as much as their mother. <3 And to my husband for PAYING for it all...

About the Author

Bridget's a lawyer, but does as little legal work as possible. She has five kids and soooo many animals that she loses count. There are for sure lots of horses, dogs, cats, and so many chickens. Animals are her great love, after the hubby, the kids, and the books. She makes cookies waaaaay too often and believes they should be their own food group. In an attempt at balancing the scales, she kick boxes daily. So if you don't like her books, maybe don't tell her in person.

Bridget's active on social media, and has a Facebook group she comments in often. (Her husband even gets on there sometimes.) Please feel free to join her there: https://www.facebook.com/groups/750807222376182 She also gives a free book to everyone who joins her newsletter at www.BridgetEBaker Writes.com

Also by Bridget E. Baker

I write romantasy and end of the world fiction under Bridget E. Baker.

The Dragon Captured Series: (dragon shifter romance!)

Ensnared

Entwined

Embroiled

Embattled

The Russian Witch's Curse: (horse shifter romance!)

My Queendom for a Horse

My Dark Horse Prince

My High Horse Czar

My Wild Horse King

My Trojan Horse Majesty

My Death Horse Overlord

The Magical Misfits Series: (paranormal humor!)

My Pigeon Familiar

My Mongrel Pack

My Itching Scales

The Birthright Series (urban fantasy romance):

Displaced (1)

unForgiven (2)

Disillusioned (3)

misUnderstood (4)

Disavowed (5)

unRepentant (6)

Destroyed (7)

The Birthright Series Collection, Books 1-3

The Anchored Series (urban fantasy romance):

Anchored (1)

Adrift (2)

Awoken (3)

Capsized (4)

The Sins of Our Ancestors Series (end of the world romance):

Marked (1)

Suppressed (2)

Redeemed (3)

Renounced (4)

Reclaimed (5) a novella!

A stand alone YA romantic suspense:

Already Gone

I also write women's fiction and clean romance under B. E. Baker.

The Irish Escape:

The Crumbly Old Castle

The Creaky Old Barn

The Scarsdale Fosters Series (standalone but interconnected romances):

Seed Money (1)

Nouveau Riche (2)

Minted (3)

Loaded (4)

Filthy Rich (5)

Old Money (6)

A standalone historical fiction:

Hungry: The Inspiring Tale of Three Donner Party Survivors

The Finding Home Series (standalone but interconnected romances):

Finding Grace (1)

Finding Faith (2)

Finding Cupid (3)

Finding Spring (4)

Finding Liberty (5)

Finding Holly (6)

Finding Home (7)

Finding Balance (8)

Finding Peace (9)

The Finding Home Series Boxset Books 1-3

The Finding Home Series Boxset Books 4-6

The Finding Home Series Boxset Books 7-9

The Birch Creek Ranch Series (women's fiction series with romance for each character that spans the series):

The Bequest

The Vow

The Ranch

The Retreat

The Reboot

The Surprise

The Setback

The Lookback

Children's Picture Book

Yuck! What's for Dinner?